Heart of the Sea

Curse of the Sea Series

Jasmine Denton

This is a work of fiction. Names, characters, places, and incidents are products of the author's imagination or are used fictitiously and are not to be construed as real. Any resemblance to actual events, locations, organizations, or person, living or dead, is entirely coincidental.

WCP

World Castle Publishing, LLC
Pensacola, Florida

Copyright © Jasmine Denton 2014
Print ISBN: 9781629891569
eBook ISBN: 9781629891576
First Edition World Castle Publishing, LLC, October 15, 2014
http://www.worldcastlepublishing.com

Licensing Notes

Cover: Lindsay Anne Kendal Graphics
Editor: Jessica Rico

The boundaries which divide Life from Death are at best shadowy and vague. Who shall say where the one ends and where the other begins?

Edgar Allan Poe

A devastating curse, an ancient witch, and a dangerous love...

How far would you go to save the life of the person you love? In another lifetime, Mykaela made a deal with the devil—a powerful sea-witch Narissa who used her to steal the souls of drowning victims. Mykaela can keep her lover Dylan alive by helping Narissa gain ultimate power using those souls.

Mykaela's been reincarnated to pay her debt to the witch. To ensure her obedience, Narissa turns the teen's life into a hellish battlefield by hurting her friends and putting her mother into a magical coma. The supernatural has been on her side up until now, but when someone close to her takes a trip down the dark side, old wounds are opened. Can they break the curse before she loses everyone she holds dear in this lifetime?

Prologue
Warrior Rising

Beautiful and dangerous, the girl rose out of the ocean a few miles from the shoreline. Dark locks of hair cascaded over her shoulders, accentuating pale skin and an elegant, almost dainty-looking heart-shaped face. Waves parted, spreading as if to worship her as she glided toward the beach. The moon poured luminance over the ocean and the girl. Her skin seemed to glow from the inside out, a silver light always complementing her beauty. A white gown clung to her shapely body, moving with the wind as she stepped onto the land.

For centuries, she'd waited patiently in the depths of the seas, searching for her opportunity to take over the land-dwellers' world. Now, she could finally make her move. Once she retrieved the souls from their storage cell, she would have everything she needed. Nothing could stop her then.

The wind around her seemed to hum, louder and louder as she spread her arms and held them straight out, as if awaiting a hug. She faced the Seaside Inn, her gaze locked on the window. Opening her lips, she began to sing,

"Blood of my blood, Keeper of my souls,
I've kept my promise, now keep yours.
I come out of the deep blue sea,
Awake and return to me."

***

Mykaela woke with a gasp, her body radiating with power. It felt like a hand was clutched around her throat, blocking oxygen and taking strength, filling her with the urge to go toward the ocean. Something was out there, drawing her toward the water.

"Blood of my blood, Keeper of my souls,
I've kept my promise now keep yours.
I come out of the deep blue sea,
Awake and return to me."

The melodic words drew Mykaela from her home, down the porch steps, and out onto the sand. Dylan and Brad followed closely behind her, calling her name and although she heard them, she didn't have the willpower to listen, to stop. Narissa waited on the shoreline and some force, some internal pull, dragged Mykaela down the beach to the sea-witch. With the moon shining up above, she went to meet her fate.

Mykaela stared in awe, marveling at the beauty, the power. Narissa reached her hand out, extending it toward her. The ocean behind her was still parted, as far as her eyes could see, but it didn't scare her. She felt peaceful...obedient and powerless. Reaching out, she took Narissa's hand.

Before she realized what was happening, Narissa grabbed Mykaela's wrist and held tight while she shoved her right hand straight into Mykaela's chest.

Pain rippled through her, as if her body was shredding from the inside out. *Not again*, she thought. She'd just felt this pain minutes ago, and now it was back tenfold. This would be the end for her, she realized.

Light erupted from her. Rays of all colors flowed from her body and into Narissa's. Opening her mouth, she tried to scream, but no sound came out. Then she dropped to the sand. She felt dizzy and disoriented, but the pain was gone. Standing up, she brushed herself off and turned to Dylan. "What the hell was that?"

Dylan, his face weighed down with worry, ran right past her and knelt on the sand. "God, no," he whispered.

She narrowed her eyes, stepping around Dylan. Her mouth dropped open and she fell back a step when she saw her own unconscious body lying on the beach.

***

He'd waited over a century for her to return to him, to be with her again, only for it to turn out so sordid. He wasn't exactly innocent—he'd been responsible for the string of murders ten years ago, the ones that caused Mykaela's dad, a hunter, to become a soul of the sea in hopes of stopping them. When Mykaela's dad set his sights on killing Mykaela for the unnatural power her soul possessed, Dylan had no choice but to destroy him.

Then, as if puzzle pieces snapped together in his mind, it clicked. Mykaela's soul hadn't been so strong because she was powerful, or reincarnated. She wasn't just the Keeper of the Vault where every cursed soul went. She wasn't just some prophesied savior who'd break the curse and set all of those souls free. She wasn't strong because she had a powerful soul, but because she possessed *many* souls. Mykaela was the vault. Her body housed thousands of cursed souls—the very souls that Kerr and his army would've stormed Harmony Harbor looking for. Now Mykaela was dead. She'd failed.

Dylan clutched onto Mykaela's lifeless body as tears streamed down his cheeks. "No, not again," he whimpered, bringing her to his chest and burying his face in her damp hair. "Don't die again."

"You lied." Dylan raised a venomous glare toward Narissa. "You promised she wouldn't die—that we'd get to live a human life again. You killed her."

"No, *you* killed her. She would have survived." Narissa's echoing voice broke through Dylan's grief and he looked up to see the sea-witch standing on the shore. "But you took her original soul. It was the only one that didn't belong to me—it would've stayed if you hadn't drained it."

"I didn't know—I didn't mean to take it all."

"I still have one more promise to keep, Dylan." Narissa knelt by his side. "I promised you'd get your soul back. Your humanity. Do you still want it?"

"What's the point?"

"You miss your opportunity. She's still the vault—an empty vessel. She could take your soul."

"Will it bring her back to life?"

"With a price, yes."

***

Mykaela stood at Dylan's side, screaming at the top of her lungs. Why couldn't he hear her? She was standing right next to him, shouting, yelling, and begging him not to do this. Hadn't they learned anything? Diabolical deals would get him nowhere—he'd already lost his soul, ruled an evil kingdom, and lost the love of his life twice all because of a deal. What good did he expect to come from this?

"He can't hear you," a voice came from behind her and she turned. A girl stood not too far away, in front of Mykaela's house. "Whatever decision he makes will be his choice."

Mykaela stared at the girl. She looked like she'd stepped out of an episode of *Xena* or something, wearing a metal pleated skirt and what looked like a pure gold tank top. A crossbow poked out of a holster draped around her shoulder, and two knives adorned each hip. She carried a jewel-encrusted sword in one hand. "I hope you're not here to fight," Mykaela said, eyeing the sword. "Because this is *not* a good time."

"I am here to fight." The girl smiled and tossed a blond braid over her shoulder. "But I'm not your enemy, and I'm not here to hurt you."

"Enough with the cryptic," she said. "In case you haven't noticed, I just died. I'm not exactly in the mood for chit-chat."

"I know you just died. That's why I'm here."

Mykaela felt a knot of dread form in her stomach. "Don't tell me you're the grim reaper. Come to take me to Heaven? Or is it Hell?"

Her lips curled in a grin, as if she'd expected to hear that. "I'm not a reaper, and you're not going either of those places. My name is Dawn. I'm a Valkyrie."

"A...a..." the word sounded so ridiculous, she couldn't bring herself to repeat it.

"When heroes die, I carry their souls to Valhalla where they prepare for the final battle, which isn't far away now that Narissa claimed the souls. I'm here to take you."

"To Valhalla?"

"Yes." Patient, kind Dawn took a few steps toward Mykaela. "You died before your destiny could be fulfilled — before you could stop Narissa from destroying your hometown, and eventually, the world. I'm giving you a second chance to fulfill your destiny; to save the world."

"But...I don't deserve it. I started all of this." Mykaela turned her focus to Dylan, who still clutched her drowned body. "All of this pain...I caused it."

"No. You were merely a pawn in Narissa's plan. She could've chosen a dozen or more other girls — you were just the one who took the bait. And you've worked very hard to atone for it, too."

"This doesn't make any sense." Her head was spinning, and she desperately craved oxygen. Would she ever breathe again? She just wanted to slip into her body, then hug Dylan, then her mother. She began to pace up and down the beach. "I don't even have a soul. Dylan drained it—that's why I'm dead right now."

"That's no match for my power. Nothing can stop me from claiming the soul of a slain." Dawn waited patiently for Mykaela to wrap her head around this situation.

"So...couldn't you just pull my soul from Dylan and put it in my body? I mean, if I'm so heroic, as you say, don't I deserve at least that?"

She shook her head and moved toward Mykaela. "It doesn't work that way. You don't belong here anymore."

"What happens?" she asked, "If I go with you?"

"You'll become immortal, nearly invincible. You'll train to fight until you're needed here. Likely, you'll never see your family or Dylan ever again. Love has no place in the warrior's afterlife."

"This isn't fair," she whispered. "I never knew I was the vault. I had no control over myself when Narissa stole the souls."

"What's more important, Mykaela?" she snapped, taking a firm step toward her. Her voice took on a bossy tone as she placed one hand on her hip. "Seeing Dylan and your family? Or saving them and the entire world? Narissa's just the beginning. She has followers, very powerful and loyal ones who are going to help her overrun humans and take this world from them. The slain and the valkyries are strong, but we need all the help we can get, and I just thought, oh maybe since you started this entire mess, you might want to lend a hand!"

Tears filled her eyes and Mykaela quickly brushed them away. This wasn't the time for tears. Turning to look at Dylan, she watched as he cried too.

As Narissa offered Dylan a chance to bring Mykaela back, he laid Mykaela's unconscious body on the beach and stood up. Turning to the witch, he wiped tears from his cheeks. "I don't care what the price is. There's no way–I'm never making a deal with you."

"He's doing the right thing. He's willing to sacrifice your relationship for the greater good," Dawn said. "Are you?"

She took a deep breath, her gaze locking on Dylan as she took in every detail she could; the bright blue eyes, his wavy blond hair, the scar on his chin. Mykaela loved it all and she'd never gotten the chance to tell him how she'd felt. But there was a bigger picture here, and she knew what she needed to do. Stop Narissa — that was the only thing that mattered now. The world depended on it.

Turning to Dawn, she nodded. "Take me to Valhalla. I'm in."

Without another word, Dawn stabbed the sword into the sand so the blade and the handle stood freely. She twisted a knob at the end of the emerald encrusted handle, and the sword began to glow a pale blue. A burst of light blinded her, and when her eyes adjusted, she saw a wavy, rippling image where the sword used to stand, like she was looking through a window and into another world. A large hall with a wolf sitting right in front of the door, his vigilant eyes looking stony and dangerous, stared back at her. Above the door, an eagle flew back and forth, screeching.

Though fear stirred in her gut, Mykaela didn't look back as she and Dawn stepped through the portal.

Chapter One

Mykaela gasped in a desperate breath, fighting, clawing, shrieking to get out of the portal, to return to her body.

"Mykaela!" Dylan's Irish-tinged voice broke through her panic. "Mykaela, wake up!"

Her eyes flew open, immediately taking in her surroundings: the antique dining room table, split right down the middle and caved in. The banister to the stairs was broken too, the poles with doves and olive branches carved into them rolled around on the floor.

Next to her, a handsome boy knelt at each side. To her right, she saw Dylan, rogue warrior of the sea and immortal beauty. On the left there was brooding and rugged Brad, a deputy by day and monster hunter by night. Dylan she'd loved for many lifetimes, but Brad had taught her to survive.

"What happened?" she asked breathlessly, looking around at the aftermath of the battle.

"When we got here, Kerr was killing you," Dylan said. "But we stopped him. He's dead, Mykaela. He can't hurt you anymore."

So caught up in her spiraling thoughts, Mykaela barely noticed the quick look Brad shot Dylan. She stood up, spinning to look around the room. Hadn't she already left the inn? She'd been on the beach only moments ago. "No," she whispered. "After that. Where's the portal? I talked to the sea-witch...and the Valkyrie and she said —"

Brad stepped up and took Mykaela's face in his hands, stopping her from rambling. "Whoa, calm down. Portals and sea-witches? Valkyries? Mykaela, you were dreaming."

"No!" She shook her head violently, pulling away from him. "I wasn't dreaming. I was dead."

"*Nearly* dead. And your brain took you on an acid trip, but it's over now," his voice was quiet, rational, as he spoke. "You're okay."

Remembering this, the situation and the fight with Kerr, she turned to look at Dylan. His betrayal flooding back to her, the violence of her death coming back in full, vivid detail. "You killed me."

His entire posture sagged with shame and regret, and he opened his mouth to speak but didn't say anything. Finally, with a hoarse, quiet voice he said, "I lost control."

Tears sprang to her eyes as she looked at him, at how torn he seemed. Remembering how heartbroken he'd looked as he'd held her limp body, with the waves crashing to the shore around them, she couldn't find it in her heart to be angry at him, even though she probably should've been. Right now, she had bigger concerns. Locking gazes with him, she whispered, "It's okay."

There was a hint of relief in his expression, but it was quickly replaced with guilt again. And knowing him, she realized, he would torture himself about this for years.

"It's okay?" Brad exclaimed, stepping up to look at her. "He almost killed you!"

"He needed the power from my soul to stop Kerr from turning this town into a graveyard," she reminded him in a harsh tone that slammed Brad back into his place. "I was more than willing to die for the cause."

Brad's gaze stayed on her, even and steady, and she couldn't tell if he was disappointed or proud. Finally he turned away, shaking his head.

"And it's a good thing I didn't." Mykaela turned from him and went to the window that faced the ocean. "Because someone much worse is on the way."

Leaning against the window pane, Mykaela looked out the streak-free glass. From the pale light of the moon, she saw the rippling tides and white ridges of water, but there was no sign of the beautiful witch she'd seen rising out of that spot. There were no dead bodies on the beach, no sign of a portal to another world. But most alarmingly, even the echoes—those stains of color on the atmosphere, created by an act of great love or great evil—were nowhere to be seen. It was as if the whole thing had never happened.

The house, however, was covered in the aftermath of the battle. Hints of swirling blue and purple energy hovered in the dining room and lobby.

She turned, surprised to see Brad knelt beside her mother's body. In all of the chaos, she'd completely forgotten her mother was there. Her voice trembled with concern and guilt. "Oh my god, is she okay?"

Running over, she knelt by her mother's side, checking for a pulse. She let out a slow breath of relief when she felt the slow, steady beat against her fingertips. "Kerr knocked her out somehow," she explained. Turning her focus to Brad she said, "Can you get her to the hospital? I'll make sure everything is safe and then come up there as soon as I can."

He nodded and scooped Blanche into his arms, then carried her out without another word. Seeing her mother in that shape had rattled her, and her hands were shaking now.

But she couldn't slow down, couldn't think about anything other than the sea-witch, her plan and the power she'd held over her. It was like she'd been powerless against the witch, and she didn't want to relive that moment on the beach again.

Dylan finally stepped forward, reaching for Mykaela's hand. "Would you sit down for just a second?"

But she just walked to the front door, opened it and looked out. She searched for anything to justify the panic she felt, wondering why there were no energetic signs of such a powerful act. "It must've been a vision," she concluded.

Stepping out onto the wraparound porch, she looked out at the vast, mysterious ocean. She wrapped her arms around herself as a cold chill blew in from the water. The night sky made the whole scene seem colder, darker and more dangerous. "The most vivid one I've ever had."

Dylan stepped out behind her, following her gaze. "Whatever it was, love, we'll figure it out," he said, his voice taught with impatience. "For now, would you just sit down? You almost died. I thought...I thought you were..." He stopped, raking a hand through his hair. "So would you just take it easy for a minute? Just a minute."

"I can't 'take it easy,' Dylan!" She spun to face him, wishing he would just get out and let her process what had happened. "I've seen who we have to face. She's...she's scary. Not psycho like Morrigan or sneaky like Kerr, but really, really *scary* in an old, powerful kind of way." Desperation and fear clouded her tone as she remembered the warnings she'd heard. She'd seen what her future held; she knew her fate. "She's going to kill me."

Just the thought of it sent her racing into a panic. "There's so much I have to do. Aside from finding Narissa and seeing if we can even go up against her, I have to convince my mom to leave town. It's just not safe for her here. Make things right with Jared…we've never been the same since I killed Morrigan," as she rambled, tears stung her eyes, "and I never told Charity's mom how Charity really died. She deserved to know that….before… There's a box of undeveloped rolls of film under my bed…they're ancient, but I want my mom to have those. And Brad, I never told…"

Dylan squeezed her shoulders, just enough to make her focus on him. "You're talking like you're going to fail." His eyes, which reminded her of the softest, most peaceful parts of the sea, locked on hers and held it evenly, certain of the truth behind his words. "I promise, Mykaela, I *will not* let her kill you. But you have to fight, okay? You can't give up now."

Taking a slow, deep breath, she nodded, engraving that word into her brain. *Fight, fight, FIGHT.*

"Good," he said, releasing her shoulders. He guided her to the porch swing. "Sit down. Regroup."

Reluctantly, she sat, resting her elbows on her knees and her head in her hands. She heard the swing chains squeak and whine as Dylan sat down next to her.   "Something in that vision scared the hell out of you, love," his soft voice was full of the wisdom and understanding that came with centuries of surviving a curse. "What was it?"

Her hands were shaking and her nerves were frayed. No matter how hard she tried, she couldn't get a grip on it. But she couldn't tell him what she'd found out, couldn't risk that information leaving her lips, just in case someone was listening or using magic to spy. She shuddered to think what would happen if anybody ever found out that her body was the vault of souls…the difference between a world overrun with monsters and a world populated by humans. The balance shifted to whoever sucked those souls from her body and claimed the power as their own. Nobody could ever know that…or their lives would be on the line, too.

"It was so real," she whispered. "It was like...like she had complete control over me. I couldn't even move. And she sang this...this rhyme...a spell maybe?" Mykaela closed her eyes, feeling a chill come to her body as she recalled the words. "I've kept my promise, now keep yours. I come out of the deep blue sea, awake and return to me."

Dylan's eyes narrowed in confusion. "What happened after that?"

Another chill ran over her skin, but she shrugged it off. "It doesn't matter," she said. "How am I alive? That's the bigger question."

"I don't know," Dylan said. "One minute, we're doing CPR and the next...there's this red light glowing...like glowing from inside you...and then you woke up rambling about a portal."

A red light? Where had it come from? Before Mykaela could voice the question, a text message rang in on her cell phone. "It's Brad," she said, opening the message. "I have to get to the hospital."

***

Mykaela rushed into the ER waiting room, hurriedly looking around for Brad. She saw a kid holding a blood-drenched towel to his nose, and an older man with a walker and oxygen tank, but no sign of her friend.

She hurried over to the check-in desk and found a woman with short red hair and thin-rimmed glasses. "I'm looking for my mom," she said, "Blanche Whindom."

"And your name is..." the woman asked as she clicked a few keys on the keyboard.

"Mykaela. My friend brought her in."

"Yes," she said, reading a file on her screen. "I see now. Deputy Baxter is waiting with her now. Come with me and I'll take you to them."

Mykaela followed the nurse through a set of doors to the exam rooms. As they passed curtain after curtain, Mykaela started to feel an uneasy sense of dread, but she couldn't place its source.

"Number eight, here we are." The woman stopped and pushed back the curtain a little.

Brad was sitting just inside the curtain, and her mom was tucked into the hospital bed. She was pale and her lips were dry, but it was the way her aura looked that surprised Mykaela the most. The wavy rays of energy were normally invisible to Mykaela, but now splotches of sickly gray hovered all around her like a raincloud. "She's really sick," Mykaela whispered, moving to the edge of the bed. She reached out, taking her mother's hand, covering it with her palm.

"I'll get the doctor," the nurse said, bowing out.

Mykaela squeezed her mother's hand, wishing she'd been home to save her. Wishing she could help.

"They've run all the usual tests," Brad said, coming up behind her. "But they haven't told me anything yet. I told them she just passed out...since I didn't know what really happened." Brad placed his hand on her shoulder, spreading warmth all through her skin. He kept his voice low, whispering to her, "When we came in, Blanche was out and Kerr was killing you. How'd you get that far in over your head?"

"I guess that's what happens when you deal with sea monsters," she said, wiping away a tear that escaped. "I found Kerr holding my mom hostage," she explained. "He said he'd kill her unless I agreed to let him change me into a siren. I couldn't let her die...so I said yes."

"You were going to let him do that to you?" he asked, his voice a shocked whisper. "You hate sirens more than anybody I know."

She looked over her shoulder at him. "What would *you* do to save *your* mom?"

He shut up then, clamping his jaw and looking at her with a surprising amount of sympathy.

The sound of the curtain sliding back drew their attention to a doctor approaching. "Miss Whindom?" he asked, tucking a clipboard against his side. "I'm sorry to admit your mother's case has us a little baffled. It's like she's sleeping and can't wake up. We have yet to pinpoint its cause." He handed the clipboard over. "If you'll sign these forms, we'll admit her for further observation. You can spend a few minutes with her if you like, but after that you won't be able to see her until visiting hours in the morning."

"Wait a second..." Mykaela said, turning to him. "Are you saying she's in a coma?"

He was hesitant to answer. "It would appear that way, but like I said, we can't determine the causing factor. Were you with your mother when she passed out? Is there any history of aneurysms in your family?"

"No," she said, shaking her head. "Not that I can think of." She looked over the forms in her hands. The stack was at least an inch thick, and the writing tiny. She had trouble paying attention in class...how would she ever finish this?

"When is she going to wake up?" she asked the doctor.

"It could be any minute, or maybe not at all. There's really no way to tell yet." The doctor paused to wait for more questions. Then, finally, he motioned to the clipboard. "Turn that in to the nurse's station when you're done. I promise, we're going to do everything in our power to help your mother."

He turned and left and Mykaela sank into the nearby chair, her gaze fixed on her mother's unconscious body. "He was a lot of help," she said to Brad.

"Maybe she's still under some kind of spell that we can break," Brad offered. "I can look into it if you want."

She nodded. "Thanks. I'd do it myself, but," she lifted the clipboard in the air. "Apparently I have the entire Library of Congress to fill out." She tilted her head down and began to fill out the forms. They started out simply enough—asking for her mother's full name, birth date and place and things like that. But then they started asking for insurance information and policy numbers and family medical histories and Mykaela found herself in over her head for the second time that night.

"I'll be back in a few minutes," Brad said, stepping around Mykaela.

She nodded again in response, focused on trying to recall if her grandmother had died of heart disease or a heart attack, and wondering what was the difference between the two.

As she worked on the forms, her mind began to wander back to the vision of Narissa. When would she strike? Was there any way to guard herself against Narissa's mind control? Or was it fate, and would she end up en route to Valhalla no matter how hard she tried to fight it?

The thought of completely losing this life...losing her mom and her brother, and Dylan and Brad, was enough to push her to tears again. But by the looks of things, she might lose her mother anyway. And anybody else could be next.

And how was she alive? What did it mean? And for heaven's sake, what was her mother's maiden name? Why couldn't she remember it? Leaning back, she rested her head against the wall and tilted her head toward the ceiling. Closing her eyes, she willed her body to relax. Her brain, especially, needed to relax or she wouldn't be able to think of anything.

But the second she closed her eyes, she saw the sea-witch rise out of water that parted to make way for her. Saw her shove a hand through Mykaela's chest and rob her body of all the souls that inhabited it. She felt that searing, burning pain all throughout her body. Saw Narissa tilt her head toward the sky and cackle menacingly...

Feeling a hand touch her, Mykaela woke with a jolt, knocking the clipboard and the pen off her lap. Startled, she looked quickly around, taking in the sight of the hospital room and Blanche still unconscious. Next to her, Jared stood by the curtain like he'd just come in, his expression filled with concern and a hint of amusement. "Heard you've had a rough night," he said, giving her a small smile.

"You have no idea," she breathed, reaching down to pick up the clipboard. She yawned and grabbed the pen from the floor. "I must've dozed off. What's Mom's maiden name?"

"Here, let me take care of that." He held his hand out for the paperwork.

She gratefully relinquished the clipboard to him and then looked over to her mom. She hadn't moved a muscle, but the machines hooked up to her showed a steady, consistent heart rate.

"How'd you know I was here?" she asked as she stood and walked over to get a closer look at the machines.

"Brad called me," he said, taking the chair. He held the clipboard up to write something in one of the dozen blank fields she'd left. "I can't believe *you* didn't. Although, I guess under the circumstances, I'll grant you a reprieve."

Turning to look at her mom, she felt tears spring to her eyes. "Kerr promised me that she'd be okay," she said. "That was the whole reason..."

The reason I died, she thought, or almost died, or whatever had happened.

"A siren broke a promise? Imagine that."

"I guess I deserved that." For the first time it occurred to her that giving in to Kerr's plan probably wasn't the best idea.

"Speaking of," he added, looking up at her, his eyes flashing with judgment. "Remind me to kick your ass later. You were going to let him *turn* you."

"Jared, I didn't have much choice. He was going to kill her!" Looking around, she fought to keep her voice quiet. "Where were *you*?"

He stood up, jaw clenched and voice quiet, but every bit of rage showing through in spite of his efforts to stay civilized and supportive. "Yeah, I should've been there. But none of this would be happening if you'd never gotten involved with Dylan. I warned you about him. I begged you to just stay out of it...but you had to go poking into those deaths last year. Before that, our lives were normal. And now look at us."

"That is *not* true," she countered, "you were a hunter for years before Dylan ever washed up on that beach. I'm not going to stand here and argue with you about the choices I've made. In case you haven't noticed, we're in the middle of a major crisis here and I can't believe you'd—"

Jared raised his hand to cut her off, like nothing she said mattered. He leaned in close, a dangerous but controlled tone in his voice. "I know what he did to you."

She stood there, speechless, so convinced that Dylan had done the right thing that it hadn't occurred to her others might not see it that way. "I'm fine."

"Have you looked in a mirror?" he asked, motioning to the sink on the other side of the room. "Because you look, well, *drained*. You almost didn't make it."

27

Swallowing hard, she started toward the mirror. Not sure if she wanted to look or not, but some morbid curiosity was compelling her to look anyway. Placing her hands on the porcelain sink, she cautiously stole a glance at her reflection.

She was shocked to see two green eyes, sunken and surrounded by dark purple circles. Pale, waxy skin only made her look more grotesque, reminding her of the dead bride in that Tim Burton movie. Her lips were bluish, but returning to normal, and her hair...well the flat ironing she'd done on it this morning was wearing off, giving it a half-curled, dull and lifeless look. And was it just her imagination, or did she look ten pounds lighter than she remembered?

Turning from the mirror, she leaned against the sink. After a moment to steady herself, she finally gathered the courage to look at Jared.

He was watching her, with a look of disappointment, concern, and anger, and she couldn't tell which was directed at her. "The next time I see Dylan," he said, locking eye contact to reinforce his point, "I'm going to kill him."

"Jared," she said cautiously, knowing this could make him blow. "I can't let you do that. Dylan's a...*valuable* tool right now. He's more powerful after...after what happened...and besides that, he's tangoed with these things for centuries. He knows things we need to know. So you can hate him all you want for what happened, but—"

"Stop calling it 'what happened'," he snapped, coming closer. "Mykaela, he took your soul. Or most of it, anyway."

"But we won," she said, as if that would somehow make everything better. "Kerr's dead."

"You call this winning?" He motioned to the room around him. "My mom's in a hospital bed and you look like you're on death's door. Oh, and there's still someone after you. Nice job. Great victory."

Mykaela crossed her arms over her chest, feeling the sudden desire to get out of there. She wasn't doing anyone any good by just standing around, fighting with Jared and trying not to cry. Her energy would be better suited geared toward stopping Narissa or finding a magical cure for this coma. But there were still a few things she had to take care of first.

"Are you going to yell at me all night?" she asked. "Or are you going to stay here and look after Mom so I can figure out what's wrong with her and how to fix it?"

He sat back down in the chair with a sigh, a look of guilt coming in as the anger faded. "The only place you're going is home to rest. Brad and I will look into curing mom, as well as making sure nobody comes after her again. *We* will take care of it. *You* just go be a teenager."

Mykaela raised an eyebrow. "We?"

He looked over at her, lips closed tight.

"Your little band of hunters is taking over," she realized.

"You think we're leaving the town's fate up to a seventeen year old girl and her bad taste in boyfriends?" He shook his head. "No."

"You can't shut me out of this," she insisted. "I'm a part of it. You have no idea how big of a part..." she let the sentence trail off, unable to believe she'd almost blown her secret. Now she really needed out of there before she blew up completely.

"Go home," he repeated. "Get yourself cleaned up, looking healthier. Everything else can wait."

Looking into his stern brown eyes, she knew he wasn't going to change his mind. So she finally nodded in agreement and turned to tell her mom goodnight. As she leaned down close to plant a kiss on Blanche's cheek, she whispered, "I promise I'll save you."

Then she stood and hurried out of there, past the nurses' station, out into the main hallway. She kept her head low, feeling like her lungs were about to explode if she didn't make it outside really, really soon. She dodged the old man in the walker and bumped into an orderly, mumbling apologies as she quickly blurred past them. Finally, the mechanical doors opened and let her out into the cool night.

She breathed in deep, then let it out and breathed in again, hoping the motions would keep her from hyperventilating. The conversation with Jared replayed in her mind. She didn't like the idea of the hunter's council getting involved...if anything, they'd just become more casualties. She didn't know much about them, but she knew there was no way they'd be okay with letting Dylan live, especially not if Jared opened his mouth about him. And for that matter, how would they feel about her? She possessed magical powers, had been reincarnated and had worked with a sea-witch to create the hunter's target. They might kill her on principle.

She needed to find Dylan and warn him...but where had he gone?

In the shadows, she could see a man leaned up against her car, hands shoved in the pockets of a jacket. At first, she thought it was Dylan. But as the figure came closer, she could make out Brad's strong jaw line and cleft chin, along with his broad shoulders. She gave him a weak smile that would've been more convincing if she hadn't been so exhausted.

"I thought you'd left," she said, reaching into her pocket for her keys.

"I was going to," he said, coming a little closer. "I just wanted to check on you again, first. Make sure you were..."

His words trailed off as she passed under the streetlight, allowing him to really get a good look at her. He looked her up and down before quietly saying, "You're nowhere near okay, are you?"

She stopped in front of him and shrugged. "Honestly, does it really matter? With everything that's going on?"

"It matters," he said, those eyes never leaving hers in a way that was analyzing and comforting at the same time. "To me."

Giving him another weak smile, she pushed past him and hit the 'unlock' button on her keyless remote. "Thanks. But I could really just use back up. Jared's trying to shut me out and let the hunter's council help mom and stop the sea-witch."

"The sea-witch. Is that ever going to stop sounding weird?" He turned, still watching her, the hint of a smile playing at his lips. Seeing she wasn't amused, he quickly said, "They'll get themselves killed."

"Obviously." She opened the door to her Jeep and climbed in the driver's seat.

"But that's what the people in this town seem to do best. My parents, your dad...and you seem so willing to be added to the list." He walked over and rested one hand on the roof of the jeep and the other on the open door, looking in at her.

"Brad..." she started to tell him she was too exhausted to talk any more. All she wanted was to go home. But something in his expression had changed. He wasn't angry like Jared or worried like Dylan. There was something else...

"Mykaela," he said, voice quivering just enough to catch her attention. "I watched him kill you tonight."

"Everything turned out okay," she whispered.

"It's a good thing that Kerr's gone," he said. "But it's not worth your life." His silvery eyes locked on hers, boring his message straight through. "You can give me your greater good speech and tell me that Dylan was just trying to save the day, but the truth is that you had no idea what he was doing. I saw it in your eyes. You were scared, and betrayed and...and *dying*."

She shifted uncomfortably as he evoked emotions she'd been trying to ignore all night.

"The guy couldn't even clean up his own mess, do the one thing that could save your life. I gave you CPR." As he spoke, his anger and disdain showed through. The more intense it became, the more his aura appeared. At first it was a dull glow, but it flashed in and out until a bright red haze surrounded him. "Because he can't breathe, because he's not human. It was me."

"You're not entirely human either, are you?" she asked, taking in the bright colors around him and trying to determine what exactly he was, or if he was even really Brad. Morrigan and Kerr had both been able to shape-shift.

He looked around, trying to follow her gaze, but he couldn't see what she saw.

"Sensing evil is my gift, Brad," she said. "Remember? And you've been putting out some serious flares. Red auras. Music. A creepy presence. What's going on?"

He was staring at her now, looking slightly panicked. "It's nothing," he said.

"You're breathing so you're not a Son of the Sea. And a siren's aura wouldn't be red. So what exactly are *you*?"

Stumbling back, he stared over at her, looking almost betrayed.

"Is this about what happened to your dad?" She tried to keep him looking at her, but he kept dodging her gaze. "And how he died?"

He shook his head. "Maybe your powers are growing. Maybe you can see the auras of humans now."

"Maybe," she said. "But I meant what I said. I need you to back me up right now. Human or not."

Looking at her a moment, sizing her up, his panic faded. Stepping up, he reached out and grabbed the keys from her hand. "You look exhausted. Let me drive you home."

Fighting a yawn, she said, "I'm fine."

He chuckled and reached out to nudge her shoulder. "Come on. We can't have you passing out on the way home. Scoot over."

Reluctantly, she slid over to the passenger seat and let Brad hop in behind the wheel.

Chapter Two

After leaving Mykaela, Dylan went to the abandoned warehouse where he and Rachel used to hide out. He found Rachael in her bedroom, upstairs, and wasn't surprised to see her packing what few belongings she owned.

How human of her, he thought. She was only turned a year ago. "I have to say," he said loudly, prompting her to jump and spin around, dark hair flying over her shoulders as her mouth dropped in surprise. He leaned against the doorway, blocking her exit. "Never thought you would betray me."

She turned, stuffing a shirt into a duffel bag. "It's survival of the fittest, Dylan. It's only smart to go with the winning team."

"Smart?" He raised an eyebrow. "You're a seventeen year old immortal swimming with the things sharks are afraid of. Doesn't seem very smart to me."

"Dylan, I'm sorry." She slung the bag over her shoulder and started toward him. "But you're on your own."

But when she got to the doorway, he didn't budge. Reaching up, she pushed at his shoulder but he still didn't move.

"Get out of my way," she said, glaring at him.

He stepped aside, but as she slipped past him, he picked her up by the strap across her shoulder and slung her all the way to the other side of the warehouse. She slammed into the wall, cracking the cement where she struck. By the time she landed on the floor, he was at her side.

Stunned and dizzied, she looked up at him.

"You're not going anywhere, darling." He snapped his fingers and created chains made of purple electric currents. They bound her wrists over her head and her feet together. With a flicking motion, he attached this magical binding to the ceiling of the warehouse, until she was suspended from it dangling and helpless.

He pointed to the spot on the floor, by the staircase. "We were standing right there the day, the *only time* I've ever given you a direct order. What was it?"

She stared at him, stubborn and reluctant—and loyal to someone else.

He shook his head, disappointed, and snapped his fingers. Blue bolts of electricity shot from the bindings around her wrists to her ankles and back up shooting all over her body until a painful scream ripped through her lips. After a minute, he snapped his fingers again and it stopped. "What was the order?"

"I wasn't to interfere with your mission in any way," she said, quoting him verbatim.

"And the mission was…"

She rolled her eyes, reluctantly answering. "Protect Mykaela."

"Exactly," he cheered, coming closer to her. "Now, if I am to protect Mykaela, I need more information on this sea-witch. You know who I'm talking about, don't you?"

Though she didn't look at him, he could tell she was hiding something.

"You warned us about her before Mykaela ever had the vision. What was it you said? 'Now the real villain is coming, and you just pissed her off'?"

"Mykaela had a vision?" Rachel asked.

"Don't," Snapping his fingers, he sent another zapping jolt of power to remind her who was in control, "change the subject. If you cooperate, this won't hurt a bit," he said, taking a standing position in front of her. "Try to deceive me, and I'll make sure it hurts like nothing you've ever felt before."

The look of fear on her face brought a slight hint of guilt, but he pushed it aside. With Kerr dead, Rachel was their only clue to finding out more about the sea-witch. "I assume you learned of Narissa through Kerr?"

She nodded.

He crossed his arms. "How long did Kerr have you spying on me?"

She swallowed hard, taking a good look at the electric chains before she answered. "Since I was turned. He thought...since I'd known Mykaela when I was alive, that I'd have an automatic in with you." She gave him a slight smile. "Looks like he was right. Your heart, Dylan. It'll be your downfall."

Stone-faced, he made another motion with his finger and caused her to be electrocuted. She screamed in pain, a ragged animal sound. He waited patiently until the screaming stopped before he went on with his questioning. "What do you know about Narissa?"

Rachel tossed her head back and laughed. "I know that if you were smart, you'd get the hell out of here before she finds you. Mykaela, too. We should all just...just *run.*"

"Why?"

Rachel was shaking, terrified of whatever she knew. Dylan uncrossed his arms and prepared himself to do whatever it took to make Rachel crack.

***

Exhausted from the tumultuous night, Brad dragged himself out of his truck and to his apartment. Unlocking the door, he slipped inside and shut it behind him without bothering to turn on a light.

All he wanted was to slip into bed and enjoy a nice, restful sleep. But after everything that'd happened — to both Mykaela and her mother — he wasn't sure he could rest.

"You look like hell." The coy, feminine voice came from somewhere behind him.

Whirling around as he pulled out his gun, he searched for the source of the voice, immediately identified it and took aim all in a matter of seconds. The accuracy and timing was enough to surprise him — he'd always had good instincts, but this was a little…inhuman.

"Always with that silly gun." Brooke was sitting at the end of the couch with her legs crossed, her head resting against her fist. "You know it's not actually going to hurt me, right?"

"I don't know," he said with a shrug. "It might sting a little."

"Why does Dylan live?" she asked, anger slipping in to her casual tone.

"He doesn't. Where have you been?"

"You know what I mean," she snapped, dropping her hand to rest on the arm of the couch. "He killed our father tonight. And you just let him walk."

He lowered his gun. "For one, I doubt Dylan's even killable right now. He fed on his soul mate or whatever tonight," he added as he turned around and headed toward the fridge. "It looks like he'll be power-boosted for a while."

He heard the chair squeak as she stood. "Good for him. So, from what I'm hearing, he's powerful and you're scared."

"I'm not scared," he said as he opened the fridge, "But I'm definitely not avenging the death of a siren. I wanted to kill him myself."

"But you couldn't, because you're too weak. Because you're still in transition." She walked over to the counter and leaned her elbows on it, looking in on him from the living room. "That's why I'm here. I can tell you haven't fed yet. I can smell your tortured soul from here."

Grabbing a bottle of water, he shut the fridge and turned to her as he opened it. "What, exactly, am I supposed to *feed* on?" He locked gazes with her over the rim of his bottle as he took a drink. "Because I've been studying this whole…incubus thing and from what the legend says, it's pretty disgusting."

She giggled a little, shaking her head. With inhuman speed, she hoisted herself over the counter and in an instant, she was sitting on top of it. She smiled at him a little, at his innocence. "Basically, you absorb certain hormones in your victim's bodies. Completely zap the adrenaline, estrogen, oxytocin. Your body needs them to survive."

"See?" he said. "Disgusting."

She shrugged.

"And I'm guessing this transfer happens during sex? That's how a siren works."

"Technically all you need is a kiss," she replied. "The sex is just a bonus."

"But your victims die," he said, "doesn't that bother you?"

"It only bothers *you*," she said, pointing at him with a long red-tipped finger for emphasis. "Because of that soul you refuse to release. Your humanity is literally killing you, and all you have to do is…let it go."

He set the water and down and walked toward the living room. "You know what? You need to get out of here before I start experimenting ways to kill you." Stopping by the TV, he added, "And don't come back."

She groaned in frustration and raked a hand through her hair. "I don't know why Kerr insisted on letting your human family be hunters," she said. "I told him over and over that it was a bad idea. You're too stubborn. Too set in these human ways."

He angled his body to face her as he slowly reached one hand between the TV and the entertainment center, clutching his fingers around the handle of a small hatchet. "Then I guess this is just a huge waste of your time," he said, moving a little closer with the weapon concealed behind his back. "You should leave."

"I can't," she snapped. "You have to join the other side. It was my father's dying wish."

"Yeah?" he asked. "And why is that? Because I heard he was just the messenger."

She stood, turning to face him. But before she could complete the turn, he lunged, arm in mid swing. Without missing a beat, she grabbed the axe and slammed him into the nearest wall. Using the handle of the axe against his throat, she pinned him there. "Listen to me," she said, her eyes glowing red with anger. "Right now, everything that's human about you is withering away. Your hormones, your energy will be gone soon. It's like the two sides of your heritage are clashing together, trying to defeat the weakest link. Do you hear what I'm saying? Unless you forfeit your humanity and feed, you're going to die a slow, miserable death!"

"Then I'll die human!" He shoved her away, but she only moved a couple steps.

She glared at him, raging, furious. Her succubus nature glowed in her eyes, rimmed with red veins. "I can't let that happen," she said. "Make no mistake. You will feed one way or the other."

He lunged for her again, but in an instant, she disappeared and left the front door standing wide open in her wake. The door was still swinging open, but he saw no sign of her.

***

Mykaela went straight home. Taking a look around the wrecked dining room and lobby made her feel even more exhausted. Bypassing the mess, she went upstairs, put on some pajamas and went to bed. Within minutes, she was asleep.

To her relief, she suffered through no more dreams about the sea-witch. It was as if her brain simply turned off, like she was too tired even to dream. When she woke again, it was light outside and she could hear seagulls squawking around the ocean outside her window.

Rolling out of bed, she stretched and walked over to the vanity mirror and gave herself a good once-over. Her skin's bronzed hue had returned, though she still looked a little paler than normal, and her lips were rosy again. The circles under her eyes had faded to a translucent blue.

Not too bad, she thought. She picked up the hairbrush and pulled it through her gnarled hair. Before she could finish getting all of the tangles out, her stomach started aching so badly she decided to just throw her hair into a sloppy bun and head to the kitchen for some food.

As she neared the end of the stairs, she heard Jared and Brad talking in the kitchen. Rounding the corner, she saw them sitting at the table, with an array of papers, notebooks and text books sprawled out in front of them. They both stood when they saw her, and Jared came rushing up to her.

"You're up!" Jared moved closer to her, examining her closely. "How do you feel? Are you okay?"

She swatted his hand away as he reached to feel her forehead. "I'm fine. And still mad at you by the way." She moved around him and grabbed an apple from the fruit bowl on the counter. Taking a peek around Brad, she looked at the stuff on the table. "What's this?"

"Work." Brad shifted into her line of vision, blocking her view of the table.

"Are you sure you're okay?" Jared said from the other side of the room.

"Yes," she said, slightly annoyed. "Why do you keep asking me that?"

He stared at her, a look of puzzlement coming across his face. "You were asleep for three days."

She almost choked on her bite of apple, and the half-chewed chunk skidded down her throat, leaving it feeling raw. She quickly poured a glass of water from the tap, drank a gulp and swallowed again. "Three days?" she looked to Brad for confirmation.

He nodded.

She started to panic. "Why didn't you wake me up?"

Jared came to the edge of the counter. "We tried. You'd just snore and roll over."

"Is Mom okay?" Mykaela asked frantically. "Do the doctors know what's wrong?"

"Mom's the same," Jared said solemnly. "And the doctors are clueless."

Mykaela shook her head, knowing she'd need to resort to magical means to save her mother. She just needed to know who to go to for help. "What about Dylan?" Mykaela asked, remembering Jared's threat. "Did...did you..."

"No," Jared said, turning back to the table.

"It turns out that with Dylan's new power boost, he's damn near unstoppable," Brad explained, then he added quietly, "Yet one more thing to worry about."

"Wait...you tried to kill him?" Mykaela asked, grabbing her brother's shoulder. "Even though I asked you not to?"

He shrugged out of her hold, but angled himself to face her. "He's fine. So you should just go upstairs and get ready for school or something. If you hurry you can still make it half the day."

"School?" she replied, raising an eyebrow. "You expect me to go to school. While mom's in a coma and creatures are preying on the town."

"I told you this wasn't your fight anymore," he said, locking eye contact with her. "Now go."

She shook her head, wanting to mouth off to him. But he was as stubborn as she was, and she didn't want to waste time arguing. So she left them to their unorganized research and went upstairs and quickly showered and dressed.

She left out the front door to avoid being seen by them. But she didn't bother to go to school. She drove straight to Dylan's warehouse on the edge of town.

When she walked into the warehouse, she didn't see Dylan at first. Then he rounded the bar that separated the kitchenette from the large open room on the other side of the space. He was sweaty, glistening in the light pouring in from a few broken and dirty windows.

"She wakes," he said with a broad smile, letting her know he was happy to see her. "Have a good nap, Sleeping Beauty?"

"It felt like more of a hibernation," she said, approaching the bar and leaning against it. "I'm surprised you knew...I talked to Jared this morning."

He nodded, leaning on the counter to look at her. "A couple hunters trying to kill me isn't going to stop me from checking on you. You gave us all quite a scare."

She smiled a little. "Well, I'm fine. It must've just been my soul regenerating."

"Still, it's good to see you up and around." His gaze lingered on hers a second, like he wanted to say more. "About your brother...I hope I didn't hurt him too badly."

"You both look fine to me," she said. "Besides, he had it coming. Thinking he can just push me out of my own destiny, no less!" she sat down on the bar stool. "The nerve!"

"He's pushing you out?" Dylan said.

"He won't let me help find a way to save mom. Or stop Narissa. So he and Brad are holed up in the kitchen, with their notes and their society of hunters and their ancient laws, and here I am, the chosen one, the Keeper, without a team."

"Hey," he said, touching her hand. "You have me. And we'll find others. But what about this bothers you so much? That they won't let you help?"

"Yeah. This is my mess to clean up," she said with a sigh. "But it's not like I can just tell him that I cursed you in a past life, and that I'm supposed to break the curse now. He'd probably just shut me out even more. And that's *if* he even believes me."

He watched for a minute, gaze lingering compassionately on her, before he finally said, "How can I help?"

She sighed, wondering where to start. "Well...after I agreed to let Kerr turn me, he touched the back of mom's head and made her pass out. He said she was just sleeping, that'd she be fine. But then she never woke up. I just figured...being Kerr's apprentice, or whatever, maybe you've seen him do this before? Maybe you know something about it."

He thought for a minute, looking confused. "I have seen him do that before, the sleep spell, but I don't think that's what's wrong with your mom."

"What else could it be?" she sat up straight, listening.

"Well, any of Kerr's ongoing spells would've broken when he died. Like the one he cast to make you think he was human. Your mom should've woken up after Kerr died. Maybe someone...intervened somehow."

"Why would anyone want my mom in a coma?" she asked, mostly to herself, but he quickly gave her a reasonable answer.

"For the same reason Kerr used her as leverage. Because you care. If she's in trouble, you're going to be distracted. Unfocused."

"So...you think Narissa's behind this?"

"Or one of Kerr's followers," he added. "It's like...they're making you look left when if you'd look right, you'd see something sneaky."

"Shouldn't this *thing* have come forward with their demands by now? I mean, assuming they want to trade like Kerr did."

"I don't know..." his gaze turned distant, like he was thinking about something, or putting puzzle pieces together. "Maybe I should go underwater. See if I can overhear anything or get someone to open up to me."

"Dylan, to them you're a traitor," she said. "I don't think they'd be receptive to you. I think they'd probably kill you on principal."

He shrugged. "Let's be honest, love, who doesn't want to kill me?" A small smile tugged at his lips. "Until a few weeks ago, even you were waiting in line."

She winced as she remembered how angry she'd been, how much she'd wanted to kill him but had been unable to. Now, she realized, that must've been because of their past-life bond. Somehow she'd always known they were connected, even back then.

"The way I see it," he continued, "at least I'd be taking the risk for a good cause."

"I can't ask you to do that," she said, wishing she could selfishly ask him to risk his life for her. If it would save her mom, she'd do anything.

"You didn't." He gave her hand a squeeze, and then stopped to listen closely, his ears perking up. "Sirens," he said.

Her entire body went still with fear, thinking he'd meant the creature. But a second later, she heard the whirling sounds of a police car's siren, and relaxed a little. Looking out the window, she saw several squad cars rush by, followed by a few ambulances. Each one headed toward the south side of the beach. "Must be something big happening."

"Looks huge."

Something wasn't feeling right, so she stood up. "I'm going to follow them. We'll talk later?"

He nodded, and she took off. Following the sounds of the sirens, she ran alongside the road, gracefully making each turn and curve, picking up speed on the straight stretches until she saw the flashing lights. Slowing down, she lingered at the edge of the road, looking in as police roped off a crime scene.

But it wasn't the swarms of police officers that intimidated her, or the paramedics dashing around the scene, or even the dead bodies scattered all along the beach. The first thing she noticed were the echoes.

Chapter Three

Translucent splotches in hues of vibrant red, deep purple and ocean blue stained the atmosphere. At the edges, near the ocean, a black haze lingered, stretching way out over the horizon. It was so intense, the way the echoes lingered like a thick, impenetrable fog.

Mykaela stood at the edge of it all, taking in the morbid, horrific view. Something very old, very *evil* had been here and left behind dozens of victims. Men and women, kids and even pets formed a scattered array of corpses along the sandy beach. There was no blood, no survivors, just a gruesome picture of life cut too short, too soon, a maelstrom of impossible to fathom violence.

Those swirling mists of energy drew her closer, just inside the edge of the scene. If she could just touch one of the dead bodies, she could see what had happened. She took another step, heading toward a man slumped over a cooler.

"Miss," a stern female voice made Mykaela stop on instinct. "This is a crime scene. You should leave."

"I realize that," she said to the cop. "But I just—"

"Mykaela!" Jared's angry voice made her jump in surprise. Then she groaned and rolled her eyes as she braced herself for his attitude. She turned to see him barreling up to her, a roll of police tape in his hand leaving a yellow and black trail behind him. Without stopping, he grabbed her arm and led her further up the hill and out into the parking lot, away from the other people. He kept his voice low, eyes on the crime scene as he said, "What are you doing here? You're supposed to be in school."

"What happened?" she asked, too distracted by the lingering feeling of evil that lurked around the beach.

"I'm not going to tell you again. Stay out of it." He locked eyes with her in a warning before he started back down the hill to the beach.

"Jared," she called. "You can't just…Jared, stop!"

But he kept walking down the hill, ignoring. Shaking her head, she started to walk away. Then she heard Brad's low whisper, "*Psst*, Mykaela."

She turned to see him walking away from a paramedic and coming toward her.

He looked around to make sure no one saw them, then leaned in and whispered, "What do you see?"

"You don't want to know," she said, shivering again when she noticed the hazy black fog lingering over the ocean. "I haven't been able to touch one of the bodies. If I could…"

"Later," he said. "For now, go home." Just as she was starting to yell at him, he quickly whispered, "Look on the table," before hurrying back down to the crime scene.

Following Brad's tip, Mykaela hurried back to the house, surprised to find that they had abandoned their research and left all their information in plain sight on the table. She shook her head at their stupidity. Even though the Inn was closed and the doors had been locked, she never would've left her work sitting out like this.

But she was glad they had. She bent over the table, surveying the mess and scanning for something useful. They had maps of the town, maps of the waterlines, maps of the sewers. There was a list of names, a chart of supernatural creatures and their powers. So far, she hadn't seen any indication they were working on getting her mom healthy again.

She moved over to a thick, old book, open to a page on Shamanism. Mykaela quickly grabbed a nearby pencil and a post-it and started writing down the topics Jared and Brad had been researching. She'd look them up on the internet later. Before long, she saw Jared's squad car pull into the driveway.

***

Locked inside her bedroom, after hours of internet research, Mykaela finally stood from her desk and stretched. The printer whirred as it spit out a few more pages onto an already thick stack of paper.

She picked up the stack, grabbed a roll of scotch tape and continued to work. Though it didn't look like it, there was order to the chaotic notes strewn all over the room. She'd posted the information on sirens and sea-witches on one wall and dedicated the wall above her desk to her mother's cure.

So far, she was looking into Shamanism as a possible solution. Supposedly, they could heal illnesses of a spiritual plane by travelling to the spirit world, which she was pretty sure would work if, somehow, she managed to get her hands on a legitimate shaman who would help. On the print-out, she stuck a yellow post-it with a note to check with Brad. Other working theories included faith-healers and of course, sea-witches. It was possible that she could strike a deal with Narissa and trade the souls for her mother's complete recovery. It would be tricky and dangerous, though, so she was saving that as a last resort.

"Wow," Dylan's voice came from behind her.

She whirled around to see him enter through the open window.

His eyes scanned the walls. "You've been busy."

Raking a hand through her hair, she turned, eyeing the progress she'd made. Shrugging, she decided she hadn't done much good. "I'm still no closer to helping Mom than I was yesterday. While I was dead *asleep*."

He studied her a moment, in that way he always did. Accepting what she said, but knowing what she truly meant and never taking her words at face value. "Have you tried coming up for air?"

Glancing over at him, she started laughing, prompting him to grin.

"What's so funny?"

Her chuckles fading, she shook her head. "I'm sorry. It just sounded funny coming from you."

"Hey, at least you smiled." He motioned to the open window. "It's beautiful outside tonight. Have you noticed?"

She stole a glance out the window. "I haven't, not really."

"Think you can spare a minute to enjoy it?"

Giving him a wry smile, she stuck one leg through the windowsill, ducked under the window and stepped out onto the roof above the porch. Dylan followed her, and they sat down, with their backs pressed up against the house, and looked out at the ocean.

Mykaela was relieved to find the waters peaceful and calming. Right now, they looked a lot less intimidating than they really were. Now, she could look at them in awe and wonder, the way she used to.

"I keep trying to fix my life," she said quietly. "But I only make a bigger mess."

Dylan looked over at her. "Remember when Charity died and you kept digging into what had happened?" He gave a bittersweet sounding chuckle. "I tried warning you. Everybody did—Jared and your mom. We tried telling you that you wouldn't want to know, but you never listened. You saw the face of evil and you just had to fight it. Of course your life is a mess, Mykaela."

"Are you saying I should've just kept the blinders on? Or like the other people in town, pretend I don't see it? All those people on the beach, Dylan, they died. Just like Charity died. Like I almost did. Someone has to make it stop."

"And it has to be you?"

She sighed, shaking her head. "I'm not good at it," she said, laughing gently and bitterly. "But I can't help but feel like I brought this nightmare to town when I saved you all those years ago. I can't just do *nothing*. But that's exactly what I've been doing."

"You're trying."

"I just..." choking on her words, she hesitated until she was sure she could keep her voice from quivering. "I wish Mom would wake up. You know? I just want her to be safe and not...caught up in this mess."

Though she tried to remain strong, tears built in the corners of her eyes and her voice grew thick as her façade frayed at the seams.

Without a word, Dylan slipped his arm around her shoulders and pulled her close. Resting her head in the slope of his shoulder, she let out a trembling breath and let his closeness comfort her.

Finally, he spoke, his Irish-brogue sounding mischievous. "I think it's time we get proactive."

"Meaning?"

Without answering, he stood, and in a split second, dashed to the edge of the roof. "Come on, Mopey. You coming or what?"

Flashing her a sexy half-grin, he jumped down onto the sand below. She scrambled after him, jumping from the edge and ready to land on the ground when he bolted underneath her, catching her elegantly in his arms.

Setting her back on her feet, he took off. She ran after him, all along the beach to where the caves began. Finally, they stopped just outside of their special cave.

She was breathless when they stopped. "I didn't know you were faster than I am," she said, leaning against the rocky side of the cave.

"I have a few other tricks, too." He held his hand out. "You got your knife on you?"

"Yeah," she said slowly, wondering where he was going with this. She pulled the knife out, handing it over.

Turning the handle, Dylan plunged the blade straight into his chest.

Mykaela screamed in surprise and shock, but the scream fell silent when the blade flashed purple and fizzled out, leaving Dylan unharmed. She narrowed her eyes, looking at the glass still lodged in his chest. "How…?"

He yanked it out, and she watched as his wound closed back up. He tossed the knife to her and she caught it. "This little thing may have worked before but it's not going to cut it now. If it won't kill me, don't use it."

"So…you're like, invincible now?"

"Relatively. For now. As much as I hate how it all happened, the power boost couldn't have come at a better time. So, before the batteries drain and I'm weak like before, I thought it's time for a new weapon."

Lifting his hands toward the sky, he spread his arms out, summoning storm clouds. Thick and grey, they rolled in out of nowhere, tumbling and roaring. Soon, bolts of lightning zipped around inside the clouds, gathering together in a thick purple stream of lighting that struck the sand between them.

Light blinded Mykaela's eyes and she raised her hand to shield them, catching a glimpse of Dylan. His shadowy figure, arms stretched out in a powerful stance, surrounded by all of that glorious light. It was enough to make her fall in love with him all over again.

Finally, the light flickered out until there was a dull glow on the ground between them. When the light went out, Dylan stepped forward and knelt beside the charcoaled and sizzling sand. He dug into the sand until he came up with a large chunk of fulgurate, shaped like a lightning bolt. Unlike her knife, this was the size of a small sword. While the glass was still hot, he used his hands to smooth and mold the end of the glass into a handle and handed it over.

She liked the way it felt in her hand, and the second she touched it, she felt overcome with power. Maybe it had something to do with how powerful Dylan was right now, or because the blade was made with the power of her soul, but she felt drunk on it, almost. Dizzied by the strong, sturdy weight of the glass in her hand.

Then she remembered the massacre this morning, and she thought of all those humans who lost their lives on the beach. Anger quickly set in. Turning, she angled her body toward the shoreline and called out, "You guys want the Keeper, right?"

Out of the corner of her eye, she saw Dylan's expression fall in concern. He stepped up, trying to take her arm but she yanked away.

"That's what this is all about, isn't it?" she cried into the water. To the average person she must've looked crazy, but Mykaela knew that someone out there was listening. "You want the souls and I'm the only one who can give them to you. Well, I'm right here!" she called her challenge out into the calm waters. "Come and get me!"

"Mykaela," Dylan's voice was rational and low as he grabbed her arm, but she could hear the hints of panic in it. "This is a bad idea."

But she only looked out at the eerily calm waters and called out another challenge, "What? You can take out an entire beach full of innocent people but you're afraid to face the Keeper?"

The surface of the water began to bubble and gurgle. The wind picked up speed, blowing with fierce gusts all around them. It seemed to be coming from every direction; from the water in front of them and the cliffs to their right. Wind even blew in from the shadowy trees to their left. Bodies began to rise up out of the water. Dripping wet soldiers wearing old, tattered clothing moved toward the shore. Mykaela wasn't sure if they were sirens or sea-souls or a mixture of both, but she decided it didn't matter. They could both be killed the same way.

Keeping his eyes on the water, Dylan's fingers dug into her arm as he tried to pull her away from the beach, but she stood her ground. She was tired of hiding and waiting and playing it safe. She wanted a fight, and she wanted it *now*.

There must've been fifty of them coming toward the shore with venomous glares fixed on Mykaela and the traitor who'd abandoned them.

"Mykaela," he said, his voice sounding unsure.

"You said you wanted to get proactive," she reminded him, raising her new weapon and planting her feet in a defensive stance. Tossing one last look over her shoulder at him, she ran down the beach and started slashing. She chopped off a couple heads and the bodies turned to water. This time, she was the one committing the massacre. She counted five creatures that went down, and she wasn't even counting the ones Dylan was taking out.

Dylan, who'd been helping her with physical combat, suddenly stopped fighting. He raised his arms in the air, calling thick, dark storm clouds. Lightning bolts started streaking from the sky to the earth, each streak colliding with a soldier. He took half a dozen out like that.

"It's taking too much power," he called to Mykaela. "We have to run!"

But she ignored him and continued to slash away at the supernatural soldiers, venting all of her anger and hatred with each powerful swing. Then, one of them knocked the sword out of her hands. He flew at Mykaela, knocking her to the sand. Dylan ran toward them, but he was struck with a bolt of lightning, immobilizing him. He fought to get free, but the bolt kept him from getting to Mykaela.

She struggled, while the sand caved and shifted underneath her. But the creature was so much stronger than her, and he had his hand aimed at her heart. He was getting ready to drain her soul.

Suddenly, he grabbed his head in pain. Screaming, he fell off Mykaela and huddled on the sand. Mykaela stood, and looking around the beach, she saw the monsters dropping to their knees. Their hands gripped around their heads, each one fell to the ground, immobilized and defeated. The lightning bolt around Dylan disappeared and he rushed over to her.

"Are you okay?" he asked, taking her by the shoulders.

"I'm fine." She searched the beach. "What's happening to them?"

Dylan nodded toward the trees to their left. In the shadows of the woods, they could make out a silhouette. Someone was in the woods, watching them. Helping them.

"Who is that?" she asked, heading toward the woods.

"We don't have time," he said, "Look."

She followed his gaze and saw the soldiers were recovering. Some of them stood, looking disoriented, while others dove into the ocean and disappeared.

"They're retreating." Dylan grabbed her hand and pulled. "We have to go, now."

Reluctantly, she let Dylan pull her away from the beach. As they left, she looked back over her shoulder. But the figure in the woods was gone.

Chapter Four

In their mother's hospital room, Mykaela and Jared waited for news from the doctor. A machine beeped, slow and steady with their mom's heartbeat. It was the only sign of life. She watched the waves on the screen rise and fall with the beat, still dazed and unable to believe this was really happening. More than anything, she wished her mother would wake up.

Finally, Dr. Sanders walked into the room. He was a tall, balding man with spectacles who always carried a clipboard and never wore a stethoscope. Looking at them, he seemed cautious and unsure.

Jared stood as the doctor entered. "Did your tests find anything?"

"I've never seen anything like this," Dr. Sanders said. "As hard as we try, we can't find a cause for your mother's condition."

Mykaela turned to face the doctor, keeping her arms crossed as she listened to him.

"I'm not sure this hospital is the best place for her anymore," he continued. "I've written down the names of a few assisted living facilities that take her insurance —"

"Nursing homes?" Mykaela interrupted with a scoff. "She's only in her forties."

"I realize this is a terrible thing for your family to endure," he said gently, so gently it was almost disrespectful and mocking. "But, I'm afraid you have to face the reality that she might not wake up."

"Ever?" Mykaela asked, her heart filling with dread.

"I don't see her recovering from this."

With the feeling of loss hovering over her like a rain cloud, she shook her head in denial. No matter what any doctor said, she would never give up on her mother.

"I know it's a difficult thing to face," he continued.

"Just stop," she whispered, feeling a crushing weight on her chest.

Jared, who'd been utterly silent since the doctor entered, finally spoke up. "So there's nothing you can do? You don't have any way to treat her condition?"

"I'm afraid I wouldn't even know where to start."

Losing her temper, Mykaela rushed forward and grabbed the doctor, slamming him against the wall with her super-strength. "You're talking like she's already dead!" she cried, holding on to him by his lab coat. "She isn't dead! She's going to be fine, do you understand me?"

He squirmed under her grasp, looking alarmed and weak. "Miss Whindom, you need to calm down."

"I need to calm down?" she shot back. "Well you need to wise up!"

Jared moved forward, grabbing Mykaela and trying to pull her back. But she was stronger than him, and he couldn't move her.

Struggling to hold the doctor still in spite of Jared's strong grip on her, Mykaela lashed out at the intimidated bald man. "You stupid doctors and all your years of school and you can't help her because you have no idea what the world's really like!"

"Mykaela, stop it," Jared warned, wrapping one arm around her waist and grabbing her wrist with the other hand, fighting to get her to release the white coat.

"You have no idea what's really out there," she yelled, "so what good are you? You're just another ignorant civilian. You're going to be someone's prey if you're not careful!"

"Is that a threat?" Dr. Sander's asked, his face flushed with embarrassment because neither of the men in the room were stronger than this enraged teenage girl.

"No," Jared said quickly. "It's not a threat. Mykaela, let him go!"

"Why should I?" she cried. "He can't even figure out what's wrong with her!"

Finally, Jared managed to wrench Mykaela away from the doctor, and wrapped his arms around her to keep her from dashing straight after him again.

Dr. Sanders scooted toward the door. "I'm calling security."

"Please don't," Jared said, trying to hang on to Mykaela as she fought to get free. "She'll calm down, we just need a minute alone."

Looking skeptical, Dr. Sanders turned his back on the mess and rushed out of the room.

Once the door shut, Jared released her. Yanked free, she whirled around to face him. Her cheeks flushed, heart pounding, breathing heavy. So angry, with no one to hurt to make herself feel better.

"Are you out of your mind?" Jared said, an undeniable scolding tone to his voice.

"Don't go all high-horse on me," she warned, shooting him a glare.

"You just attacked a doctor!" he exclaimed, coming closer. "You almost told him everything. Have you completely lost all sanity and reason?"

"Maybe if people knew about the evil that lurked around, things like this wouldn't happen!" She motioned to their mothers still, listless body for emphasis. "Or maybe they would learn how to treat magical comas if they knew they existed."

"If you went on rambling about sea creatures and supernatural beings, you'd be staying upstairs in the psychiatric ward." Jared grabbed her shoulders. "I know this is hard to handle, but you've got to keep your cool."

"How can I do that?" she cried. "He just told us she'd never wake up!"

"From a scientific point of view," Jared corrected, his gaze boring down into hers to drive the point home. "You and I know that a lot more than just science goes on around here."

Calming down, she looked up at him as he continued to try to reason with her.

"Mykaela, I promise you," he whispered, his voice steady and certain, "if it's the last thing I do I will find a way to cure Mom."

"How?" she pleaded, not sharing his hope. "Another deal with the devil? That's what got us into this mess!"

His brown eyes narrowed in bewilderment as he looked down at her. "What do you mean 'another deal'?"

Then Mykaela realized that, yet again, her life was full of lies. Jared didn't know about her past life, that she was responsible for the curse. Just like he didn't know that the vault all of the sirens were searching for was Mykaela's body. "I...I just meant the Kerr thing," she said quickly, without sounding very convincing. "I told him he could turn me if he let mom go. He put her to sleep and she hasn't woken up."

Skeptically, he gazed down at her, still clutching her shoulders. "Are you sure that's what you meant?"

"What else would I mean?"

"I don't know, you tell me."

She pulled away from him, rolling her shoulders to loosen them up. But her body was still tense, every muscle taut and aching. "I'm all wound up," she explained, stepping toward the door. "I'm going to go blow off some steam."

He turned, following her with a knowing, disapproving gaze. "By killing something?"

Pulling open the door, she hesitated. "Nothing human."

With that, she walked out, closing Jared and his disappointment in the hospital room.

***

Tossing her head back, Rachel let out of a scream of pain. Her arms were marked up with burns and abrasions, but in the entire time he'd had her held hostage, she hadn't told him much. She was tied to a chair now.

"You must really be afraid of someone." He pulled a barstool across the room and positioned it in front of her chair. "Putting yourself through all of this, when I've told you before I'll let you go once you tell me what I need to know."

Even though she looked weakened, there was a ravenous look to her sea-blue eyes. "If I talk, I'm as good as dead anyway."

"Not if you help us kill Narissa."

She laughed. "Kill Narissa. It can't be done, Dylan."

"Everything has a weakness," he said. "I will find a way. The question is…will you still be alive when I do?"

Lifting her head, she met his gaze. "Just look at you," she said, her voice low and taunting. "All drunk on power. A far cry from the starved rogue I met last year."

"This isn't about me. This is—"

"About Mykaela," she finished. "It's always about her, isn't it? You're always dedicating yourself to saving her or protecting her or making her remember what you mean to her. But what do you think she'd say if she saw this? How do you think she'd feel?"

He pulled Mykaela's small knife out of his pocket. By now, Rachel was weak enough for it to hurt her. He moved it back and forth in front of her, the glass blade glinting in the dull light from a swinging bulb above them. "What does Narissa want with the souls?"

"Speaking of souls." With her arms still bound to the chair, Rachel leaned closer to Dylan. "What did it feel like to drain Mykaela's?"

He narrowed his eyes in a warning.

"Because I was there," she said. "And you totally lost control. What should've been a quick juice-up almost got her killed. Kind of takes dating violence to a whole new level, doesn't it?"

His anger got the best of him and he shoved the glass blade of the knife straight into her knee. The skin around the wound started to sizzle and burn as she cried out, gritting her teeth to keep from screaming again. Then, she started chuckling again, soft sarcastic sounds. "Looks like Kerr got what he wanted all along," she said. "Once again, you've embraced the monster inside."

He yanked the knife out of her leg, allowing her a reprieve from the pain. "This is about protecting Mykaela," he said, his voice thick with anger. "If embracing the monster is what I have to do to keep her alive, then that's exactly what

I'll do. Now you're going to start talking, or I'm going to start getting creative."

***

In the darkest edge of the woods, Mykaela stood on the cliff where it all began, in both lifetimes. The place Dylan had jumped from to commit suicide and escape Morrigan. The same place where, centuries later, Morrigan tried to kill Mykaela and her best friend, Charity. Out of both those tragedies, Mykaela was the only one to survive.

And all of it was because of some ancient witch who wanted...what? Mykaela didn't even know, but something told her Narissa's desire for the souls was about more than just power.

As waves crashed against the sides of the cliff a few hundred feet below, Mykaela hoped her plan would work. Closing her eyes in concentration, she yelled in a powerful, demanding tone, "*Narissa!*"

Her voice carried over the cliff, echoing down to the waters below, where she hoped the sea would carry her summons to the witch. She waited, but nothing changed.

"I'm right here," she cried, her voice echoing. "If you want me, come and get me!"

A thick, jagged bolt of lightning dashed across the sky, its presence marked by a loud clap of thunder. Mykaela jumped, taking in the gathering storm clouds, the rising gusts of wind. She knew evil was near even before her ears picked up the sounds of a soft, melodic hum, like a dark lullaby of vocalizing.

Suddenly, she saw swirls of black smoke beginning just a few feet away from her. Flowing in fluid, gentle motions, this dark mist began to form the image of the woman. Even when Narissa appeared, this black smoke—or dark energy—continued to curl around her like a hazy fog.

The woman had long, flowing hair as dark as the energy around her, and she wore a sparkling silver dress. She looked the same as she did in the visions, and the memories of her past life. She hadn't aged a single day in the last century.

Narissa's ruby-red lips curving in a smile, she clasped her pale, damp looking hands together and looked Mykaela up and down. "Mykaela, so good to see you again. Although, I have to say, you looked much better as a southern belle."

Mykaela looked the woman up and down, feeling like this was all surreal. It was the first time she'd ever met Narissa face to face in this lifetime, and the woman seemed different than she'd imagined. Prettier, more delicate, but with danger lurking behind those seemingly friendly eyes. "What did you do to my mom?" she asked, not bothering to draw a weapon. She knew none of them would be strong enough to help her, anyway.

"Skipping the formalities? You used to be so polite."

"I'm not the same girl who made that deal with you. She's dead and gone."

"Our deal tells a different story."

"And where does my mother fit into this story?"

Narissa gave a sick little smile. "She's my little insurance policy, your mother. It's pretty simple actually. You obey, she lives. You disobey, she dies."

Mykaela felt something tug at her gut. She'd suspected that was why Narissa was holding her mother captive with a spell, but hearing it made the situation seem more hopeless. "If you want the souls so bad, why don't you just take them?"

A hint of annoyance flashed across Narissa's face.

Reading between the lines, Mykaela felt a sense of relief. "You don't know where they are."

Clenching her jaw, Narissa moved toward the girl, walking slowly. "It's annoying, really. I go through all the trouble to create that curse for you, but because your love powered it, the souls went to you. Magic has a funny way of…trying to keep you on your toes."

Mykaela watched, cautiously.

"Give me the souls and we'll call this a day, shall we?"

Taking a step back, Mykaela shook her head. "Never."

Narissa's hand shot out, clutching around Mykaela's throat and squeezing. "You humans drive me crazy. Always feeling guilty. Always looking for the easy way out." With swift, angry motions, Narissa lifted Mykaela off her feet. As her words lashed out at Mykaela, Narissa moved the two of them across the clearing with ease, while Mykaela dangled, helpless and at the mercy of the witch's hand around her throat. Narissa shoved her straight into a tree, pressing until the bark dug into her back. "Where was your morality when you traded Dylan's soul to save your relationship?"

"I loved him," Mykaela choked out. "I was trying to save his life."

The slimy wet hand clutched the area just around her windpipe, making it difficult to breathe. "You were such a spoiled brat that couldn't stand to lose, so you let thousands suffer. I admired you for that, it took guts."

"That's not true!" Mykaela pushed at the witch, trying to buy her some breathing room, but the woman wouldn't move. "You tricked me. You preyed on my love for him."

Bringing her face close, her lips snarled in a dangerous look of disgust. "You ignorant fool. You know nothing of true love. True sacrifice! You got off easy. And yet, here you are, backing out on your bargain!" With a grunt, she tossed Mykaela across the clearing like she weighed nothing. The girl slammed into another tree and then smacked against the ground so hard she could've sworn she felt a bone crack. Waves of pain shot through her body.

In a blur of black smoke, Narissa appeared at her side. Lifting the shimmering skirt of her dress just above her knees, she knelt by Mykaela's stunned body. Her voice was a taunting whisper and each word was clipped and emphasized. "Give me the souls."

Her voice trembling, she whispered, "No."

Rearing her fist back, Narissa swung as hard as she could. When her knuckles collided with Mykaela's face, it slammed her head back into the earth, sending bone-shattering pain shooting through both sides of her head. She tasted blood and the world started to spin out of focus. While the girl was dizzied and stunned, Narissa stood and moved back a couple steps. Stretching her hand out, she spoke a low, dull chant and the black smoke started swirling around Mykaela. The wisps wound themselves around each arm and bound her legs together, then started to trail up toward her throat. She was completely enveloped by the shadowy wisps, and the more she struggled to break free, the darker the shadows became.

Mykaela spit out a mouthful of blood and looked up at Narissa through teary eyes. "What are you going to do?" Her voice a painful whisper as the shadows tried to strangle her. "Kill me? You'll never get the souls then."

A look of pure rage filled Narissa's pretty features. With a scream, she hit Mykaela with another burst of shadows. Wrenching her hand to the left, she jerked Mykaela to her feet with her magic and came closer. Bringing Mykaela's mangled, bloody face to hers she said, "You're right about one thing. I can't kill you, but I can make you suffer. I can make you *wish* you were dead." Her voice was a loud, booming echo in the stormy clearing, "Give me the souls or I swear to you, no one in your life will ever be safe again!"

Flinching, Mykaela struggled to get free. The hold around her throat seemed to loosen, allowing her some breathing room. "Why do you want them?"

Narissa froze, a raging look in her eyes. It was as if her concentration snapped, and the shadows that held Mykaela captive dissipated and vanished. Mykaela fell to her knees as the force disappeared. Slowly standing, she studied Narissa closely and knew she had hit a touchy subject. "Why are the souls so important? What do you need their power to do?"

"I'm not playing games!" She threw Mykaela again, not clear across the field this time, but far enough to hurt. "Give them to me now!"

"That's never going to happen," Mykaela said, for the last time.

Rage completely took over Narissa's eyes and she lunged for Mykaela, grabbing her by the throat again. Just when Mykaela was sure her windpipe would cave under the pressure, a burst of white light hurtled toward them out of nowhere. It smashed into Narissa and tossed her body all the way across the clearing.

Stunned and surprised, Mykaela sat up and searched for the source of her help. At the edge of the woods, she caught a flash of golden blond hair, but then it was gone. Hearing Narissa huff and stand, she turned back to the sea-witch in dread and terror. Her entire body was aching and she couldn't stand up, all she could do was wait for what happened next.

But the witch wasn't looking at Mykaela. Her gaze was fixed intently somewhere beyond her, toward the woods. Mykaela watched, curious and intrigued as to what the stare down was all about. Then, she slowly lowered her gaze to look at Mykaela and gave her a creepy, ominous smile. In a burst of dark smoke, Narissa vanished.

Mykaela turned, looking once again for whoever had saved her from Narissa, but there was no one in sight.

Alone in the clearing, Mykaela struggled to stand, but fell back down on the soft ground. Pain shot through her ribs, her throat hurt and her eyes felt swollen. Blood oozed from a cut on her lip and she was pretty sure she'd fractured her ankle.

Lying still, Mykaela took a minute, trying to calm herself down, trying to gather the strength to stand and pull herself out of these dark woods. But every part of her ached, and she could barely move.

She hated to admit she needed help—especially for something like physical pain—but right now she did. Grabbing handfuls of grass, she pulled herself up to the edge of the cliff, grunting in pain. By the time she reached the ledge, she was winded and tears streaked her cheeks.

Taking in a deep breath, she cried out into the night, "Dylan!"

She fell back against the ground, hoping her desperate plea would float across the sea to summon him in however the ritual worked.

A few seconds later, like magic, Dylan was running out of the woods and into the clearing, looking alarmed. Seeing her, his expression fell into one of pure concern and he dashed to her side.

Grabbing his hand, she smiled up at him, so thankful he'd heard her.

"Mykaela, what happened?" Dylan's frantic voice asked as he carefully tilted her face to look at it in the moonlight. "Who did this?"

"Narissa." She coughed as fresh blood leaked into her mouth from the cut on her cheek, and it felt like she had one on her lip, too. Clutching his hand tight, she managed to pull herself to a sitting position. But the motion made her dizzy and she swayed.

Reaching his arm out, he cradled it against her back, supporting her weight as he helped her to her feet. "Let me carry you," he said, his tone soft and worried.

"It's not that bad," she insisted. "I'm just a little…dazed, is all."

He rolled his eyes, reached out and scooped her into his arms.

She opened her mouth to protest, but as her body settled against his, she felt a warming comfort come over her. Easing her stubbornness away, making any protest die on her lips as she realized that Dylan really did make her feel complete, no matter what was happening around her.

Without another word, he zipped them out of the forest to safety.

Chapter Five

Sitting in the kitchen of the inn, Dylan dipped a white wash cloth into a bowl of warm water. In the chair next to his, Mykaela sat with her knees pulled up, her arms wrapped around them to brace her body against the pain. She was unbelievably sore, *everywhere*.

In the window's reflection, she'd seen her eyes bruising all different colors, with an abrasion thrown in on her cheek and lips. There were also fingerprints around her neck and it hurt to swallow.

"What were you thinking?" he whispered, shaking his head. Gently, he dabbed at the cut around her lip, washing away the blood. "Did you forget about the vision you had? She kills you, love. It could've happened tonight."

"Yeah," she said with a dismissive chuckle. "Thank God for my guardian angel. That's the second time I've been mysteriously saved."

"You got lucky," he said. "By the way, I'm going to be keeping twenty-four hour surveillance on you, at least until you decide to stop trying to get yourself killed."

"I wasn't —"

"Don't even try to deny it," he said. "First the other night on the beach and now this? You might have a death wish, but some of us like you better alive."

Looking at him, at the sincerity in his eyes, made her remember that there were people who still cared about her, even if it didn't seem like it. "I'm glad I summoned Narissa." She winced as Dylan brought the rag to the scrape on her cheekbone. "It made me realize something."

"What?"

"She isn't like the bad guys we've fought before. Her motivations aren't power and greed or even hate." Impatient, she grabbed Dylan's hand and pushed it away from her face so he would listen to her. "It's love. *That's* her driving force."

He narrowed his blue-green eyes in doubt. "She's an evil witch, Mykaela. I don't think the word *love* is in her vocabulary."

"But tonight, she said I didn't know anything about true love or sacrifice. And the way she said it...it was like..." consumed in the memory, she tried to sort it all out. "She said it the way I would say it to Jared...about you."

She saw his head tilt, his gaze shift to meet hers. Darting her gaze away from him, she continued to ramble. "And before, when I dreamt about our past life, I remember asking her if she'd ever loved someone so much she couldn't stand to live without them. She looked like she'd literally been slapped across the face—an ancient sea-witch, mind you—and it stunned her. It's all gotta mean something, right?"

"I know the bruises on your face mean you shouldn't go up against her alone."

Choosing to ignore him, she picked up an ice-pack he'd gotten from the freezer earlier and pressed it against her swollen eye. "It's good news," she insisted. "It gives her a weakness."

He leaned toward her a little more, curious. "You think love makes you weak?"

She gawked at him. Given everything they'd been through together, she thought they would be on the same page about this one. "Don't you?"

Shaking his head, he rinsed the rag out in the bowl of water, staining it red. "I think it makes her more dangerous. A person motivated by love will stop at nothing, pay any cost, hurt anyone." Using one hand, he gently tilted her chin so the left side of her profile faced him, and dabbed at the long scrape across her neck. "I pray Narissa's never known love at all."

She shuddered at his touch, at the soft, Irish-tinged whisper. "But if she has, maybe we could use it against her. She's definitely done that to us."

"That she has," he said with a bittersweet chuckle.

His gaze turned distant, and he dropped his hand. She studied him so closely it caused him to look up at her. "What?" he asked, a nervous smile tugging at his lips.

"I was just thinking...Narissa was surrounded by all of this black energy tonight. They always are—every creature. They have a color and a song that tells me what they are, but with you...there's nothing." Still studying him, she searched for any of those signs now. "There never has been."

"What do you think it means?"

She smiled at him, reaching out to take his hand. "I think it means you're definitely not evil." She gave his hand a squeeze. "And I'm really glad you were here for me tonight."

He leaned closer, a patient, but concerned look on his face. "Just promise me you won't do something that reckless again. Okay? I can't lose you again."

Before she could answer, the kitchen door opened and Jared came in, his arms full of paper-bagged groceries. He kicked the door shut behind him and dropped the bags on the counter. "I bought 'em, you put 'em away."

As he turned to her, taking in the scene—first aid on the table, the guy he didn't approve of nursing Mykaela's bruised and swollen face—his mouth dropped in his standard look of worry and disappointment. "What happened to you?"

Mykaela bit her lip, wincing slightly at the pain. It didn't help her case any.

Dylan turned to Jared. "She summoned Narissa."

"You did *what*?" he exclaimed, crossing the room to stand beside her. "How could you do something so stupid?"

"Hey," Dylan said, looking up at Jared. "She was only trying to help her mother."

"Yeah, and I thought I told you I never wanted to see your evil face around here again." Eyes flaring with anger, Jared took a step toward Dylan. "You're the reason she's in this mess."

"Jared, just calm down," Mykaela said.

"Calm down?" he repeated, chuckling. He turned, walking away from them, bringing a hand to his mouth. Turning, he started shouting, "Mom's in a *coma*, and every time I turn around you're trying to get yourself killed, and you expect me to just *calm down*? Just what? *Roll with it*?"

"And you expect me to just sit on the sidelines and I can't do that either," she snapped. "So I guess we're even."

"Here's what you're gonna do," he said, coming closer, his tone turning bossy and demanding, barking orders she was expected to follow. "You're going to stop falling for creatures, you're going to stop summoning evil witches. And you're going to start," he added, pointing to Dylan. "By getting this thing out of our lives."

Mykaela glared at him, pushing to her feet. "I know you're scared, but—"

"You're damn right I'm scared," he shouted. "Just last week this guy almost killed you! I come in and you're holding hands with him? It's so far beyond messed up. It's not even anywhere in the realm of acceptable."

Crossing her arms, she tried not to let his words bother her. But they made her feel an inch tall, ashamed for loving Dylan in spite of everything he'd done. "You don't know the whole story." Just for a moment, she considered telling him. But she had no proof that letting him in would help matters any.

"And I don't care." He grabbed Dylan by the arm and pushed him toward the door. "You get out." Turning to Mykaela, he pointed. "You go get some rest. You look like hell."

Dylan left without a word, but tossed one more look over his shoulder. Catching gazes with Mykaela, he gave her a slight nod, barely noticeable, but it was enough to tell her that he wouldn't let Jared keep him away.

Once they were alone, Jared turned back to the counter and began to put the groceries away. He roughly shoved a loaf into the breadbox, slammed a few cans of Spaghetti-O's into a cabinet.

"Jared," she started, but he went on slamming food onto shelves and paid no attention to her. "Come on. The cold shoulder's a little childish, don't you think?"

Without a word, he turned to the fridge and put away a gallon of milk.

"I know things are bad right now, but you can't shut me out like this," she said. "You can't expect me to be able to walk away."

"From what, exactly? From an unhealthy relationship? From your sick hobby? Which one can't you walk away from?"

"Sick hobby?" She shook her head. "What are you talking about?"

"You know what just…drives me crazy about this whole damn thing?" he asked, turning to her with one hand balled into a fist at his side. "You have the nerve to call yourself a hunter."

She tilted her head, waiting for him to continue, but the stinging pains of insult and wounded pride were already starting to set in.

"I've been training for this kind of thing since I was five," he said, his voice deep and offended. "Every weekend. Every summer vacation. Every spare minute of my life was spent preparing for the day the monsters would try to take over. You go on one revenge-driven killing spree after you get your heart broken and you think you have what it takes? You're kidding yourself."

"Whether I have what it takes or not, I have to try," she said. "This is my destiny."

"I don't believe in destiny," he spat, like he was fed up with the word. "There's no greater purpose, no grand design. Just chaos and evil and humans getting caught in the crossfire."

"Why do you think I'm doing this?" she asked. "I'm trying to stop them, once and for all."

"How Mykaela? Because you don't seem to be doing anything besides making deals with them and trying to get yourself killed."

"If you're so perfect and if you're such a good hunter, then how did two sirens slip past you undetected?" she shot back, crossing her arms and leveling an icy stare on him. "First Morrigan twisted you around her finger and you didn't even notice. And Kerr lived in one of the bedrooms upstairs for months and you were completely oblivious. But *I'm* the one who's kidding myself, right?"

He glared at her, the other hand balling into a fist.

"And if you're so much better than I am, what did you do to try to save mom? When Kerr was going to kill her, what did you do?" she asked, her voice cracking. "Because I'm the one who was willing to give up my entire life just to save her and you…you weren't even here!"

His jaw clenched and his eyes narrowed into an even colder glare.

"So where were you, Jared?" she asked, her voice half-taunt, half-plead, "While he was *killing* me, where were you?"

He stared at her, his expression so cold and angry, but with something softer brewing beneath the surface. Still, his lips stayed clamped shut, refusing to part and explain.

So many times lately, she felt like she was seeing him for the first time and she realized he might have secrets of his own. It was likely that he did, and her curiosity was piqued. Did this secret have something to do with his frequent absences? "Where were you?" she repeated.

He turned back to the grocery bags on the counter and reached inside, but found it empty. Wadding the bag up with one hand, he tossed it into the recycling bin across the room, landing it square in the center.

"Is this about the hunter's council?" she asked, watching carefully for a reaction. "What are they, anyway? Who are they? What do they do?"

"You're asking a lot of questions that no seventeen-year-old should know the answer to."

"It's like talking to a brick wall," she exclaimed, grabbing two handfuls of hair in her hands. It was so frustrating, the way he wouldn't give a straight answer. "You never really answer anything!"

"Then take the hint," he snapped back.

"Why can't you just work with me? We're on the same side, here."

But he just shook his head and went upstairs, once again leaving the issues between them unresolved.

***

Wearing a pair of dark sunglasses to cover the bruises from the fight with Narissa, Mykaela pulled her jeep into the parking lot of Brad's apartment complex. When she pulled up to the row in front of his apartment, she saw him standing at the side of his truck, getting ready to open the door.

Pulling up behind him, she called out the open window, "Bad time?"

He glanced over at her. "I got a minute for you."

"Great." She pulled up next to his truck, parked and hopped out. "Don't freak, okay?"

He raised an eyebrow. "Why would I..."

But his words trailed off as she pulled the sunglasses away from her face. "Before you say anything, let me point out that I'm fine. It doesn't even hurt. And I think I'll be perfectly healed in a day or two, so —"

"I thought you didn't bruise," he said slowly, still taking in the swollen and puffy discoloration.

"Normally, I don't," she said. "But we're not going up against just the sea-souls anymore. We're up against the thing that *created* them. I'd say the normal rules don't apply."

He looked like this worried him. "Are you okay?"

"Yeah." She lifted herself up to sit on the hood of her jeep. "I'm fine. But I could use your help."

"Looking like that," he said, leaning against the bumper, "how can I say no?"

Shaking her head, she fought a smile, trying to stay focused on what she'd come here to discuss. "I summoned

80

Narissa last night—by myself, which was stupid, because I realized she's so much more powerful than I'd thought. And she's scary, like in this…determined, unstoppable way. Not to mention she threw me around like a ragdoll. I can't go up against her by myself, and Jared definitely can't do it. But he's trying to push me out of the way, telling me to have nothing to do with any of it. If we all teamed up, we would stand a better chance."

"All teamed up? As in…"

She nodded in determination, her goal finally out in the open. "As in Dylan, you, and Jared working with me to stop Narissa once and for all. The problem is," she leveled a scolding look on him, "I can't get the three of you in the same room without someone threatening to kill the other."

He tilted his head, a reluctant look on his face.

"Last night Narissa told me that if I didn't give her the souls, no one in my life would be safe. And if everyone is always picking each other apart, you're easier to pick off. I don't want to see anyone else get hurt, so we have to work together. Safety in numbers."

"The problem is we don't trust Dylan."

She sighed, shaking her head. "You can trust that he wants Narissa destroyed as much as we do."

When he cut his gaze to meet hers, she saw his reluctance fade, and she knew she had him. "We'd be a team," he said. "Equal partners. I'm not 'taking orders' from anybody."

"Of course," she said, to appease his pride.

"Even if I was willing work with Dylan—and I'm not saying I am—Jared still poses a problem."

"I know. I was hoping you could talk to him." She looked up at him through her eyelashes. "Convincing him to work with Dylan and me won't be easy. You up for the challenge?"

He thought a minute. "I'll try, okay? I can't promise I'll do any good."

"If anyone could get through to him, it's you," she said. "You're practically brothers."

***

Shadows stretched out from the granite headstones as Brad walked along a path paved through the cemetery. Clouds partially covered the moon above, casting little light on the graveyard. Once upon a time, it would've spooked him, but not anymore. Now, he liked his cemeteries just like this. Quiet and desolate and dark, the type of place an ordinary human would cross the street to avoid at this hour. That way, he could talk to Charity in peace and quiet.

Earlier, he'd tried to talk to Jared like Mykaela had asked, but the conversation hadn't gone well. He'd only been a third of the way into his 'work with Dylan' speech before Jared shut him down and insisted they work together, like they always had. But Brad was feeling out of sorts and frustrated, so he took the night off from hunting. Instead, he'd come here, to the cemetery.

In his hand, he carried a small bouquet of wildflowers he'd picked from a field near the house where Charity had lived. He remembered a very distant time ago last year when he'd picked her a bouquet of these very flowers right before he'd sneak in her window at night. Her bright blue eyes had lit up with a smile and her blond hair had fallen over her shoulders as she'd dipped her nose into the brightly colored bunch of flowers to smell them. He closed his eyes a moment, allowing the picture of her to linger in his memory. If he concentrated hard enough, it was almost like she was walking right next to him.

He passed a large stone crypt on his way to his ex-girlfriend's grave, and for a second, he could've sworn he heard something move inside. *Just a rat*, he told himself as he moved on. Finally, he came to the slab of stone that marked Charity's grave and knelt down.

His heart felt heavier as he looked at the set of angel wings in the center of the headstone. Each one was engraved with part of a name. *Charity Cavanaugh*. He rested the flowers against the middle of the stone and then leaned his back against it and heaved a heavy, hearty sigh as his body relaxed.

"Everything just keeps getting crazier and crazier," he said, and even though he knew he was only talking to dirt and stone, he liked to believe she was listening somehow. "I'm going through all these...*changes* and Mykaela's being blackmailed pretty hard by some scary sea-witch. She and Jared are barely even speaking now, and they used to be so close."

He absent-mindedly plucked blades of grass as he spoke. "The two of them...they're all I have now. You know? Everyone I've ever loved is gone...and I just wish they would get along."

He heard a noise somewhere to his left and he looked over his shoulder, stretching to see above the headstone. A couple plots away, he could make out a dark figure wearing a hooded sweatshirt. Slowly, he stood to his feet and turned to face his stalker.

"Who's there?" he shouted, not liking the idea of being spied on, here of all places.

At the sound of his voice, the hooded person took off running. He bolted after them, weaving around headstones and dodging flower arrangements as they both raced through the cemetery, straight toward the old crypt. He finally caught up just outside the stone steps and latched on to the black cotton sleeve, and then clamped his hand down hard around a thin arm. With his free hand, he yanked down the dark hood.

The first thing he saw was the hair, golden blond and flying everywhere in the wind like some luminescent candle flame. Then he took in her hauntingly familiar blue eyes, widened with anticipation and braced with fear. Stunned, his gaze raked slowly over the familiar heart shape of her face, all the way down to her full and rosy lips, set in a straight, tough line. A sound of shock caught in his throat as he stared at someone he never thought he'd see again.

"Charity," he whispered, his voice husky with doubt. He held her tightly with a hand on each arm now, his fingers digging into the cotton fabric of her hoodie. Somewhere in his mind, he wondered if this was hurting her, but he was afraid to let go, in case something tried to steal her away again.

Finally, her lips curved upward in the subtlest of smiles. The sound of her voice sent chills all over his body when she whispered, "Hi, Brad."

Chapter Six

Standing in the darkened cemetery, Brad looked at Charity in disbelief and wonder. Hearing her soft, loving voice again sent a cold chill through his arms, spreading all over his skin. Overcome with joy, he pulled her against his chest. Winding his arms around her, he squeezed tight with gratitude and relief. As he closed his eyes to enjoy the feel of her body against his, he felt a few thankful tears slip down his cheeks. He heard her inhale a sharp breath, and then shudder it out again. When they parted, he saw she was shaking.

And finally, the questions began to surface. At first, he couldn't voice a single one, and then, "But...how...?"

She looked up, her mouth parting to answer. Then she broke away and fled into the crypt, slamming the heavy stone door shut behind her.

She vanished from his sight so fast it made his heart leap into his throat. "Wait," he cried. He ran after her, pushing open the door. He walked into the dark, cold crypt and searched for a sign of her, but he could see only shadows. They stretched out from every corner toward the center of the room.

"Charity," he called, but was only answered by his own voice echoing back at him. Then, he started to think it was all some kind of hallucination, or a siren playing a trick on him. These days, he couldn't even trust his own mind. Maybe this…transition, as Brooke had called it, was messing with his head and making him see things that weren't there. But then, maybe this was entirely real, too. "Charity, come out!"

He stood at the entrance to the crypt, staring into the shadows and searching for any sign of Charity. Listening carefully, he could hear the soft, shallow sounds of her breathing and hope sparked inside him again. "You're really here, aren't you?" he asked, taking a step inside. "I've seen crazier things," he said, mostly to himself, as if to justify his hope.

Then she stepped out of the shadows. As his eyes adjusted, he could see she still looked very much the same as she always had. She stood just over five feet tall and had soft hair and soft features that would make anybody think she was a pushover. But there was something different about her, too. It took him a minute, but he finally placed it. That joy, the warmth that had always shone like a light behind her eyes seemed to be missing. Instead, there was something much colder about her and he couldn't place it. Still, he stared in awe, relieved to see her again.

"It's really you," he whispered. "How can this…?"

"It's like you said," she said, and her voice sounded hoarse and stiff, like it hadn't been used much in a while. "Crazier things have happened."

"How long have you been back?" he asked.

But she only shook her head, keeping her lips clamped tight.

Confusion began to overwhelm him as more questions piled on top of each other. Where had she been all this time? Why hadn't she come to see him? Why was she just standing there right now, acting like she didn't love him anymore? "It doesn't matter," he said as he realized it. Stretching his arm out, he held his hand out for Charity. "Let's just get out of here. We can—"

"Brad..." she hesitated with her mouth partway open as she tried to find words. "I can't."

"Can't?" he asked, squinting at her. He came closer, until there was only about an arms-length between them. "Can't what?"

She stared at his outstretched hand in longing before she finally said, "I can't go with you, and I can't explain."

This only confused him more. "You've been through a lot," he said, trying to reason with her. "It's normal that you'd be afraid to go back into the world again—" His digital watched beeped at the top of the hour and Charity jumped.

Looking down at his wrist, her eyes were wide with fear again. "What time is it?" she asked, but before he could answer, she grabbed his arm and looked for herself. Then with in a soft, fearful whisper, "It's midnight."

He barely heard her, too distracted by the feel of her fingertips against his skin. It was such a calming sensation, her touch. But then she dropped his hand, raising a stern gaze to meet his. "You have to go."

"What?"

Taking him by the arms, she ushered him toward the crypt door. "You have to go, now."

"Go?" he exclaimed. "Why?"

"Please, Brad," her voice was desperate as she maneuvered both of them toward the door. "Just trust me and do what I'm asking you to do."

He put his hand against the edge of the door to keep himself from being pushed out. When he really stood his ground, she couldn't do much to move him. "What's going on?" he demanded. "I just got you back; I'm never letting you out of my sight again."

She gave a frantic look around the crypt before she finally turned to him, her expression full of resolve. "Okay, okay." Sounding a little breathless, she cupped his face in her hands. "Come back tomorrow at sunset and I'll answer all your questions, okay? But right now, you have to *leave*."

"Do you promise me you'll still be here?" he asked, his eyes searching hers for answers.

"I promise." Stretching up on her toes, she planted a kiss on his cheek. Then she gave him one last shove out of the crypt. The door slammed shut, even though no one had touched it. Not knowing what to think, Brad lingered outside the crypt, looking up at it. His mind swirled with confused thoughts and rationalities as he staggered out of the graveyard that night. But no matter how confused he was, or how many questions were unanswered, nothing could trump the joy he felt. Charity was back, and now the human in him had something to fight for.

***

When Mykaela woke the next morning, the house was empty. There was a note of the fridge from Jared.

Went to work. GO TO SCHOOL!

Rolling her eyes, she tossed the note down on the counter and headed back upstairs to get dressed. On her way to school, she decided she'd stop by Dylan's warehouse. She needed to ask him to find out anything he could on whoever had saved her from Narissa. Whoever it'd been, they'd made Narissa flee and for that, she wanted to be on their side.

As she pulled up outside the warehouse, the shrill pitch of a female scream ripped through the morning, causing Mykaela's heart to jump in surprise. On reflex, she jumped out of her Jeep and pulled out her weapon.

She crept up to one of the dirty windows and peeked inside. Through a thick layer of dust, Mykaela could see flashes of purple. Her eyes focusing, she detected Rachel bound to a chair and Dylan in the middle of shooting one very long stream of power at her.

She didn't even stop to think. Rushing in, she sped up to Dylan and grabbed his arm, cutting off the power flow. Her eyes studying him, searching for signs of a monster, she demanded, "What are you doing?"

The sounds of Rachel's scream cut off, leaving her shuddering in the aftermath.

"Mykaela, I know how this looks—" Looking at her, his eyes were wide in surprise and guilt.

Do you?" she asked, stepping away from him. "Because it looks like you're torturing my friend."

Turning from him, she looked over at Rachel. Bound to the chair by dancing electrical currents, she was wounded and covered in burns and bruises. Her heart filling with sympathy and confusion, she walked over to Rachel.

"Mykaela, she's not that teenager you used to know," his voice was desperate with warning, "She's a monster."

She shot him a glare. "That's what they say about you." Turning her attention to Rachel, she asked, "Are you okay?"

Rachel looked at Dylan with a glare. "Your boyfriend's gone off the deep end," she said. "He's kept me locked in here since the night Kerr died."

Her mouth dropping, Mykaela turned a look of betrayal on Dylan. "How could you?"

"She was working with him," he said. "She was playing us the entire time."

"He's crazy," Rachel said. "Mykaela, I'd never betray you."

Looking into Rachel's eyes, Mykaela didn't see a monster. She saw a friend in need, someone she had let down. Reaching out, Mykaela touched the electric current binding Rachel to the chair, but it zapped her. She leveled her gaze on Dylan. "Let her go."

"That would be a mistake, love."

"Now, Dylan!"

He rushed forward, grabbing her shoulders. "You're looking at this with your human eyes. Just look with your powers, okay?" His fingers digging into her skin, he pleaded with her, "Just *look*. Do you see anything around me? Any signs this was an act of evil? Look at me and look at her. Which one of us is evil?"

Even though he begged her, she refused to try. She was too afraid she would finally see his echoes, the stains of his evil nature. So she only narrowed her eyes into a glare and repeated, "Let her go."

Dropping his hands to his sides, he shook his head in disappointed. "Just once," he whispered, "I wish you would trust me." Snapping his fingers, he made the ropes around Rachel's wrists disappear.

Finally released from her magical hold, Rachel stood, but wavered on her feet. Weakened, she fell against Mykaela for balance. Wrapping an arm around Rachel's waist, she supported her weight and helped the girl stand.

Leaving Dylan behind, Mykaela drove Rachel back to the inn. When she entered the back door, she found Jared and Brad in the kitchen, talking. Rachel was limping and leaned against Mykaela as they entered the kitchen.

"What happened?" Jared asked, standing from the table.

"Wait a second." Brad reached out and grabbed Jared's arm. "She was working with Kerr. Mykaela why are you helping her?"

Ignoring both of them, she guided Rachel to a chair and gave her a bottle of water. The thirsty sea-creature drank it in a split second, but Mykaela pretended not to notice. She knew the odds that Rachel wasn't who she used be but she couldn't help but try. "Dylan was torturing her," she said. "He was—"

Suddenly, Brad reached out and grabbed Mykaela's arm, yanking her away from Rachel to stand by him and Jared.

She didn't have time to question, before Jared stepped up. "Why?"

"What?" Mykaela tried to shrug out of Brad's hold, but he was stronger than usual.

"Why was he torturing her?" Jared asked. "Did she know something?"

Rachel shifted nervously in her seat as the hunter approached her. Though wounded and obviously weakened, Rachel still had an almost rabid look in her eye that was intimidating.

"This is crazy," Mykaela said, "If she was on their side, she would've killed me while we were alone."

"Not necessarily." Keeping his gaze on Rachel, he taunted, "You're too weak to take on Mykaela, aren't you? How long's it been since you fed?"

Rachel looked up at Jared, looking helpless. "Look, I'm not—"

"Not a monster?" he asked. "Yeah, I've heard that one before."

Without warning, Rachel flew at Jared, her hand outstretched, trying to drain his soul, with a ravenous and hungry look. Adrenaline kicking in, Mykaela tried to go help, but Brad grabbed her arm again. "Just watch," he whispered.

Without even moving or flinching, Jared grabbed Rachel's arm and twisted it behind her back, then gave her a shove. Thrown off balance, Rachel stumbled through the open doors and into the dining room. Moving with the speed and stealth of a ninja, Jared came up behind her and with a solid punch, knocked her into the middle of a circle of fulgurate chunks. As Jared pulled the last chunk out of his pocket and tossed it into place, Rachel's presence activated the trap. Pink bolts of power shot up all around her, locking her in a magical cage.

Stunned, Mykaela tried to speak. "I…I've never seen you fight before," she said.

Straightening out his shirt, he glanced up at her. "I've been doing this a lot longer than you."

She stepped up and eyed Rachel in the cage. "She was really just playing me the whole time?"

Rachel glared at Mykaela, a look of pure hatred in her eyes. Her voice echoed off the magical walls surrounding her. "For someone with psychic vision, you're surprisingly blind."

"Tell us what you know," Jared said, crossing his arms. "And maybe we'll toss you a little snack."

Rachel laughed at him. "I just spent weeks being tortured by a sea king," she said. "You can't break me."

"Oh please," Brad exclaimed. "He was king for a whole summer. We've been hunters for years."

But Rachel said nothing.

"Dylan's going to tell me anyway," Mykaela said. "Either way you're dead."

"That's right," Jared said. "You've got nothing to lose."

"But you do," Rachel said, her eyes on Mykaela. "And you're going to lose it all."

Mykaela felt her body stiffen in dread.

"You're going to get exactly what you deserve," Rachel said menacingly.

Her heart started pounding as she realized Rachel knew the secret of her past life, and now she was in the same room as Brad and Jared. She could blow the lid off this whole thing, right now.

Rachel opened her mouth to speak, but a knock at the door made them all freeze.

Mykaela edged over, peeking through the lobby at the front door. Through the glass window, she could see a woman standing outside with a briefcase.

"It's probably just a guest," Jared said, stepping up and nudging Mykaela toward the door. "Go get rid of her."

"Why me?" Mykaela asked as Jared shoved her out into the lobby.

He grabbed one of the doors and closed it, then grabbed the other one. "We voted and you lost. Now go."

With that, he shut her in the lobby. Seeing her through the door, the woman waved and smiled.

Mykaela tried to smile politely as she opened the door just wide enough to say, "We're closed for renovations, but there's a motel downtown—"

"Oh," the woman chuckled lightly. "I'm not a tourist."

She shifted to lean against the doorframe. "Then who are you?"

"My name's Jill," she said. "I'm from Social Services."

Chapter Seven

Mykaela froze, looking at the woman with a feeling of dread she couldn't get rid of. She'd never dealt with social services before, but if a social worker was here, she knew it could not mean anything good.

The woman was tall and slender, with her brown hair pulled into a neat and tidy bun. "Aren't you supposed to be at school?"

Mykaela suddenly realized why the woman was standing on her porch. "Yeah," she said with a shaky laugh, "I'm just running late, that's all."

"I see." She had a sympathetic smile that made Mykaela feel uneasy. "Is your brother home?"

"No," she said quickly. Too quickly, she realized. She needed to play it cool, and act like nothing was wrong. Most importantly, she needed to act like she didn't have a teenage girl locked in a magical cage just ten feet away. "Maybe you should come back later."

The woman ignored this. "We've heard about what's happened to your mother, and we'd like to help."

"Help?" Mykaela repeated nervously.

The woman opened her mouth to answer, but she was interrupted by the sounds of a crash from the dining room. Hearing the noise, she gave Mykaela a questioning look.

A hideous nervous laugh escaped Mykaela's lips as she stepped out onto the porch and closed the door behind her. "Like I said," she said, "Renovations."

"I see," she repeated, and this made Mykaela nervous. What did she see, exactly?

Folding her hands together, she looked Mykaela up and down. "Is that why you haven't been to school since your mother was hospitalized?"

"I know I shouldn't skip school," she said, crossing her arms defensively. Then she quickly added, "In fact, Jared's been on my case about it every day. But with everything going on with Mom, I...I just can't concentrate."

She nodded knowingly. "You've been through a lot. That's why I think your family could use some extra support right now. And your brother certainly has his hands full," she said. "Is there another relative you could stay with? Someone a little older?"

"No," she said, feeling the desperation in her voice. "There's only Jared."

That's why you can't take me away, she wanted to add, but knew it wouldn't help her case any.

Jill nodded again and pulled a business card out of her pocket. "Have your brother call me and we'll see what we can do."

Reluctantly, Mykaela took the business card. "We're fine," she said, as the woman started toward the steps. "Really....this whole thing is unnecessary."

"Just tell Jared to call me." With that, she went down the steps.

Mykaela went back inside the house. As she entered the dining room, she saw a large puddle of water in the middle of the trap. Her eyes widening, she looked up to Jared, who was putting his knife away. There was a coldness in his eyes that looked new, much different than the light-hearted party animal he'd been last summer. It reminded her of the way sadness lingered around their family and their lives like a fog, sometimes you couldn't even see through it. He didn't seem bothered by the fact he'd just killed a former-friend of hers, a girl he'd passed in the hallway by their bedrooms on more than one occasion. To Jared, it was just business.

It seemed ironic that just a few weeks ago, he'd been swearing he would never be a hunter again. And now, he was so eager to take her place. The saddest part was that they were all better off with Rachel in that puddle. And with that almost animalistic look in his eye — the look of a true hunter — she really didn't want to be the one to deliver that business card. "Really?" Mykaela asked, trying to stall. "You couldn't have waited five minutes?"

"No reason you needed to see it," he said. He grabbed a towel and dropped it into the puddle of water. "Who was at the door?"

She laughed a little, but instead of breaking the ice, the sound fell flat and awkward. Crossing her arms, she reluctantly admitted, "A social worker."

He glanced up at her. "What?"

Next to him, Brad looked concerned, but stayed respectfully silent.

"I think…" she hesitated, biting her lip a little. "I think the school might've called them."

"Because you've been skipping?" he asked, but she could tell it wasn't really a question. More like a disappointed statement, or an accusation. "That's great, Mykaela. Just great."

"Would you give me a break?" she exclaimed, cringing at the thought of yet another argument with him. "That puddle of water right there used to be one of my closest friends and that's all that's left of her!"

It was all her fault. Rachel had been cursed in the same way Dylan had, and all because of her. She pulled out Jill's business card and held it out to Jared, hoping he'd take it and go away. "I never wanted any of this to happen."

"But it did." He swiped the card from her hand. "And it's not like I can tell them you have to skip school because you're destined to fight sirens and sea witches. So what do you suggest I tell them, Mykaela? Come on. You seem to have all the answers lately."

He waited, like a total jackass, knowing she had no answer. Finally, he said, "I don't care what comes up, you're putting in a full day of school tomorrow."

Shaking his head, he walked past her, into the kitchen.

Brad looked at her a second, as if deciding if he should say something. "Are...are you..."

"I'm fine," she said, keeping her gaze away from his. Her gaze focused on the towel in the floor, soaking up the puddle of water that used to be Rachel's body. Remembering how just last year, she and Rachel binged on cake after Charity's funeral, and then the time before that when the three of them had modeled homecoming dresses in this very room. "I just need some air."

Turning, she headed out the front door, grabbing her keys.

"Don't do that," he said, following her out onto the porch. "You don't have to be so tough."

"Yes, I do," she said, whirling to face him. "With my life, and the things that happen, if I'm not tough, I'll get torn apart."

His eyes searched over her, drinking her in. His expression marked with compassion yet again, he reached out pressed his palm against her cheek. "Believe me," he whispered, his voice soft. "I get it."

She remembered all the people Brad had lost, and all the death he'd seen. Not knowing what to say, she turned and went back to her Jeep. Even with all the fuss about school, she couldn't find the strength in her to go. All she wanted to do was cry.

So she went to the one person she knew would understand, the one person who loved her no matter what. She drove back to Dylan's warehouse.

He was outside when she pulled up, just sitting in the sun. Hopping out of her car, she walked up to him. "I'm an idiot."

His eyes were inquisitive as he looked at her. She knew he could tell that something bad had happened by the concern on his face.

"I just took that rabid monster who used to be friend into my house full of hunters," she said, plopping down to sit beside Dylan. "Guess what happened."

"They killed her," he said, his eyes lingering on hers in sympathy.

She nodded, resting her elbows on her knees.

"I'm sorry, love," he said.

"I know all you guys see is a girl who was working with Kerr," she said, shaking her head gently. "You didn't know her like I did. She was the one who taught me how to do a cartwheel and the splits. She's the one who encouraged me to go for you when I thought it was bad timing."

He wrapped his arm around her shoulders, and suddenly, Mykaela didn't feel like she needed to be so strong. Suddenly, she knew it was alright to cry over this.

"She was my friend," she whispered, tears stinging her throat. "And she was cursed by the spell I cast. *That's* what turned her into the monster."

"Mykaela…" he said softly, but he knew better than to tell her this wasn't her fault. "She knew about the curse. She chose to jump, rather than die at Morrigan's hands. And she knew exactly what it would do to her."

"If I'd known she did that, I could've helped her. She hadn't been around humans since she died," she said, "Maybe if she'd been able to blend in, like you did, she would've been okay. We could've taught her how."

"But Kerr found her first," he said. "And not everyone holds onto their heart when they turn. The only reason I did was because I loved you so much. If Rachel didn't have anything like that here to hold on to, she would've easily been seduced by the evil. This was just a terrible tragedy, Mykaela."

"I know," she whispered, leaning her head against his shoulder. "I just wish I could've helped her. It doesn't seem like I can help anybody anymore."

***

It took every bit of Brad's strength not to go right back to the cemetery. All night long, he fought the urge to go check on Charity every five minutes. All throughout the day, while he was working with Jared or talking to Mykaela, he wanted to blurt out what he'd discovered, but he knew he couldn't do that yet. Not until he had answers to the questions everyone would undoubtedly ask.

He did exactly as she'd requested and didn't murmur a word about her mysterious reappearance. Though it was absolute torture, he waited until sunset to return to the cemetery. This time, he brought a backpack full of supplies and carried it over one shoulder as he headed into the graveyard.

He walked straight to the crypt, only pausing to look over his shoulder and take in his surroundings. The heavy door gave a loud creak as it opened. Stepping inside, he took a slow look around. Like before, he saw nothing at first. With the fading daylight behind him, he could only make out nameplates arranged in rows all along the walls, and it occurred to him that he was surrounded by dead bodies.

He wondered, not for the first time, why Charity would choose to stay in a place like this. "Hey," he said cautiously, then listened for any noise.

"You came back." Charity's voice echoed around him right before she stepped out of one of the shadows to the far right. Today, she was wearing a white sweater and a pair of blue jeans, and her blond hair was fixed up in some sort of twist. She looked much more like the girl he'd remembered and loved so much.

"Of course I came back." He stepped up, shutting the door behind them. He closed them off in the darkness of the crypt, then searched through his backpack for the lantern he'd brought. Once the small light lit up the space around it, he could see her more clearly.

"Did you..." she hesitated, looking at him with skeptical eyes. "Did you tell anyone?"

He shook his head. "No."

Her lips spread in a warm, relieved smile. "I knew you wouldn't."

Turning, she led him over to the corner, where he saw an open door hidden in the floor of the crypt, leading to a downward sloping staircase. He followed her down the steps to a large room below the crypt. The entire room was bathed in the bright yellow glow of old-fashioned torches.

On the farthest wall, he saw a small cot made up with blankets and throw pillows. To his right, there was a large table stacked with books. Shelves lined the rest of the room. Though more books were on them, they were also stocked with little vials and trinkets.

"Wow," he said, taking an observatory look around the room. "This is where you've been staying?"

"I know. It's dark and creepy and it has a funny smell." She wrinkled her nose as she looked around the room. "Last year my skin would've crawled at the sight and there would've been no way you would've gotten me down those stairs."

"That's true." He chuckled with her, and it felt so good. When the laughter died down, he gave her a long, studying look of admiration. "You're so different," he said. When she gave him a cautious glance, he added, "In a good way."

He set the lantern and his backpack down on the table. "So you've just been…hiding here?" he asked. "For how long?"

"Since the beach massacre," she said. "A lot of souls crossed over that night. During the chaos, I slipped through."

He nodded, studying her in curiosity and intrigue. "Can anybody do that?"

"Do we have to talk about that?" she asked, turning to him. "I'm back, isn't that what really matters?"

She looked at him, her expression hopeful and wary. "You're right," he said, reaching out to take her shoulders. "That's all that matters."

He took a moment to enjoy the feel of her shoulders in his hands, her flesh-and-blood body right in front of him. Her indigo-blue eyes softened as she looked at him, reminding him just how much they'd cared about each other. And though there were so many things he didn't know; like how and why this happened and what price Charity had to pay, he didn't let himself ask. It was enough to just be here with her.

"I brought you something," he said. Still leaned against the table, he broke one hand away from her and used it to open the flap on his backpack. Reaching inside, he pulled out a can of Pepsi.

Her eyes lit up like the blue can was a diamond ring. With a bright, thankful smile she took the soda from him and cracked it open. She took a small, tentative sip, then tilted her head back and gulped. When she finally lowered the can, she took a deep breath and started laughing.

"God, that tastes good," she said.

"Good, cuz there's more where that came from."

A few minutes later, they were outside, enjoying the quiet, peaceful night. Brad spread a blanket down on the grass outside the crypt. They'd chosen the side that faced the cemetery, so the crypt hid them from the town's view. The sun had set by now and the night sky pitched the cemetery into darkness.

Brad and Charity nestled underneath the great shadow of the building and began to set out their picnic. He'd brought cheeseburgers, fries and cheesecake all fresh from the diner. He also brought a six pack of Pepsi. He set the lantern on the far corner of the blanket for light.

"So, you don't want to talk about how this happened," he began, absently dipping a fry into a glob of ketchup. "But what about why you didn't come find me? Or Mykaela?"

By the time he finally spit out the question, she had a mouthful of food and she took her time swallowing, which made him think she didn't want to give any answers on that subject, either. She picked up her soda can and took a long drink.

"You're stalling," he said, giving her a small, reassuring grin. "What's going on, Char?"

Her voice was quiet and meek, reminding him a small, scared child. "I used to think Mykaela was my friend, but she's not. She left me to die, Brad." Her gaze held his, and he could see tears shine in her eyes. "Do you have any idea what it was like...to *drown*?"

He watched her go silent again, watched a look of tortured pain cross her face, and he realized how horrible it must've been.

"The water was so cold, freezing cold. And it was surrounding us from every side," she said, her voice growing scared and emotional. "You try to fight, but with each desperate, useless motion, you dig your own grave. You can see the surface, but you can't reach it, and the whole time you know that if you could just break your face above water, you can buy yourself a few extra moments."

The picture she painted made his heart swell with pity for her, and he would've done anything to help, but what could he do? Even though it didn't seem like enough, he slipped his arm around her shoulder and squeezed her body against his.

"I knew I was coming up on my last breaths," she said, keeping her head tilted down as she told her story. "I could see Mykaela trying to reach me, but she was getting weaker and weaker. Then suddenly someone blurred right past me, like I wasn't even there. He went straight for Mykaela and whisked her away." Her voice cracked and she stood, putting some space between them. She lingered at the edge of the blanket with her back to him, looking out at the darkened graveyard. "I didn't want to die, Brad. But he didn't save *me*. He saved *her*."

"Charity…" He stood, reaching out to place his hand on her shoulder.

She turned to him, taking his hand. "Walk with me," she said with a gentle tug. Together, they began to stroll down the path toward Charity's headstone.

"When I came back," she said, speaking the words slowly as if this was the abridged version of the story, "I didn't have anything to do but walk the cemetery. And then I found this."

They passed Charity's grave and stopped at the one beside it. Brad remembered who was buried there and felt the compassion fill him.

"My mom's dead," she said, her voice cracking with tears. "And my best friend betrayed me." Turning to Brad, she looked up at him. "You're all I have now."

He wrapped his arms around her and pulled her tight against his chest. "And I'm right here," he whispered, pressing his lips to the top of her head. "I'm not going anywhere."

She hugged him back, holding on as tight as she could. But when his watch beeped, she quickly pulled away. Looking up at him, she whispered, "It's midnight, isn't it?"

He checked his watch, then looked up at her with suspicion. He remembered last night, at the top of the midnight hour, she'd forced him to leave the crypt in a panic. "What happens at midnight?"

"You have to leave." Her eyes looked damp.

His eyes narrowed. "Why?"

She started walking back toward the crypt, but he grabbed her arm and turned to face her. "Charity, what's going on?"

"I can't tell you," she said.

"You won't leave this cemetery," he said, clinging to her arm. "And you make me leave every time the clock strikes twelve like some twisted fairy tale. Tell me what's going on."

Her eyes were wide and fearful as she looked around the cemetery, trying to pull from his grasp. "I told you I can't explain."

"Is someone doing this to you?" he asked. "If you're afraid of someone, I can help."

"It's not like that," she said. "Just come back tomorrow morning, okay?"

"No," he said, "I'm not leaving you."

"You have to." She grabbed his arms, looking deep into his eyes. "I know this is crazy, believe me. I would tell you everything if I could, but you have to trust me when I tell you that I just can't right now. And right now, you need to *leave*."

He started to protest, but she stretched up and kissed him. Wrapping her arms around his neck, she pressed her body against his and let the kiss deepen. When she pulled her lips away, she whispered, "Please, Brad. Just come back in the morning."

She seemed so desperate and distressed and he wanted to make her happy. So he nodded and let her slip away. She went to the crypt and shut the door behind her, but he didn't leave the cemetery.

He headed back over to the picnic and packed everything back up. Then he sat down beside the crypt and waited. But all through the night, no one else came to the cemetery. And when the sun finally started to peek over the trees, the tomb opened once again. Charity came out and gave a smile at the sunrise. "I forgot how beautiful those are."

Brad stood from his place beside the crypt and walked over to Charity. He looked her up and down, feeling even more confused. "You're okay," he said.

She looked at him, her eyes hiding something, and nodded. "You never left, did you?"

"I thought you were in danger," he said. "I couldn't..."

Reaching out, she took his hand and led them inside the crypt again. "It's okay now," she said. "Now I can tell you everything."

Chapter Eight

The next morning, Mykaela did as Jared insisted and went to school. In the two weeks she'd been absent, someone had taken her favorite desk in homeroom and Mr. Evans had assigned three books in English class. Even though at one time she'd cared very much about grades and academic performance, now she couldn't find it in her to care about any of it.

The whole time she was there, all she could think about was her mother. She was lying in a hospital bed, as she had been for the last two weeks, and Mykaela had no idea if she would ever wake up. Even if she could find a way to kill Narissa, how did she know that would make the spell on her mother wear off? What if she surrendered the souls via mind control, like she'd seen in her vision? Then she would lose her leverage, condemn numerous souls and practically sign her mother's death certificate all at once.

There was so much to think about and so much to worry about, and by the time she arrived home, her body was aching to hit something. She called Brad to see if she could come over and use his punching bag, like she always did when she had a bad day or needed to vent. But he didn't answer, so she decided to use the one in Jared's room instead.

She spent the better part of the afternoon using his exorcise equipment. The steady, vigorous movements of lifting weights helped to focus her frustration, which she later channeled on the freestanding punching bag.

She wasn't aware Jared had come home until she heard his voice ask, "Bad day?"

Turning in mid-punch, she saw him standing in the doorway looking in on her. Still wearing the earth-toned deputy uniform, he leaned against the frame and watched her with a look of curiosity and amusement.

Without dropping her arms from the punching position, she shrugged her shoulders and then turned back to the punching bag. "I did what you wanted," she said, giving the bag a solid punch. "Normally I do this at Brad's, but he's been avoiding me for a while now."

"You can use the equipment whenever you want." Walking into the room, he stood in front of the dresser and placed his badge and gun on it. "But don't you have boatloads of homework you should be doing?"

"Don't push it," she said, shooting him an annoyed look. "I have plans tonight and it doesn't include pencil and paper."

"I'm gonna take a shot in the dark here and guess that your plans do include hunting."

She rolled her shoulders to loosen them up, but whenever she was around Jared, her body filled with tension and she knew no amount of punching would help. "Dylan's going with me," she said, then realizing it didn't help she immediately began to argue her case. "So I won't be alone, and say what you want about him, he wouldn't let anything happen to me."

"Unless his batteries run low," Jared said as he unbuttoned the khaki colored shirt and shed it, revealing the black cotton A-tank underneath. His voice was tinged with sarcasm. "With the essence of his soulmate being a quick, powerful fix, well, what could go wrong?"

"We both agreed not to do that again," she said, fighting her annoyance. "It's too risky."

"Good."

She left it at that and headed out to meet Dylan. Together, they patrolled along the beach, but didn't find anything. This went on for the next two weeks. She played her part for Jared and put in the work at school, and at night she and Dylan would search the town for Narissa's followers. But it seemed like every supernatural creature had fled the town or found a really good hiding spot. Every time she tried to use her powers to sense their evil trails, she saw so much evil all over town that it was hard to keep track of which stains were fresh and which were old. It was as if the whole town was marked with it.

"I just can't wait until I put this whole school stuff behind me," Mykaela was saying to Dylan as they walked along the town square. Sirens liked to frequent bars for victims, so they stayed close to the saloon on most patrols. "It doesn't seem as important as it used to. If it weren't for Jared, I would've dropped out already."

"I always pictured you going to college," Dylan said.

She shook her head. "If things go the way they did in my vision, I won't live to see graduation."

"Is that vision still bothering you?" he asked, angling to face her as they walked down the sidewalk together.

"I saw my own death," she said, "and afterlife. I still have nightmares about it."

"You've managed to prevent your visions before, haven't you?"

She thought a minute. Sure she had, when she was dealing with some kind of minion or lackey. But this was Narissa. She didn't want him to worry or accuse her of having a death wish, so she thought it was best to steer their conversation away from the vision. "I haven't had a vision since that night, either," she said. "And one would really come in handy right now."

"So would the Mirror of Truth," Dylan said, "but Narissa made sure we wouldn't have access to that."

"You don't think she's found some way to block the visions, do you?" she asked as the thought suddenly occurred to her.

He shrugged. "It's more likely she's cloaked her actions with some kind of spell."

"Sounds like something she would do," she reasoned.

Up ahead, the cemetery came into view. She could see the tall, wrought iron gates that guarded a field full of granite headstones. But there was something different about the graveyard tonight. Above the headstones, a hazy white mist lingered. It was thick like a fog, but on the energetic level.

"Do you see that?" Mykaela asked, just to make sure. She'd never seen a *white* stain before.

"No," Dylan said, stepping up beside her. "What do you see?"

"Echoes," she said. She pulled out her weapon and they headed toward the cemetery. He walked alongside her, allowing her psychic senses to lead the way. Following the trails of white mist, she walked along the stone path in the cemetery. The color led her to the door of a crypt. At the top, above the large stone door, was written the word *"Cavanaugh."*

That was Charity's last name, she remembered, but it was also the last name of many people in town. Half the people in this cemetery were from the Cavanaugh line. "It's coming from in here," she said.

Dylan stepped up and pushed open the door. She followed him into the dark, creepy stone room. Inside, she couldn't make out anything but that white haze against the black shadows.

"It looks empty," she said, "but the echoes are everywhere."

But Dylan's eyes were fixed on the far corner of the room. "Over there," he said, nodding slightly in that direction. "Two people."

She saw something in the shadows move. "Come out," she warned, just once, before she charged in to find out who was hiding.

There was a tense moment of silence, and then one of the figures moved forward. Brad stepped into the small square of moonlight coming through the open door behind them. Mykaela looked around the tomb in surprise. "Brad?" she asked, lowering her weapon a little. "What are you doing here?"

"Mykaela, you might want to brace yourself."

Just the suggestion was enough to make her body immediately go tense. "What?" she asked.

He waved to the corner, motioning for someone to come out. A girl stepped out of the shadows. She was petite and thin, around Mykaela's age. She had the heart shaped face and rosy cheeks of Charity's, but that was impossible. Charity was dead and had been for a long time. She fell back a step, stunned by the impact of seeing that face again. That girl, standing in front of her, had once been her best friend.

Rage filled Mykaela like a giant tidal wave. She leapt, tackling the girl and pinning her to the cold granite floor. Charity flailed her arms in surprise as Mykaela fought to keep her pinned to the floor. "You're wearing her face," she shouted, fuming as she positioned her sword at the girl's throat. "What is this? Another one of Narissa's mind games?"

"Mykaela, stop!" Brad grabbed her by the waist and surprised her when he succeeded in pulling her away from whoever had the audacity to pretend to be her fallen friend.

"Let me go," she said, fighting against his hold. Dylan whooshed up to them, wedging his body between the two of them in an instant. He gave Brad a warning look and he stepped back, turning to kneel beside Charity.

Helping her sit up, he looked up at the two of them. "It's *really* her."

Chapter Nine

Standing perfectly still, sure she was hallucinating, Mykaela lingered against one wall of the crypt, staring at the blond girl in awe and disbelief. The friend she'd thought was dead for almost a year was now huddled in Brad's arms. She looked every bit as vulnerable and scared as the day she died, and it stirred up all of those horribly vivid memories of nearly drowning. If it hadn't been for that expression — the same one she'd seen while they were both drowning in the ocean together — Mykaela wouldn't have believed it was really her.

But, in spite of all the laws of physics and nature, her friend was alive again. Traumatized, frightened, but *breathing*. She looked like an average teenage girl in a denim skirt, knee-boots and a white blouse, with her long blond hair trailing around her head in some kind of intricate braid. But how was this *possible*? How had her friend escaped the clutches of death, when Mykaela had attended the funeral?

So filled with relief and gratitude, she rushed forward, kneeling at her friend's side, and squeezed her into a tight hug. Tears of joy sprang to her eyes at the feel of Charity's warm, living body. She looked up at Dylan over Charity's shoulder, her gaze asking the question she couldn't speak. *How?*

He just shook his head, but she could tell by his expression that his brain was working on it, and he was concerned.

Suddenly, Charity shoved Mykaela back onto the stone floor and stood, crossing the room to the entrance of the tomb. "Don't touch me," she warned, her voice taught as a wire.

Stunned, she looked up at Charity from the floor.

Charity glared at her with ravenous eyes. "You just tried to kill me."

"I thought you were—"

"A siren?" Charity finished, raising her eyebrows. "Like the one who killed me? You wouldn't have anything to tell me about *her*, would you?" She held Mykaela's gaze in a challenge, waiting.

Mykaela stared at her friend, wondering what she was implying. How much did Charity know? And just how deep did this anger go? Standing, she faced her friend. "Yeah. Actually, there's a lot we need to talk about."

"There is," Charity said, her pitch rising. "The problem is I don't *trust* you."

As the words sank in, a horrible thought occurred to Mykaela. "How long have you been back?" she asked, and when Charity didn't respond, she looked to Brad for an answer.

He just shook his head and lowered his gaze to the floor, refusing to speak a word.

"You couldn't even let me know you were alive?" she asked.

"Why should I?" she asked. "When you left me to die?"

Her mouth dropped and her body lurched forward to embrace Charity again, and clear up this whole misunderstanding. But Charity held her hand up in a warning and Mykaela thought it was best to keep her distance. "I didn't leave you to die, Charity," she said, pleading, "Please, you have to believe me."

"Right," she said with a nod. "At best, you left my body to drift around the ocean and my family to wonder what had happened to me."

"No." She shook her head as her mind swirled with all the ways Charity had misunderstood this. What she'd done may have seemed heartless, but she'd been a coward back then. Too afraid to face the disbelief in people's faces when she told them what had happened. "No, I would've told them. I would've come clean and then..."

"It was your stupid idea to go to that spot and have a séance anyway," Charity spoke with an icy, mean tone. "You just had to try and contact your father's spirit. You were so desperate to talk to him just once. I guess that's what daddy issues can do to a person. But wait...didn't your father try to kill you?"

Hearing such hateful, brutally honest words speak to her in Charity's voice cut her through to the core.

"Maybe those issues are why you fight so hard for *him*." She pointed to Dylan. "Think about it. He's the same kind of monster your dad was. He's definitely old enough to be your father. Nothing says well-adjusted like dating a man in his hundreds," she said, doing a clicking sound with the side of her cheek. She looked at Mykaela in mock surprise. "Wait...didn't he try to kill you, too? I'm really seeing the resemblance here. You need some serious help, sweetie."

"This isn't you," she whispered, unable to bear hearing any more.

"No," Charity shouted, the sound echoing in the small tomb around them. "This is what you did to me! And all I have thought about since the moment I came back is how much I *hate* you."

The words lashed at her, quick and sharp like tiny whips. On the verge of tears, Mykaela fought hard to maintain composure. "I made a mistake, I know I did—"

"You've made more than one but I am done wasting my time rehashing the past with you." She turned, stepping out of the tomb, outside, she stopped, looking over her shoulder just a little as she called, "Brad, let's go."

Brad stepped up, walking past Mykaela. He caught her gaze with an apologetic look, but she couldn't help but feel betrayed. Betrayed by him, by her friend, but deep down, she knew she'd performed the biggest treachery of all. Her worst fear had come to pass. Now Charity knew about that betrayal and hated her for it. She turned to Dylan, distraught and barely able to form words. He stepped up and wrapped an arm around her shoulder.

"Did that really just happen?" she asked in a breathless whisper as she collapsed against his side.

He helped support her as he led her out of the cemetery and took her back home.

***

Brad's fingers fumbled with the key nervously as he slid it into the lock on his door. "The place is kind of a mess," he warned, turning the key. But she didn't respond, so he pushed open the door.

She walked inside, her arms still wrapped tight around her middle, as they had been since she'd left the cemetery.

"Are...are you sure you're not hungry?" he asked, locking the door behind them. Even to him, it sounded stupid. She'd just had a painful non-reunion with her former best friend and he didn't think food would help much. He moved to the coffee table, scooping up a stack of books and straightening up loose papers. "Or thirsty, maybe?"

"What's all this?" she asked, looking around at the notes he'd taped to the walls.

He looked around nervously, wishing his obsession about his past and his heritage hadn't consumed him so much. "It's...it's just research."

"About those monsters?" Charity asked, moving to read a page he'd torn out of a book.

He nodded.

"You fight them?" she asked, turning to look at him.

He crossed his arms, nodding again. "I have for years. Even before..."

Her eyes widened a little, but she looked like she admired him instead of resenting him.

"I can teach you...if you want," he offered.

She shivered. "Are you kidding me? I *never* want to see one of those things again."

He chuckled, remembering how she'd squealed at the sight of a spider or a crab. She'd always been girly like that.

"What's so funny?" she asked, fighting a grin.

"Nothing," he said, the laugh fading to a feeling of complete happiness and calm. "It's just...good to have you back."

She smiled, her gaze lingering on his. "Do you have any soda?"

"Yeah, I think so." He went to the fridge and grabbed a can of Dr. Pepper. When he turned back around, she was taking a seat at the bar between rooms. Cracking open the can, he handed it to her.

She took a sip, but at the taste, she tilted her head back and started gulping it down. "God, I missed that," she said, her cheeks flushing a little like she was embarrassed. "It's like crack or something."

He laughed and she finished off the rest of the can. "You want anything else?"

Tilting her head, she thought for a minute. "Yeah. A do-over with Mykaela."

Moving forward, he leaned against the counter to talk to her. "Yeah, you said some pretty…vengeful things to her."

"I couldn't help it," she said, covering her face with her hands. "I saw her again and all of those feelings came rushing back. This is exactly why I didn't want her to know about me until I had my anger under control."

"It's okay because if you want a do-over, Mykaela will give you one. She missed you so much, Charity, and since she betrayed you, all she's wanted was to make it right."

She shook her head, dropping her hands to her lap. "I have to stay away from her."

"Why?" he asked. "She's your best friend, and always has been."

"She's a lot more than that," she whispered, her eyes turning dark with secrets again. There was so much she wasn't telling Brad, so much he needed to take on faith. "I know I need to forgive her, but I can't."

"Forgiving takes time," he said, placing a hand on her cheek. "I hated her for months after you died. I blamed her…but in the end, it wasn't her fault."

He could see she didn't look convinced, and he couldn't imagine how deeply rooted her anger toward Mykaela was. It made sense…Mykaela had been rescued while Charity died. And even though she was back now, what did she really have to live for?

"I have an idea. How about we stop talking about Mykaela?" He cupped her face his hand, curling the other one

120

around her waist. Pulling her close, relishing this feeling of her—something he'd never thought he'd experience again. When he kissed her, it was so much better than he ever remembered. It made all of the other memories seem like a fading dream, inadequate by comparison. He knew, without a doubt, that he never wanted to lose her again.

Then something dark started to build inside him. Fighting to make its way out, fighting to act on the lustful urges, to seduce her...turn her into a victim. He pulled back suddenly, stepping away. She kind of stumbled, like she'd been leaning completely into him, and looked up at him, her eyes full of question.

"Sorry," he said, clearing his throat. "Maybe we should just take it slow."

"I was dead, Brad," she said, a bitter chuckle in her throat. "I think we've moved...slowly enough."

"Yeah, I know." Embarrassed and flushed, and still fighting the darkest parts of himself, he turned to the dishwasher and started putting dishes in the cupboard. "It's just...I missed you, you know? Just you being *here* is enough. Isn't it?"

He stooped to place a few pans in a lower level cabinet.

"You know, before..." she hesitated, then decided to skip finding a way to phrase her death and resurrection, "you were always too noble to sleep with a minor. Does coming back from the dead tip the scales any?"

His hand fumbled the skillet he was holding, and it clattered to the ground, making him even more flustered and embarrassed. He didn't want Charity to think he didn't want her—it was quite the opposite—but he still had no idea what he was capable of, what kind of changes this transition was making to his body. If he let himself get that carried away...there was a strong possibility he could hurt her, kill her, even.

But he couldn't tell her any of this, not after she'd made it perfectly clear how she felt about "those monsters." If she found out he was one of them, he could lose her all over again. If he lost her, there would be no way he could fight the transition.

He stood up, trying to put this in a way that didn't sound like a brush-off. "You've been through a lot tonight. There's no need to rush."

***

"She hates me." Mykaela paced across the floor parallel to her bed, walking all the way to the bathroom door before turning around and doing it all over again. "She was my best friend, now she's somehow resurrected and she hates me! With good reason. I was only the worst friend in the world."

"No, you weren't." Dylan was leaned against the desk, watching every nervous and fidgety move Mykaela made. "You were just a scared girl."

"So what?" Mykaela asked, turning at the bathroom door to head back across the room. "Scared or not, I still lied. For months, every time someone asked me what happened to Charity, I lied. I said I didn't know. But I was there, I watched it happen and then I just ran. What kind of person does that?"

Dylan stepped up, taking Mykaela by the shoulders to keep her still. "You'd nearly died, and you watched your friend die. No one should expect you to be thinking clearly after something like that."

"I just ran away," she whispered, ignoring him. "She's right. I just left her body to rot in the ocean and get eaten by fish while her mom went crazy with worry. If Morrigan hadn't left her body on the beach like some present, no one would've even known she was dead!"

"Everyone does things they wish they could take back," he said. "But now you have time to make it right with Charity. Okay? So clear your head, get some rest and go see her tomorrow."

Mykaela nodded slowly, closing her eyes as he stroked his fingertips back and forth across her temples to soothe her. She let out a steady breath, trying to calm her speeding thoughts.

"Just talk to her," he said. "Explain your feelings and listen to what she says. I'm sure everything will work out."

"I don't know how you can be so optimistic." Bringing her fingertips to his, she opened her eyes. "You've always been like that."

He gave her a small smile. "I could think of nothing worse than living an eternity without faith."

***

After Dylan left Mykaela at the inn, he took his time walking back to the warehouse. He was trying to make sense of everything that had happened tonight.

A few feet in front of him, he saw traces of black smoke. The swirls grew thicker and thicker, until they formed to a woman's shape. Even though he'd only met Narissa once before, ages ago, he instinctively knew it was her. Somewhere deep inside, he could feel it—he belonged to her.

Fully formed now, Narissa gave him a coy smile as she eyed him up and down. "Dylan, is it? I can certainly see why Mykaela was so determined to keep you."

"So you're her, huh?" he asked. "You don't look evil."

"Evil." She wrinkled her nose in disgust and scoffed at the term. "It's all a matter of perception."

"That's why you tracked me down?" He raised an eyebrow in question, a hint of sarcasm to his tone. "To talk about perception?"

"No." Turning to look at the ocean, Narissa toyed with the charm to her necklace. "It's about Mykaela. She's backing out of the deal, and it's annoying me."

"Well, we're sorry to inconvenience you."

"Dylan..." she sighed, dropping her hands to her hips. "I know you love her. She's the one who makes your eternity worthwhile. The reason you've been hanging on to this world all this time. So please, talk to her. Convince her to do the right thing so you two can finally be together. Before someone else gets hurt."

"Whatever plan the two of you cooked up had nothing to do with me, darling. Count me out." He started to walk away, but as he passed her, she reached out and grabbed his arm.

"Dylan, wait." Stepping closer, she looked up at him with a gaze that was almost pleading. "I saved your life. You owe me."

"You saved me?" He gave a loud, sarcastic chuckle. "Is that how you see it?"

"That siren would have bound you to her forever. That's an eternity of being forced to do what she says, of being away from the woman you really loved. She would have made you forget all about Mykaela, would've wiped her from your mind completely. Yes, I saved you!"

"And you did that out of the goodness of your heart, did you?"

Her expression shifted, heating with impatience. "I arranged for you and Mykaela to have a second chance. Now, the least you can do is pay up!"

"Why are those souls so important to you?" He moved in closer, showing her he wasn't about to be intimidated. "What do you need them for?"

Her only response was a glare, but her fingers once again returned to the necklace. From this angle, Dylan could see it was a silver dolphin.

"Because it seems to me like you're too romantic to be the power-hungry type. That's why you picked a couple in distress as your victims, right? That's why you saved me. So what's your endgame?"

She let go of his arm with a shove and turned away from him. Her silvery silk skirt flowed in the wind as she went a few paces down the beach, tilting her head to the sky. "You answer to me, not the other way around."

"Fine," he said. Knowing he needed to keep her talking, he continued, "Answer this one thing then. Does love make you strong or weak?"

"And if I answer this question, you'll convince Mykaela to give me the souls?"

"I'll think about it."

Tossing an impatient glance his way, she sighed and crossed her arms. "I suppose it depends. If the lovers are together, they can be invincible. But separated, they are vulnerable."

"So where is he, then?"

Slowly, she turned to face him with a warning look.

"Your lover. The one who makes your eternity worthwhile." He started down the beach toward her, speaking casually. "I'm guessing he's trapped somewhere pretty bad because this is one huge, long-term plan you have going on here. I mean, two centuries worth of collecting souls for power? What door do you have to bust open to get him out?"

She flew at him, a blur of shimmering silk and black as night hair. Shoving her arm straight into his chest, she wrapped her fingers around his cold, lifeless heart and squeezed. Pain ripped through his body, agonizing and rendering him stunned.

"I think it's about time you shut up and relay a message for me." Slamming his body down on the sand, she pinned him and leaned in close. "I'm being nice by keeping Blanche in that coma. But if Mykaela doesn't give me the souls soon, someone close to her will die. Maybe it'll be her brother, or that cop, or maybe I'll just take you. Rest assured that I will pick each and every one of you off until Mykaela's so alone she's begging to die, but I'll make sure that doesn't happen. Maybe I'll whip up a new curse, who knows?" Rambling, she grinned wickedly. "She's pushing me to desperate measures. Do you get my point?"

Though he glared at her, he nodded and she yanked her hand out of him. He grabbed his chest, surprised to find it solid and unharmed. The pain faded, and when he looked up, Narissa was gone.

***

Mykaela couldn't sit still. She'd been worried about Charity since she left. The fact that she was alive again also meant she could die again, and she didn't know how to defend herself from the supernatural predators that seemed to love this town. Aside from that, it'd taken a lot of power to resurrect Charity—she'd seen that from the echoes in the cemetery—and no one would do something like that without a good reason. Mykaela had a nagging feeling it was all another part of Narissa's plot to steal the souls. But she didn't know for sure, and it was driving her crazy.

So, after a good half-hour of pacing around her bedroom, her mind racing with wild, panicked thoughts, she finally drove to Brad's house. As suspected, his truck was parked outside.

Mykaela knocked, then waited. Her mind awkwardly wondered what was happening on the other side of that door. Emotions were high tonight, and for some reason Brad seemed more seductive than usual lately. Was it possible he and Charity were...

Brad opened the door, revealing the living room and kitchen, but no sign of Charity. Without a word, Mykaela barged past him and took a look around.

"Where is she?" she demanded.

"Sleeping." He motioned to his bedroom.

She had to check, just to make sure. The door at the end of the hallway was open a crack. Nudging it open further, she peeked inside. She smiled a little when she saw Charity curled up underneath a cozy pillowed quilt. The steady rise and fall of her chest indicated she was sleeping peacefully.

Walking back down the hall, she marched up to Brad and gave his shoulder a hard punch. "What the hell was that about?"

"Ow! What?" A little stunned from the punch, he grabbed his shoulder and shot her a *what-the-hell?* look. "What'd I do?"

"Do?" she repeated, glaring at him. "You didn't do anything! You didn't say anything! You didn't bother to tell me she was alive, you didn't even try to get her to listen to me. You just took Charity and left. That's what you did!"

He just shook his head at her. "She asked me not to tell you."

"Why?" she demanded, hands on her hips. "Why has she been hiding from me?"

"I don't know exactly," he said. "I just know what she tells me and it's not much. She's not as open as she used to be...she's become really secretive."

She roughly dragged a hand through her hair in frustration. "Are we all supposed to pretend this doesn't mean something bad? She's been *resurrected*. That's gotta be bad news, right? It's just not…not natural."

"In this town, what *is* natural?" he asked. "It doesn't have to mean something bad."

"You didn't see what I saw," she pointed out. "There were some serious echoes."

"Echoes?" he asked. "What, like, music?"

"No." Shaking her head, she leaned against the counter as he crossed the room to the refrigerator. "There was a trail of color that led me straight to her door. That doesn't happen with humans. So either she's not human, or something pretty powerful is helping her."

He reached inside the fridge and pulled out a beer. Cracking it open, he lifted the bottle as if in a toast. "If there is a catch, I'm sure it'll reveal itself soon enough." He drank, giving her a bitter smile. "Just enjoy it while you can."

She took a second to look him up and down before she asked, "Are you okay? You're not usually the drinking type."

"It's been a long night." Easily avoiding her gaze, he moved across the room to sit on the couch. "A long few weeks, really. That's how long I've been hiding this from you, by the way."

Turning, she kept her skeptical gaze on him. "It couldn't have been easy filling Charity in on everything that's happened."

Glancing at her, just for a second, he took another long drink from the bottle. "She lived in the cemetery, Mykaela," he said. "So any deaths I would've told her about, she discovered on her own. Before I even found her. I didn't have to tell her much."

"I assumed she'd been staying here," Mykaela said. "You mean she'd been living in that crypt?"

He nodded. "Every time I asked her to come with me, she just said she couldn't leave the cemetery yet. She would never tell me why."

That didn't sound suspicious at all, she thought.

"Did you tell her the other thing?" she asked, tilting her head to look at him more closely, so she could determine for herself if he was telling the truth. "The *us* thing."

"There was never an 'us'," he said, "there was a 'maybe-us' or a 'not-really us'—"

"Yeah, that's why I called it a *thing*."

"Whatever it was…" he glanced over at her again, then leaned his elbows on his knees and locked eye contact with her. "Whatever it was is over, okay? It has to be."

"You think I want to give her yet another reason to hate me? But I can't lie to her either, she deserves better than that."

"You don't understand. One way or another, those evil bastards have killed everyone I've ever loved. Everyone, Mykaela." He leaned back again, nodding in determination. "But now Charity's back, and I don't care what it takes, I'm never going to lose her again."

Chapter Ten

"You're just trying to postpone going to school," Jared said as he pulled into the hospital parking lot.

She rolled her eyes in response. When she'd woke up this morning, Jared had insisted on escorting her to school — in his squad car — just to make sure she would actually go this time. She figured Brad had filled him in on the Charity situation and Jared was already prepared for Mykaela's desire to head straight to Brad's and try to make amends. With the social worker breathing down their necks to ensure Mykaela was 'properly cared for', she couldn't blame him for being vigilant, but wondered why he always gave her the third degree. "I just want to see Mom for a few minutes," she said as she unsnapped her seat belt. "It's barely after seven. We have plenty of time."

Climbing out of the car, she met up with Jared at the bumper and they started walking across the parking lot together. "You know," she whispered to him, "Most guys wouldn't make their sister go to school the day after her friend is mysteriously resurrected."

"As creepy and intriguing as Charity's restored life is, it's not a good enough excuse to cut class. You can see her after school."

"You're a drill sergeant," she said, shaking her head. "It's total dictatorship."

He chuckled as he pulled open the large glass door. "It's called *guardianship*."

"Still, you're being a little unreasonable about all of this," she said as they walked inside. "Considering the evil I'm up against, social workers and principals don't scare me very much."

The hospital hallways were crowded with orderlies, nurses and patients as Mykaela and Jared weaved their way through the crowd in search of their mother's room.

"They should," Jared said, keeping his voice low so no one could hear. "Because when this all over, they're the ones who can affect the outcome of your *human* life."

He had a point there, but she refused to admit it. Luckily for her, they were finally entering their mother's room and out of respect, ceased arguing. Jared stopped suddenly in front of her, causing her to bump into his back. She stumbled back, looking around him, and saw the bed was empty.

Jared looked around the room for a second. "Did they take her to get some tests done?"

Mykaela moved toward the bed. The blanket was pulled back, revealing a small yellowish lump on the starch white sheet. As she drew closer to the bed, she could make out what it was, and a knot formed in her stomach. "I don't think so, Jer," she whispered.

He turned to her as she held out the small cone-shaped seashell that'd been left on their mother's bed. He was confused at first, then realization settled in and anger came with it. "Stay here," he said, then quickly darted out of the room.

Dazed, Mykaela looked down at the seashell in her hand. She knew this seashell was a message from Narissa. Instinctively, her gut told her exactly what that message was.

No more playing nice. Narissa wanted the souls, and she wanted them now.

Jared came back into the room, followed by the doctor with that stupid clipboard. With wide, puzzled eyes, he looked from the paper on his clipboard, to the empty hospital bed. "This can't be right."

"Are you telling me that no one in this hospital can tell me where my mom is?" Jared demanded, his eyes flashing with outrage.

"We'll get to the bottom of this right away," the doctor responded as he left the room.

Jared turned to her, looking worried and shaken.

"How long did you really think she'd be safe here?" Mykaela asked, her voice quiet and whispery. "Didn't you have someone guarding her?"

"Of course I did," Jared snapped. "And of course they're nowhere to be found now!" He pulled out his cell phone and dialed someone. To Mykaela, he said, "Just go home."

Mykaela nodded and left the room, knowing she had no intention of going home. Rushing out of the hospital, she stopped on the sidewalk.

Above, dark clouds rolled into the clear blue sky out of nowhere. The clouds raced across the sky, like an army conquering a nation, and bathed the entire town in one giant shadow. With a loud crack of thunder, rain poured down in torrents.

Through the pouring rain and the shadowy clouds, Mykaela could see the black stains on the atmosphere, the signs that this was all Narissa's doing.

In minutes, the streets were flooded and the rain showed no signs of letting up. Mykaela just stood in the downpour, clutching that seashell in her hand, thinking about her mom.

At least an hour later when Jared came out of the hospital, Mykaela was still standing in the exact same position. She hadn't been able to move, or act or even really think straight. It was as if she was frozen in complete terror.

"Mykaela!" Jared exclaimed, immediately shrugging out of his jacket. Coming closer, he slid it around her soaking wet shoulders. "What are you doing?"

The rain still poured down in torrents, splashing into her eyes when she tried to look up at him. His hair and uniform were getting wetter by the second, but still they stood in the storm.

"I can't lose her, Jer," she said, her frightful voice barely above a whisper. "I...I just can't." Then the tears came, mixing with the rain on her cheeks.

His expression filled with compassion and understanding. Wrapping an arm around her shoulders, he squeezed tight. Without a word, he led them to his squad car.

***

He took her home. In a daze, she changed into some dry clothes and then went back down to the kitchen.

When she got there, Jared was on his cell phone, pacing back and forth across the floor. "Yes, sir," he was saying. "I understand how important her education is, but as you can see, our family crisis just keeps getting worse."

He paused, listening, as Mykaela quietly took a seat at the table.

"I think that would be a great solution," he said finally, with a small smile of triumph. "I'll come by and sign the paperwork first thing in the morning."

As he hung up Mykaela said, "I take it that was the school."

"Yep," he said. "We decided that, until life gets back to normal, you'll meet with a tutor."

"A tutor?" Mykaela repeated, surprised.

"Don't complain," he said, holding up his hand. "It's a good deal. You only have to worry about school once or twice a week, for a couple hours."

She was quiet as she realized that at least, he was compromising.

He took a seat at the table. "That gives us plenty of time to figure out a way to stop this sea-witch."

Glancing up at him, she raised an eyebrow. "Us?"

Shrugging, he sighed. "You've made it clear you're not going to stop hunting," he said. "The least I can do is have your back."

"Finally," she said.

"The good news is Mom's likely still alive somewhere," he said, getting straight to business. "If they wanted to kill her, they would've done it in the hospital. They just wanted to keep a closer eye on her body."

"Oh, is that all?"

"It's not ideal," he said. "But it's better than the alternative."

"True."

"How did you summon Narissa?" he asked suddenly.

She eyed him suspiciously. "I called her name out into the ocean," she answered. "But, even if you tried, there's no guarantee she'll answer. She only answered me because I'm the Keeper."

"Then I guess the Keeper's going to have to summon her," he said decisively.

"That's suicide," she said, "all she's going to do is gloat and beat me up again."

"Look, Narissa is expecting you to contact her. She wanted to steal Mom to rattle you, and you have to let her know it worked. Summon her, tell her you've found the souls and you'll give them to her, then lead her to a trap," Jared explained. "I'll do the rest. And I'll be right there with you, the whole time."

"What kind of trap can hold an ancient sea-witch?" she asked, leaning forward to listen.

Reluctantly, he explained, "A long time ago, before I was even born, the hunter's council worked with a witch to create a room that could hold any supernatural being."

"Seriously?"

He nodded. "Once they go in, they can only come out after they're dead. And here's where things get a little tricky." Leaning his elbows on the table, he explained, "Your powers qualify you as supernatural. So, under *no circumstances* can you lead her in. She has to go in alone."

She was quiet as she tried to wrap her mind around this new information. A room that could trap *any* supernatural being, no matter how powerful? It was more shocking than the fact Jared was actually letting her help. "Why am I just now learning about this?"

"Because it's on a need-to-know basis."

She let him have that dig for free and moved on. "Say we do get her into the room. Then what? We'll have a pissed off sea-witch in a cage."

"We make a deal. Barter her freedom for Mom's health and safe return. Or locate Mom some other way while she's trapped. The point is she won't be able to hurt anybody else. She won't be able to hurt you."

So far, it was the best idea she'd heard and their only real option. "It's worth a shot. But there's something I need to do first."

***

Balancing a disposable aluminum pie-plate on one hand, Mykaela raised her fist to knock on Brad's door. When he opened it, he didn't look surprised to see her.

He hesitated before he spoke, as if choosing his words with caution. "Look, Mykaela…I'm not sure she wants to see you."

Mykaela braced herself against the stings of pain, trying to keep the signs from leaking into her expression. "Can she tell me that herself?"

He studied her a minute, then stepped aside and let her in. She saw Charity standing a few feet behind him, dressed in an over-sized t-shirt of Brad's and the pair of sweatpants. Charity's pale blue eyes watched Mykaela carefully as she approached.

It felt so good to see her again—even if she was looking at Mykaela like she was a total stranger—that it made tears sting her eyes. Blinking them back, she stretched out her hand to offer her the pie plate. "I brought you a cheesecake," she said, her voice sounding insecure. "Your favorite."

Charity's unimpressed gaze travelled from the pie to Mykaela. "Really? You think bringing me a desert is going to make up for what you've done?"

"Of course not," Mykaela said, flinching at how hateful her friend sounded. "But you've been dead for how long? Are you really going to tell me you don't want it?"

She bit her lip, debating. Finally, she took the plate from Mykaela's hands and went over to the island. As she pulled the plastic lid off, Mykaela turned to Brad.

"Not to kick you out of your own house or anything, but can we have a minute alone?"

He looked to Charity for approval.

"Okay, you guys can both stop acting like I'm going to murder you," Mykaela snapped, fed up with both of them acting like she was the enemy.

"You mean again?" Charity quipped as she dug into the middle of the cheesecake with a spoon. She took a hefty bite and then closed her eyes in pleasure. Finally, she looked to Brad and nodded. "You can go. I'll be okay."

He nodded and opened the door. "I won't go far."

Once they were alone, Mykaela took a seat across from Charity. Suddenly, it was like the whole speech she'd cooked up on the way over disappeared. She never actually thought she'd get this far without being kicked out, and now she didn't know what to say.

Charity let the silence linger as she ate the cheesecake.

"I don't know how I can ever apologize for what happened," Mykaela finally began. "I swear, Charity. It's haunted me every day."

"You felt guilty," she said, swallowing. "Good."

Mykaela drew in a slow breath of patience. "You can hear the term survivor's guilt and think about how awful it would be…but it's a hundred times worse. You don't know until you live through it."

"But you did live through it," she said. "And you abandoned me to do it."

"I never wanted to leave you there," she said. "When I woke up on the beach, I just ran. I'd planned on getting help, but once I got home…I didn't know what to say. And before I could come clean…we found your body." Tears sprang to her eyes at the memories, and she wiped them away, clearing her throat. "I know there's no excuse. It's unforgiveable. But I

138

never thought I'd see you again...and now that you're here...I have to fix things between us, Charity. I have to make it right."

Charity was excruciatingly quiet. "Even if I wanted to forgive you, even if I could," she said quietly. "It doesn't change the fact that everyone around you dies."

It was one thing for Mykaela to say that about herself — she did it all the time, but hearing those words come out of Charity's mouth somehow made the fact more concrete. It hurt more, because she knew it was true — she knew no one around her would ever be safe. Still, it was such a coldhearted thing for her friend to say that she could only gaze back at her with a look of disbelief.

"Rachel, Susan, Gabby. How many more? They're all dead because these...things, these sea creatures, want *you*. Death and destruction follow you everywhere."

Mykaela swallowed hard over a lump of tears and cleared her throat, trying to protect herself from the pain.

Charity shook her head, looking down. "I like being alive, Mykaela. I want to stay that way."

"Then you'll need my help," she said. "I might attract evil, but I can fight it too."

Charity lifted her eyes to look at Mykaela's for a moment, then shook her head again. "I don't need your protection."

"I can't imagine you would, with Brad as your own personal body guard." As much as she tried, she couldn't keep the jealousy from slipping in to her tone. She tried to tell herself to be happy about Brad and Charity being together — they deserved it — but on the other hand, it was hard. Brad had been her friend, her confidante, her mentor. Now everything had changed and he instinctively took Charity's side, no matter what.

Charity held her gaze in question.

"Look, whether you want me around or not…the fact is people don't just come back from the dead. That's a supernatural thing. In this town, I handle the supernatural things. So I'm going to need to ask you a few questions."

She chuckled lightly. "So, I'm just another one of your cases, is that it?"

"Not just," she said. "But like you said, these things want me. Now I want to know what they want with you."

"I'm afraid I can't help you."

Mykaela leaned her elbows on the island's surface. "Do you remember anything about…where you were before you came back?"

"All I can remember is waking up in my coffin," she said with a bitter smile. "I was kind of panicked about being buried alive, so everything around that is a blur."

"How did you get out?" she asked. "Most people can't dig their way through six feet of earth with their bare hands."

She shrugged. "Willpower? Luck? Survival instinct? I don't know."

"And there was no one waiting for you when you surfaced? Someone who explained why they resurrected you, maybe?"

"No," she said. "And I couldn't care less why or how this happened. The point is it did."

"You say that," she said, "but someone did this for a reason. They want to use you for something or they need you. Maybe it's related to this whole sea-witch thing and maybe it's not. I don't know. One thing's for sure: You're not safe."

She pushed the plate away and leaned in close, her blond hair falling around her shoulders as she locked gazes with Mykaela. "What does this sea-witch want with *you*? I mean, last summer you were just a regular girl getting spooked by shadows in the woods, and now…you're what? Some kind of

Van Helsing? You've got psychic powers and you kill those sea-souls. How did *that* happen?" Seeing the look of question on Mykaela's face, Charity explained, "Brad filled me in."

"I don't know how it happened," she said, hating once again the need to lie. If only she and Charity were close like they used to be, then she could divulge her secrets and finally get them off her chest. But right now, Charity was an x-factor. There was no telling what she would do with Mykaela's darkest secret. "I guess it's just...destiny."

"I don't believe in destiny."

"I hear that a lot," she said with a faint smile. "I guess I didn't believe either. Until it happened." Awkward silence fell over them again, and she broke it by clearing her throat. "Anyway...you have absolutely no idea who could've done this? Think really, really hard, Charity."

Charity busied herself with replacing the plastic lid on the pie-plate, then taking it to the fridge. "I've told you. I don't know anything."

Mykaela studied Charity. She had her back turned to Mykaela, but her posture was stiff and tense. As she turned around, she wore a relaxed but very fake smile, giving Mykaela the nagging sense that Charity was lying. Studying her a little more deeply, she examined Charity's aura. There were no colors that hinted of an evil creature, no song that signaled she'd been turned into a siren. It was definitely the real Charity standing in front of her, but she seemed so different. "If you find anything out, will you tell me?"

She hesitated, crossing her arms. Reluctantly, she nodded.

Mykaela stood. "I won't take up any more of your time." She headed over to the door, then turned, glancing over her shoulder at Charity. "I'm really glad you're okay."

***

Charity watched as the door shut behind Mykaela. She waited a few seconds for good measure, and then hurried over to a nearby cabinet. From it, she took a large glass bowl and filled it with water. Then she quickly dug around in the cabinet until she found a box of sea salt. She dumped a grainy handful into the water and stirred it with her finger. While the mixture was still swirling, she pulled a tiny cone seashell out of her pocket. Dropping the shell into the water, she whispered the activation words.

The water started bubbling and the seashell floated to the surface, open end up, signaling the connection to the other side had been made. "I did everything just like you said," Charity said into the bowl. "But I can't stand it. How long do I have to keep lying to her?"

"We have no time to waste with guilt," a mix of voices came from the still churning waters. It sounded like a hundred of them, intermingling with and talking over each other. "Mykaela has been lying to everyone for a very long time."

"I know. I gave her a chance to come clean just now, and like always, she'd rather hide the truth." Charity sighed, leaning her hands on the counter. "You were right. She can't be trusted."

"That's why she can't know about our plan until the time is right," the voices echoed from the bowl. "Mykaela has her destiny. And you have yours."

Chapter Eleven

When Mykaela entered her bedroom, she went straight to the adjoining bathroom and washed her face. Then she headed to her bed, but jumped when she saw Dylan sitting by the bay window.

She pressed a hand to her speeding heart as he gave her a charming little smile.

"You scared me," she said. "Why didn't you say anything when I came in?"

"Just thought I'd give you a minute to process...whatever was obviously on your mind." He shifted toward her. "I heard about your mom. I'm so sorry, Mykaela. How are you holding up?"

The weight of her mother's disappearance came rushing back to her and she let out a worried sigh. "Honestly, I feel like if I think about it, I'll break in half."

"We'll find her," he promised.

Looking into his eyes, she believed him and it filled her with a sense of relief. "Do you have any news?"

"Actually," he said, taking a seat at the bay window. "Narissa paid me a visit."

"She did? Why??"

"She wants me to convince you to give her the souls. Said I owed her for saving my life. You were right though," he said. "She's in it for love."

"How do you know?"

"Just something she said. She's desperate, Mykaela. I think he's trapped somewhere, in another dimension, maybe. That's why she needs the souls. It takes a lot of power to crack open those doors."

"You got all of this from one run-in with her?" she asked.

He nodded and stood, shoving his hands in his pockets as he walked around the room, looking at the notes she's pinned all over the walls. "We've been looking at this the wrong way from the start. We've been acting like this is some desperate grab for power and authority but it's not. Narissa's been powerful for centuries—if she wanted a take-over she easily could've managed one. Instead, she used us…and the curse to continually store power for all these years. Not because she wants it, but because she *needs* it."

"Needs it?" she repeated, turning to look at him as he moved around her room. "For what?"

"You remember Nerina?"

Mykaela nodded. "Narissa's sister. She helped you control your…cravings."

"She also taught me about magic," he said. "She said that some spells, the most powerful ones, need an even bigger power source. Something to fuel the magic."

"So she used me to create a power source," she asked, to clarify. "That doesn't sound good. What does she want?"

"No matter how powerful someone seems, there's always something out there that's stronger. For Narissa, it was her father, Poseidon. Nerina used to tell me this story, about Poseidon's greatest warrior, Delphinus. He was so adored he became god of the dolphins, sat at Poseidon's right hand.

Until he was banished to the stars—to another world of complete torment—for betraying Poseidon. I used to wonder why she told me…and now I realize it was because her sister was planning on using us to break him out."

She hesitated, still trying to make sense of this. "How can someone be banished to stars? And how do you know Delphinus is who Narissa is after?"

"I got most of it from Rachel," he said, looking away when Mykaela glanced over at him. "She said that all of them, Morrigan, Kerr, Narissa, they all swore to serve the dolphin god." He stood, walking around the room in a loop. "You didn't notice Narissa's necklace? The silver dolphin. I think Delphinus was banished for being in love with Narissa, so she put the curse on me, on the ocean, to steal enough souls to break him out."

"That makes sense," she said. "As much as anything lately makes sense. But what's going to happen if she succeeds? I mean…surely yanking someone from the sky will have repercussions."

"That's anybody's guess," he said. "But I came up with a plan."

"A plan?" she asked.

He nodded, but took a step forward. "You're not going to like it, but I think you should give the souls to me before Narissa can find them. Then, the next time she shows up, I'll be powerful enough to kill her."

It sounded good in theory, but if the vault was drained at all chances were Mykaela would die. Of course, she couldn't tell him that without revealing the souls' location in the process. "Dylan, I can't do that." She took a step back, shaking her head. "There has to be another way."

"You say that about every plan," he said. "This is the only other option. The one that doesn't end with anybody but

Narissa dead. But it would require that you trust me, so why you're hesitating."

"It's not that I don't trust you, Dylan. I just *can't* give you the souls," she said. "I'm supposed to set them free."

"I don't want to be set free, love," he said. "I want to be with you."

"But you're not the only soul in there." She moved past him, avoiding his gaze. "You're looking at them as a power source, but I see cursed humans. Victims."

"If you set them free, I'll die," he said. "And more importantly than that, Narissa's going to be furious. She'll kill anybody you've ever cared about."

She knew that, already. Narissa had made that abundantly clear when she declared war on Mykaela's life. But it changed nothing. The only way out was to break the curse, or align themselves with someone even more powerful than Narissa. "That's it," she exclaimed, following her train of thought. "We have to summon Poseidon."

"Wait...what?" he asked.

"He's her father, isn't he?" she said, "Can't he...I don't know, ground her or something?"

"Maybe," he said. "But I doubt he's oblivious to what she's been up to. If he wanted to help, he probably would've."

"Did Nerina ever say how to contact him?" she asked, ignoring his doubts. "Will calling his name out work, or is there something more specific we need to do?"

"No one has seen him for centuries," he said, "I tried summoning him once and he never answered. I searched for years and never found a trace of his involvement in anything. It's like he just vanished."

"What made you desperate enough to summon a sea god?" she asked, taking a second away from her questions to look at him carefully. Realizing, yet again, he had this whole other life that she knew virtually nothing about.

His blue-green eyes cut to meet hers, shining with secrecy and something else, that sorrow he always carried around. She knew he didn't want to tell her, but he would. "When you died."

She drew in a sharp breath of surprise. Even though she'd known about her past life, she hadn't thought about it long enough to wonder how it had ended. Now, several burning questions emerged, but she couldn't voice a single one, because Dylan's own reaction was so much more distracting.

Sorrow was filling his features, but a resolve was creeping in, too. Finally, he stepped up and took a seat next to her. "I tried everything to bring you back," he said.

She was quiet a minute. "How…how did it happen?"

"There's a lot you don't know, Mykaela." He quieted as his gaze turned distant. "I think I should fill you in."

Chapter Twelve

After that fateful night in 1857, when she'd caught Morgaine coming out of Dylan's room in the middle of the night, Mykaela and Narissa devised their plan.

The full moon was tonight, and after she gathered the last of the ingredients, they would have everything they needed for the spell. Mykaela walked along the forest, a basket dangling around her arm, looking for fresh sage. It was easy enough to find, but it had to be harvested today or it would be useless.

Finding a patch, she knelt down and began plucking the robust, green herb. After hearing a few footsteps, she felt Dylan approach. Keeping her back to him, she glanced over her shoulder.

"Mykaela," he said gently, his accent still fresh and thick, not faded over time. "You've barely spoken to me since the other night. It's more than I can bear."

"I'm sorry this is difficult for you," she said, sarcasm thick in her voice. "Be sure to tell me how I can make it easier."

"Please don't act that way." He took another step closer. "I've apologized countless times."

She stood, dusting off the skirt of her dress, and kept walking. "And you have yet to be forgiven. That should tell you something."

"Then what? It's just...over?" He followed after her, deeper into the woods. Both of them oblivious to the dark witch who watched from the trees above.

With a sigh, Mykaela stopped and turned to face him. "Tell me why it should continue."

"I love you," he said genuinely. "You're my soul mate."

"And yet, I wasn't the one leaving your room in the middle of the night."

"I know I betrayed you, Mykaela," he said, moving forward, his voice cracking with guilt. "I'm begging you to forgive me. Please don't turn your back on us."

She sighed, shaking her head. "You know nothing about me if you think I could ever do that." Tears filled her eyes and she didn't bother to fight them back. "Dylan, I love you with my whole heart. You're my entire world and I would never let another man come between us the way you've let Morgaine into our lives."

"I never intended to —"

"I know," she whispered, cutting him off. "But the truth is, if she were to walk by right now, you would forget all about me. Every time you see her, I cease to exist. And the hardest part is that it's not your fault. She's doing this to you. To us."

He narrowed his eyes in confusion.

"The necklace she gave you." She pointed to the strand of seashells around his neck. "It puts you under her spell. It lets her control you."

His lips parted, like he might laugh but thought better of it. Speaking gently, he stepped forward. "You shouldn't talk like that. Someone might think you're…"

"I'm not insane," Mykaela snapped, frustrated. "This is not some…delusion. It's real. She's a siren, and she has you under her spell. She plans to kill you Dylan."

"Morgaine would never hurt me," he said. "You don't really know her. Maybe if you did, you would see she's no witch."

Mykaela shook her head, pitying him. Knowing his protectiveness was just part of the spell, but unable to stop the pain it ignited. "If you truly believe that, take off the necklace."

"This is silly," he said. "I'm not under any spell."

"Take the necklace off, then."

Sighing, he reached up, his fingers stretching toward the clasp. But he hesitated, then dropped his hands again.

"See?" she said. "She won't let you take it off. She's controlling you."

"I know what I did is hard for you to accept," Dylan said, stepping closer, taking Mykaela's shoulders in his hands. "But no one is controlling me. I'm acting of my own free will. As...idiotic and thoughtless as my actions were, they were my own."

Looking into his bright green eyes, she felt sorry for him. Reaching up, she cupped his cheek in her hand. "I'm not angry, Dylan. And I'm not jealous. I'm only trying to save you."

"Save me?" he asked, looking concerned, but for her sanity.

"Morgaine's going to steal your soul and bind you to her for eternity," she said, tears clouding her vision. "Unless I do it first."

"This is crazy-talk," he said, sounding desperate. "Tell me this is some joke and you don't actually believe it."

Letting her hand fall, she stepped back. "You'll see."

"You tried to warn me," Dylan said, "But I wouldn't listen."

"Because you were under her spell," Mykaela pointed out, as if this were the only thing that made the situation bearable.

"Sirens will always attack the heart," he said, bitterly. "But after you and Narissa intervened, I had no idea what was happening."

She settled back against the window seat as he began to tell the rest of the story.

"My body washed up on the beach," he began.

The first thing he noticed was that he was freezing and soaking wet. Vague memories of drowning in the ocean tried to surface, but he forced them back down as he struggled to stand.

And though his mind was finally free from Morgaine's control, he could tell something else was drastically wrong. His body felt different...empty.

Suddenly, the pain he'd caused came back to haunt him. Magnified tenfold, he was consumed with regret for betraying Mykaela. He blamed himself for letting Morgaine control him, and he needed to make it right with Mykaela before he lost her for good.

So even though he was freezing and disoriented, the only thing that mattered was finding her. He'd washed up at the edge of the cliff, and had to make his way to the inn.

When he reached it, he saw a shadowy figure standing at the top of the house, enclosed by the widow's walk. He would recognize Mykaela's silhouette anywhere, and seeing it filled him with an overwhelming amount of love.

She saw him too and quickly hurried back into the house. She came out the front door only moments later, holding the hem of her skirt off the ground as she ran out onto the sand to meet him by the porch steps.

Coming eye level with him, she stopped in her tracks, her expression filled with joy. "It worked," she whispered. "It actually worked."

He didn't fully understand what she meant, but he didn't care. Wrapping his arms around her, he pulled her into a kiss, hoping the act of love would convey just how sorry he was, and that he would spend a lifetime trying to atone. Looping her arms around his neck, she welcomed his kiss and he felt his body fill with passion and strength. He was connecting with her, opening up to her on a level he never would've been able to do under Morgaine's control. It felt so right, like this...loving Mykaela was what he'd been born to do.

He felt her strength go into his body, energizing and restoring him in a way that was almost magical. He'd never felt closer to her in his entire life, and he never wanted it to end. But then, she started to struggle in his arms, and he was so lost in the pleasure *that for a moment, he didn't even notice. Finally, he broke his lips away from hers and she stumbled back dizzily.*

In the moonlight, he could see she'd grown five shades paler than she'd been only moments ago. Worse than that, she looked weakened, sickly. Slowly, she touched her hand to her lips and looked up at him with widened, confused eyes. Her voice was a low, bewildered whisper, "What did you do to me?"

He was shocked, too, because he felt more alive than ever before. That emptiness and confusion he'd felt when he woke up on the beach was gone. His mind was sharp, his ears were picking up the sound of branches breaking miles away. In the house, he could hear Mykaela's parents snore in slumber, and noticed the light scratching of mice running along the house's darkest corners.

Focusing on Mykaela, he listened to the frantic beating of her heart, her sharp intakes of struggling breath. With his heightened vision, he could see the tears building in Mykaela's green eyes, the beads of nervous sweat gathering around her hairline. Even weakened, she looked more beautiful than ever before, and all he wanted to do was kiss her again. Remembering how she'd nursed him back to health, how faithfully she'd defended their relationship, only intensified this feeling.

"There's so much I have to say to you," he whispered. These instincts driving him, he leaned in again, cupping her face in his hands. The second they touched, a dull light shined from between the palms of his hands and her cheeks, glowing brighter and brighter. Something, he wasn't sure what, was flowing from her to him, and the weaker Mykaela became, the stronger he grew.

Realizing he was hurting her, he yanked his hands away, then took a few steps back just to be safe. He couldn't understand what was happening. In this moment, all he cared about was Mykaela — as if she were the very reason for his existence, and yet, he couldn't touch her without hurting her. Why? What had happened to him in that water?

Something Mykaela said earlier suddenly registered, causing him to look at her in a suspicious way he'd never needed to do before. "What worked?"

She went suddenly still, her expression changing into one of realization.

"Your salvation." The strange female voice came from behind him.

Turning, he saw a beautiful young woman standing on the shoreline. Long black hair blew in the wind as she glided toward them.

"Narissa," Mykaela exclaimed desperately, running to meet her on the beach. "What's happening to him? Is he a siren? Did the ritual fail?"

"Ritual?" Dylan repeated, stepping up.

"No, it didn't fail."

"But if he's still human, then why — "

The woman only gave Mykaela a pitying smile. "I said I would save him. I never promised he would remain human."

Mykaela fell back a step, her gaze meeting Dylan's in shame. He stared back at her, his mind swirling with so many confused thoughts he couldn't fix his attention on one.

Narissa took a step closer, turning to examine Dylan. Looking him up and down in a mix of curiosity and pride. "He's my masterpiece, a new breed of sea creature. We drew from the magic of the ocean to make him, so he controls water and it controls him. His soul is gone, trapped in a magical tomb where it, and all the other souls the curse collects, will stay until it is time for you to give them back to me."

"Other souls?" Mykaela stared at the witch in horror and disbelief. "You never mentioned anything about collecting souls or creating a new breed or any of this!"

"This is all just logistics. I beg you; do not forget what's most important here." Narissa came closer to Mykaela, her gaze persuading as she motioned to Dylan. "For the rest of his immortal *life, he will be devoted to you. Only you, forever. That's what you wanted isn't it?"*

"Not this way," Mykaela said. "Not because of magic."

"The love was always there," she corrected. "On that cliff tonight, Dylan had a choice. Morgaine was trying to turn him, so do you know what he did? He jumped into the ocean and took his own life. That was a choice he made all on his own, to escape her." Keeping her gaze locked on Mykaela in a way that was almost scolding, she leaned in closer, lowering her voice. "He would rather kill himself than face an eternity bound to another woman, an eternity without you. So I saved him, but you are foolish to think this would come without a price."

Mykaela drew in a shaky breath, bringing her hand to her mouth as the realities set in and her heart became conflicted.

Turning, Narissa started toward Dylan.

As she came closer to him, he looked at the woman with fear and disgust as all of this information sank in.

"You're weakening Mykaela because you're stealing her soul," she explained quickly, matter-of-factly. "It's a side effect of the curse, I'm afraid. Your lack of a soul will make you crave it forever. Find others to feed on and the power from them will sustain you and give you the strength you need. In time, you will learn to control the instinct to kill and touching her will no longer pose a threat. Just remember, the more intimate you get, the higher the risk of killing her."

In his stunned state, he could form no reply, not even a scowl. Before their eyes, the woman vanished into a swirling burst of black smoke. Dylan looked over at Mykaela, his heart full of question and betrayal. His Irish brogue was thick with anger as he shouted, "What have you done?"

Flinching, Mykaela gently started to cry, until her knees buckled. Dropping to them, she leaned forward, the sobs rocking her body.

"I betrayed you," Mykaela said quietly when Dylan finished his story.

As he looked over at her, there were no signs of anger, no blame or resentment. Only undying compassion and understanding. "All you wanted was to free me from a siren," he said.

"If I'd known all I had to do was strangle her with the necklace," she whispered.

"Narissa manipulated the situation. Manipulated you. There's no way you could have known what would become of your deal."

"Is that what you've spent the last century telling yourself?" she asked. "That I was just a victim?"

"Weren't you?" he asked. "You've got to stop being so hard on yourself, Mykaela. What you did, you did out of love."

It was hard to believe she'd loved him so much back then, and now those feelings were buried by duty and regret. She wondered if there was any part of the girl she used to be still inside of her, or if she'd lost her faith in love completely. Taking a slow breath, she shifted the subject to another topic. "So, what happened next?"

His gaze turned distant yet again. "After I turned, I fled to the ocean where I lived in seclusion for two years. Away from humans, trying to control the soul-thirst. I missed you so much, but I couldn't return until could I no longer hurt you. I was so determined to protect you that I didn't realize I was hurting you already."

Consumed with grief, Mykaela stepped up to the edge of the cliff and called for Dylan, but like so many times before, he never came. Because she was human, and he was a son of the sea. As long as she possessed a soul, he could kill her with a single touch.

She'd spent the last two years delving into magic, trying to undo the horror she'd committed and reverse the spell, but with no luck. Now, it seemed like there was only one way to ensure she and Dylan could truly be together, with no tricks. If she let the water steal her soul, then loving Dylan would no longer put her at risk.

In the dark of night, the waves tumbled and roared underneath her, each one lapping against the other, the sound of it echoing all around the cliffs.

Closing her eyes, she thought of Dylan. Remembering fondly how she'd been sitting on the front porch, reading Shakespeare, when her father and brother carried the wounded Irish boy out of the woods one foggy Saturday afternoon. As she and her mother tended to the wounds from a long journey to the south, he'd been so shy and timid, barely making eye contact. It'd taken her a good month to start a real conversation with him, and even longer for the two of them to overcome the social boundaries that kept them apart. He was an Irish immigrant and she was a southern belle, but once they admitted how they felt, love bloomed. The once shy and submissive worker bravely stood up to her father and won him over with a speech she could still remember to this day. At their engagement party, people had congratulated and wished them well with sincere smiles and toasts.

Now it was all gone, and she'd had to live with the whispers that her foreign lover ran off with another woman just weeks before their wedding. Worse than that, she'd been forced to live with the emptiness, with that gaping hole in her life and the sorrow of being separated from her one true love. The regret of knowing others would suffer at her hands tormented her daily. Innocent people as distraught and disoriented as her would lose their souls, their chance at an afterlife, and be stripped of their humanity. Their bodies would be forced to wander in hiding, preying on the very thing they used to be. It was more than she could bear to live with, but her only solace came in knowing that soon, she would suffer from the curse as well.

Without opening her eyes to the harsh world around her, she stepped forward and clung to the good memories as her body plummeted into the ocean. The water engulfed her, swallowed her up in its shadowy depths immediately. As little bubbles of oxygen escaped her mouth and nose, she made no attempt to struggle. She simply waited for death to come, and her new life to begin.

***

On a small sailboat in the midst of the Atlantic, Dylan let the body of the fisherman fall to the rocking floor of the boat. His lips curved in pleasure as the last of the man's soul flowed into his body, turning to power.

Kneeling, he focused his attention on listening for a pulse and squeezed his eyes shut in relief when he found it, weak but still beating. Looking around, he made sure his previous victims, two other men, were still alive. Though their bodies were unconscious lumps around the boat, he hadn't killed anybody. He'd lost control and drained more than he should've, but the men would heal in a few days. He'd have to be more careful next time.

He was about to dive back into the water when suddenly, he felt a chill ripple over him. It tugged at something in his gut, making his mind immediately think of Mykaela. He couldn't understand how or why he knew, but he knew she was in trouble, and that she was in the ocean.

Diving in, he swam without thinking, simply allowing his primal instincts to drive him and trusting they would lead him to her. Flying past coral and leisurely wildlife, he kept his ears open for sounds of Mykaela. Soon, they picked up the sound of her fading heartbeat.

His heart filled with horror and worry when he saw her limp body floating underneath the water, not far from the spot where he'd died. Taking her in his arms, he swam her to shore and carried her body onto the beach.

He felt so useless because all he could do was push on her chest, he couldn't even offer her breath. Maybe it was desperation, or just his love for her, but soon, she was coughing and spitting up water.

The sight of her alive and breathing filled him with a sense of relief, but it didn't take long for the anger to kick in.

Through puffy and swollen eyes, she looked up at him, her expression changing from confusion to one of disbelief and hope. "It's you," she whispered.

Even though he was mad at her, he smiled. It was so good to see her again, that for a second, he forgot about everything else.

Sitting up, she reached out to touch him. "I thought I'd never see you again."

He pulled back before her fingers could touch his cheek. "Don't," he said softly, "We don't know what will happen."

But she only leaned in closer, her eyes full of love and longing as she moved in for a kiss. "I no longer care," she said, touching her lips to his.

His love for her overrode everything else – even his instincts to protect her and the passion she ignited woke the soul-thirst as well. Before long, he felt her essence soaking into his body; warm, alluring...fulfilling. Forcing himself to push her away, he stood, putting some distance between them.

Still sitting on the beach, soaking wet and looking dizzy and weakened, she looked up at him.

"What were you doing in the water?" he asked finally, keeping a compassionate, yet stern look on his face.

She looked out at the water as waves lapped in on the shore. "I was trying to join you."

Rage swept over him. The idea of Mykaela being a monster just like him, he could think of nothing worse. "Have you lost your mind?"

"Yes," she exclaimed, standing. Tears made her eyes shine, even in the darkness he could see them. "I've lost everything, Dylan.

It's made me this weak, pathetic girl you see standing in front of you."

Compassion made the rage edge away. Taking a step toward her, he wished he could reach out. "I know this...this is a tragedy," he said. "But to turn into a monster would be even worse. You don't want to be this, Mykaela, trust me."

"What I want," she said, her voice quivering, "is to be with you."

"And do you think it's right to enjoy our love, knowing the damage it has caused?"

"Is that why you've stayed away?" she asked, her voice sounding frail and pitiful. "Because you think we're...wrong."

Cautiously, he reached out and took her hand. Trying carefully not to hurt her, they both waited to see if the soul transfer would happen, but it didn't. Now at least, he had a little more self control. His eyes, which had once been as green as hers but now shone a bright, sea blue, gazed steadily into hers as he whispered, "Right or wrong, I would follow you to the ends of the earth."

Tears finally fell, trickling slowly down her cheeks. She tried to look down and hide her face, but he squeezed her hand in reassurance.

"For you, Mykaela, I'd do anything. Even let you go."

"You don't have to," she said, her voice pleading. "We can manage this."

"You think I haven't thought about it? Of course I have. But how would we hide who I am from people?" He motioned to the sand at their feet. "I don't have a shadow. It's like I'm not even really here."

Still, she shook her head in denial, clinging to the thought of them.

Her faith, touching as it was, made him push harder. "I'm frozen in time. I can't have kids or grow old with you. And you deserve someone who can do those things. You deserve it, Mykaela. Don't you realize I can't even kiss you without trying to kill you?"

"Why do you think I was trying to drown myself?" she said. "If I'm like you, those problems don't even matter. You just have to swallow your pride and let me do it."

"No," he shouted, his voice coming out harsher than he meant. Shaking his head, he dropped her hands and stepped back. "No."

"This is the only way," she whispered.

"She has a point, Dylan." The sassy and familiar voice sent a chill through both of them, and they didn't have to look to know the voice belonged to Morgaine. He'd searched high and low for her, wanting to kill her for what she'd done to them, but he never could find a trace. Until it was convenient for her, of course. Morgaine was a diva that way.

Angling his body toward the voice, he put himself between Mykaela and the dangerous, seductive siren. Her hair was still damp, like she'd just come from the ocean, and she wore a blue silk dress that made the color of her eyes look an even purer shade of blue.

Morgaine leveled her vicious gaze on Mykaela. "You poor, pitiful thing," she said, her voice full of mocking sympathy. "Your sorrow sent a ripple throughout the entire Atlantic. You came so close to joining us."

Behind him, he felt Mykaela's body stiffen in response, and he looked over his shoulder at her, his heart once again feeling for how badly she was hurting.

"You really messed up my plans with your little curse," Morgaine said, strolling closer. "You may have freed Dylan from my control, but I was willing to forgive you because I thought you'd let him go. Now I find out you were willing to join him in eternity." Stopping, she turned a determined glare on the girl. "Well, I just can't have that."

Morgaine lunged for Mykaela, but Dylan grabbed her and tackled her to the ground. Using his heightened strength, he pinned her to the shifting sand, struggling to keep the ancient siren down.

She only grinned wickedly in response. *"We'll have time to play later."* With that, she disappeared, causing him to fall to the sand. Turning, he saw she'd reappeared at Mykaela's side.

He dove for Mykaela, but ran straight into something. It was like his body couldn't go any further and kept running up against an invisible barrier, forcing him to watch helplessly as Morgaine grabbed Mykaela by her throat and began to squeeze.

She didn't even bother to drain her soul, and instead watched with a grin as she strangled the life out of her human victim. He screamed in protest, but could do nothing to stop it. After what seemed like hours of excruciating torment, the barrier dropped. He stumbled forward as Morgaine dropped Mykaela's lifeless body to the sand.

"I'll kill you for this," he cried as he rushed to Mykaela's side and pulled her body into his arms. *"I swear it."*

"To do that, you'll have to steal souls. Soon, you'll enjoy it," she said menacingly. *"So either way, I come out victorious."* With one last, vicious laugh, she dove into the ocean.

Once he was alone with Mykaela, he looked down at her. Bruises were starting to show around her throat, and her body was getting paler. Her heart wasn't beating and he could tell by the vacant look in her eye that the girl he loved was gone. Pulling her body close, he wrapped his arms around her and held her tight. Closing his eyes, he felt tears escape as his mind swam with all the reasons this was his fault, with everything he could've done differently. Holding her close, he sat like this until the sun started to peek over the horizon and her body had long gone stiff. He couldn't bear to let her go.

***

"After that, your parents came out and saw me holding your body on the beach," he said, "They assumed I killed you, so they gathered all the men in town and formed a group to hunt and kill me, and all the others like me. The hunter's council."

Her ancestors had started the hunter's council, she thought. Of course they had. "Did anyone know that I was the one to curse you?" she asked, wondering if the legend still floated around today.

"I have no way of knowing if you ever confessed to anyone," he said.

Shifting in her seat to look at him, she felt the lingering feelings of sadness from their tragic tale. "Why didn't you tell me any of this sooner?"

"When I met you again, you didn't recognize me. You had no memory of us ever being together," he said. "What was I supposed to say? Hey, remember me, your past-life lover?"

She laughed a little. "No, I guess not at first. But what about after?"

"You were reeling. Your friends were dropping like flies all around you. And you had all of that survivor's guilt from what happened to Charity. I guess I thought I could protect you from it somehow. It's a lot to put on someone's shoulders...I wanted to spare you as long as I could."

"It must've been so hard to keep it all to yourself," she said, studying him closely. "To pretend like we just met."

"Yeah, to be honest," he said slowly, with a hint of a smile. "That part kind of sucked."

She scooted over to the space next to him, resting her head on his shoulder. He looped his arm around her, letting her settle against him. They stayed like that for the rest of the night, just enjoying each other's company and embrace, and knowing their time together was limited.

***

Mykaela was halfway to the spot on the beach where she was supposed to meet Jared. For the last few hours this morning, she'd been mentally going over the plan she and

Jared cooked up. It was three easy steps. Summon Narissa, strike the deal, then lead her to the trap. If she was convincing enough, the plan would go off without a hitch.

All of the sudden, her Jeep rolled to a stop. Puzzled, she checked the dashboard for any warning lights she might've missed and made sure the gearstick was still in drive. She turned the key all the way off and then tried to crank the engine again, but nothing happened.

Her lips curving downward in an annoyed frown, she put the car in neutral, then got out, and moved to the back bumper. With a few steady pushes, she eased the jeep over to the side of the road and then got back inside to put it in park. She put her flashers on just to be safe, and then took out her phone to call Jared.

Just as she was about to hit send, a Nissan pulled up next to her and the tinted passenger window rolled down to reveal her English teacher, Mr. Evans. He idled in the middle of the road and gave her a greeting wave. "Having car trouble?"

She gave him a polite smile in return, but he made her feel nervous inside. It was like seeing him reminded her of everything she was missing out on — school, dances, tests…all those other things normal teenage girls took for granted. "Well, yeah," she said finally. "But — "

Before she could finish, he was pulling his car forward and parking it in front of hers. As he climbed out of his vehicle, she saw he was wearing his trademarked black suit with the blazer open, showing a blue shirt underneath. He never wore a tie and kept his sandy blond hair just messy enough to look young.

Mykaela stepped out onto the ground and met him at the front bumper. "I'm sure you have somewhere more important to be," she started, but he only gave her a wave of dismissal.

"I can spare a few minutes to take a look at your car," he said. "My dad was a mechanic, so I picked up a thing or two. You want to pop the hood?"

He was using that same tone he'd always used in class, indicating that she really had no choice. So she reluctantly did as he instructed, then lingered around the front bumper while he lifted the hood and propped it open.

"It's a shame you haven't been able to make it to school," he said as he leaned over to look at something. "We've missed you."

"I doubt that," she said.

"You're pretty cynical for someone your age," he said, glancing at her. "But then, considering what you've been through, I don't think anyone can blame you."

She didn't know what to say to that, so she slid her hands in her back pockets and surveyed the road. There were no other cars in sight, just a stretch of fields on each side.

"What I mean to say is, come back when you're ready." He stood up, then nodded toward the car. "Give it another try."

It took her a minute to realize he was now talking about the Jeep and not school, so she pulled open the door and reached over to turn the key. She cranked it, but nothing happened. Just as she turned back around to tell him, she ran straight into his chest. Trapped between his body and the small triangle of space created by the open car door, she was caught completely by surprise. Before she could voice a word, he clamped his hand over her mouth and she felt the sharp prick of a needle in her neck.

What the hell? she thought, struggling to pull her face away from his grasp. But her body was weakening by the second, and her vision was turning blurry. Within seconds, the world around her dimmed out of focus.

Chapter Thirteen

When Mykaela woke, she was groggy and lightheaded. Her entire body felt heavy and her mind couldn't form a coherent thought. Through her fuzzy vision, she could make out a dimly lit room with dark cement walls. She tried to stand, but her body caught on something. Looking down, she realized her arms and legs were bound to a bulky metal chair by thick, heavy chains. She gave her arm a good tug, but the chains didn't budge. Focusing her strength, she tried again, but she couldn't break free.

"You woke a lot sooner than I expected." Mr. Evan's voice echoed from somewhere behind her. It sounded colder, less charming than usual. "It just confirms what I've suspected all along."

She craned her neck, trying to see him, but the edges of the room were shadowy and she couldn't spot him from this position. "Help!" she screamed as loud as she could, praying someone would hear her. "Somebody help me!"

"Your throat will go raw before someone hears you," he said casually. "The room's soundproof."

"What's going on?" she asked, her voice still slurred from whatever had been on the other end of that needle. "Why are you doing this?"

She heard his footsteps against the stone floor as he came closer. As he came into her line of vision, she saw he'd ditched his blazer and was now rolling up the sleeves of his blue button-down. As he tucked the fold in at the elbow, the muscles in his forearm flexed and she struggled to break free again.

"I've been watching you for a long time, Mykaela," he said, turning his attention to the other sleeve. "At first I thought you were just following in your family's footsteps. Training with Brad, playing the big hero. Then I realized, you're not exactly the average hunter, are you?"

Her gaze cut to meet his at the word *hunter*, and she felt her entire body go cold. "Is that what you are?" she asked cautiously. "A hunter?"

He gave her a sideways glance as he finished rolling up his last sleeve, but continued with his train of thought. "Then, in my research, I came across this." He reached into his breast pocket and pulled out an old, yellowed newspaper clipping.

A picture of Mykaela and Dylan stared back at her. Dressed in a fancy dress and an old-fashioned suit, they made quite the stunning couple. *In 1847.*

She studied the article — their engagement announcement — with a poker face, being sure her expression revealed nothing.

"She has your face, your name," he said, leaning down to look into her eyes. "But I've watched you grow up so I know you're not immortal. It begs the question…what exactly *are you?*"

"The resemblance is uncanny," she said, fighting to keep her voice steady and convincing. "But the name has been passed down through my family for generations. I'm sure it's just a coincidence that I look like my namesake."

"Right," he said. He walked over to one of the dark corners as he spoke. "All sorts of things are passed down through your family, aren't they? Like that bed and breakfast your family runs. Have you ever considered getting a security system? Because with all the time you and your brother have spent away from the house lately, anybody could just walk right in and snoop for hours undetected."

She felt anger spark inside her and she twisted her head to look at him. "I don't know who you are, or what you think you're doing, but—"

"I'll tell you who you are," he said, coming back into view again. This time, he had an oversized, hardcover book in his hand. Standing in front of her, he opened it to reveal handwritten, cursive lettering on egg-shell colored parchment. It had Mykaela's name, and the year 1847. "You're the girl who wrote this. A hundred and sixty years ago."

"I've never seen that before," she said, clearing her throat.

"I'm sure you haven't. In this lifetime," he added. "I found it tucked away under some loose floorboards in the attic. From the looks of it, I'd say it hadn't been touched in at least a century."

"You sound crazy. How could I have written that?" she asked, trying to reason with him. "You said yourself, you've watched me grow up."

"I've come to learn that in this town, if something sounds crazy, it's probably true." He pulled a chair up and sat down in front of her. He crossed his leg and propped the book up on it, the way he always did in class.

It was creepy, Mykaela thought. All of this was so very unsettling.

"It's a fascinating read. You wrote everything down in vivid detail," he flipped through pages as he spoke. "From

Dylan being seduced by a siren to the diabolical deal you made with a sea-witch and how horribly it blew up in your face. It's Hans Christian Anderson meets *Faust*."

She only glared at him, too alarmed for words at this point.

With his head lowered, he read aloud from the journal. *"The witch told me that when the time comes, I will be reincarnated."* Looking up, he caught her gaze. *"Only then can I pay my debt and finally be free from this nightmare."*

Mykaela felt chills crawl up her arms. All this time…the truth she'd been searching for was hidden away in her attic. What other undiscovered information was written on those pages?

"Like I said before," she said, her voice turning a little shaky now. "I have no idea what you're talking about."

"No idea," he repeated, lifting one eyebrow. "That's the story you're going with? You're just going to act like I haven't seen you sneaking around all over town to meet this guy?" He held up the photo from 1847 again and pointed to Dylan to emphasize his point. "You're going to pretend that this isn't you. That people haven't been dying around you for years. Come on, Mykaela. Give me a little credit." He tucked the newspaper clipping inside the book and slammed it shut. Leaning forward, his voice was quiet, yet somehow very intimidating as he said, "We wouldn't be having this conversation unless I was absolutely sure that you're the Keeper."

***

Though Harmony Harbor was a picturesque town, parts of it were dying and not in the supernatural way. In the lower-class side of town businesses were shutting down left and right, houses were popping up with real-estate signs in the front yards and hardly any cars travelled the streets. As

Dylan walked down the docks, he passed at least four boats for sale. He guessed Narissa was scaring off the fish.

Finally, he reached the taller end of the dock and hopped down onto the sand below. A few feet away the tide rushed against the shoreline, but right now he wasn't very interested in the ocean. What he needed was waiting for him up ahead, just underneath the dock.

The man was about Dylan's size and wearing a pair of swimming trunks. His brown hair was disheveled and damp and he sort of bounced from foot to foot, like he was full of energy.

"Thanks for meeting me," Dylan said. "I know it's risky."

Bay shrugged, a playful grin on his face. "I owed you a favor anyway."

"What can you tell me?"

"Narissa's kept everything pretty under wraps, but…" he gave a furtive glance around, then stepped further away from the water. Lowering his voice, he filled Dylan in. "Word in the big blue says we'll have a new leader real soon. All the dolphins are excited. Everyone's preparing to welcome Delphinus back. Everyone except you two star-crossed lovebirds."

"Well, we've never been big on conforming," he said. "I was right then? She is after Delphinus."

"Looks like it."

"Are you rejoicing with the rest of them?" he asked.

"Definitely not, mate," he said. "I'm more of a peacekeeper. The last thing I want is some ancient warrior released into today's world."

"Good," Dylan said. "Then maybe you can help me."

"I'm going to have to politely decline," Bay said. "Like I said, I'm a lover, not a fighter."

"This doesn't require any fighting," he assured him. "This is strictly search and retrieve."

"I'm listening, mate."

"When Nerina was killed, the mirror of truth went missing," Dylan said. "At first I thought Narissa had gotten Kerr to steal it, but then I remembered the protection spell. Nerina cast it on her most powerful items, in case anything ever happened to her, the item would be protected."

"So, Nerina dies and the item just goes...poof?" Bay asked, looking confused.

"I think it would automatically transport itself to a safe, predetermined place. Finding it, though, has been tricky."

"Yeah, especially since you've turned your back on your aquatic ways. Apparently you prefer the earth girls, although I can't for the life of me figure out *why*."

Dylan chuckled. "Maybe if you met Mykaela, you'd know. So, will you help me?"

He considered this. "I don't know, Dylan. I've managed to fly under the radar this long. Suppose Narissa finds me and blasts me into a million pieces?"

"If Narissa was after the mirror, we would know," he said. "I don't think it's even occurred to her. She's so egotistical, she thinks the battle's already won."

"I'll look," Bay said finally. "If it's not too dangerous to retrieve it, I will. But then you'll owe me."

"Deal." Dylan reached into his pocket as Bay started to leave. "One more thing."

He turned, waiting.

"If something goes wrong and Narissa succeeds...I'll die," he said. "But you're not cursed, so you won't."

"Is this the part where you ask me to look after your girl in the event of your demise?" he teased, always ready to make light of a serious subject.

"This is the part where I ask you to give her something."

Bay sighed, taking a few steps closer. "Look, Dylan, if there's one thing I've learned about you, it's that you're a survivor," he said. "I'm sure you don't have to worry."

"Just in case, I'd feel better knowing you have this." He handed over a small seashell. "So, if something happens to me, just make sure she gets it. Tell her to drop it in some seawater and — "

"And your heartfelt goodbye message will play," Bay concluded, looking a little solemn at the thought. "I'll make sure she gets it. If something happens to you, which it won't."

"Thank you," Dylan said.

He slipped the seashell into the pocket of his swimming trunks and headed back out toward the ocean. "I'll summon you if I find anything," he called over his shoulder.

Dylan waited until Bay disappeared in the ocean to leave. Next, he'd find Mykaela and make sure nothing else terrible had happened.

***

The confinement of the chains was really making Mykaela feel squirmy. Thick links were wrapped around each arm four times and the weight was heavy. She couldn't move and her leg was itching but she couldn't reach it.

"Tell me what you know about your past life," Mr. Evans said. He was leaned back in his chair again, one foot resting on the other knee as he looked causally at her. It was as if this was some pop quiz or oral test and not a forced interrogation.

"Who are you?" she challenged. The frustration was getting to her and she couldn't keep from lashing out. In the time that had passed, she'd realized that Mr. Evans had sabotaged her car and then pretended to help all so he could ambush her and bring her here. Making him just one more person she'd trusted who betrayed her. Like Dylan, like Kerr, like her own father. All any of them ever cared about was the souls. "What kind of teacher admits to stalking one of his students? And then kidnaps her to ask crazy questions about past lives and sea witches?" As she was ranting, she realized something, and her words slowed. "Wait...you're with the hunter's council, aren't you?"

He only gave her a small little smirk, as if proud she'd finally figured it out.

"How many of you are there?" she asked. "And why are you so worried about me, when more dangerous things have been preying on the town for months? Where have you been, huh?"

"Well, at least you're finally admitting you know something," he said. "What else do you know?"

"Why should I tell you anything?"

"Because maybe I can help you," he said.

She started chuckling lightly, shaking her head. "I've heard that one before."

"I know you have," he said. He locked his gaze on hers, and in it she could see something resembling sincerity, but she didn't trust it for a second. "But think about it. If I wanted to hurt you, I could have. Are you hurt?"

"I'm chained to a chair in..." she hesitated, narrowing her eyes into a glare. "Where the hell are we, anyway?"

"I'm afraid the restraints were a necessary precaution. I've seen what you can do, Mykaela." A small grin played at his lips. "I'd hate to get my head ripped off with a necklace or wind up on the other end of your knife."

"I only hurt people who deserve it," she said.

"I'm not your enemy, Mykaela," he said. "You've obviously been trying to pay some kind of...penance for what you did. Clearly you don't want to fulfill your bargain or you would've given the witch what she wants by now. You're risking a lot by disobeying her, and yet, you do it anyway."

"You know all of this just by slinking around in the shadows?" she asked, shifting uncomfortably in the hard metal chair. "Just how long have you been watching me, anyway?"

"Long enough."

Suddenly, the door opened and Jared rushed into the room. Seeing her, his face contorted in a mixture of shock, horror and something else, something Mykaela couldn't quite place.

Seeing her brother, her heart filled with hope and relief. "Jared, thank God!" she cried, struggling against the chains. "He ambushed me with this needle and when I woke up, I was in here and he won't let me go..."

The words died on her lips when Jared turned and shut the door, locking the three of them in the room. Feeling her heart drop, she watched in disbelief as he turned to face her, a stone cold look in his dark brown eyes.

"You went a little off plan," he said to Mr. Evans.

"I had to," he said. "There was a hitch and the plan needed adjustments."

She couldn't form a single word as a thousand questions flooded her mind. Why was he doing this? How much did Jared know? Why wasn't he saving her?

He made no effort to move forward and unchain her, and he didn't give Mr. Evans a second look. As he stared emotionlessly back at her, she realized that he was in on this just before he said, "You need to tell us where to find those souls, Mykaela."

Chapter Fourteen

Brad's engine rumbled, slow and steady, as his truck idled in a parking space just outside the bar. With his hands gripped tight around the steering wheel, he peered through the windshield at the quiet autumn night and wondered how he'd ended up here.

Though the clock on the dashboard told him it was 1:00 a.m., he didn't remember getting out of bed. Glancing down, he saw he was fully dressed in a pair of jeans and his leather jacket, but he didn't remember picking any of it out. His pulse raced and his heart struggled to pump blood through his body. Even over the sound of the engine, he could hear his heart thump in desperation to survive. The exertion made beads of sweat gather around his hairline and the edges of his vision were blurry.

It was the transition, he realized. His decision to die had been so concrete before. He'd known what he wanted, and really, he'd had no reason to survive. But now that Charity was back...he was more tempted than ever. How could he leave her all alone and unprotected in a town like Harmony Harbor? And so soon after getting her back? But at the same time, how could he expect to be with her if he completed his transition to monster? Even if he did somehow manage to control the urge to kill her, Charity had made it clear how she felt about anything that wasn't human.

Just as he was about to shift gears and drive home, his ears picked up the sound of a door swinging open, then music drifted out from the bar across the street. His hand hesitated on the gear stick as he continued to listen, hearing the annoying click-clack-click-clack of high-heeled shoes against the cobblestone sidewalk. The footsteps were unsteady and offbeat, like the girl was drunk.

His grip tightened on the steering wheel as an alluring smell drifted through his open window. The pheromones enticed him, called to him. It was coming from her, he realized, and even before he saw her, he felt the overwhelming urge to kill her.

When he looked out the window and saw the scantily clad girl stumbling down the street by herself, the urge magnified. He clutched the steering wheel tighter, focusing all of his attention on the grip to keep his body inside the cab of the truck. Then she turned down an alley between two buildings and his mind thought it was the perfect opportunity to complete the transition and ensure that he would be around to protect Charity forever.

"It's not the way," he muttered through clenched teeth, desperately trying to break through his survival instinct. But the more he fought, the more tired he became. And the weaker he grew, the stronger the urge.

Soon, it was as if he possessed no control over his body. There was just the urge, his primal nature. Feed. Survive.

These instincts driving him, he slipped out of the car and made his way across the dark street with quick motions. Stepping in to the alley, he saw the girl's shadow stretching out across the pavement up ahead. Mustering up the last of his strength, he forced his feet to stop and tried to convince himself to get back in his truck.

He could fight this, his mind argued, he *needed* to fight this. It was better to die after twenty-one years as a human than live forever as a monster.

Just as he was about to win the battle, the girl turned, pushing a wave of pheromones across the alley and straight toward him. At the scents, his hunger reactivated like a flipped switch and his control disappeared.

In an instant, he dashed across the alley and grabbed the girl by her shoulders. As her lips parted to scream, he leveled his gaze on hers and felt this force come out of him, like a *push*. "Don't scream," he ordered, his hand clutching her shoulders tight. "Don't make a sound."

The sound died on her lips, and the girl stared back at him with wide and confused eyes. Seeing the fear on her face, smelling the signs of it emanating from her body made guilt tug at his heart. Still, it was no match for the ravenous hunger. "I don't want to do this," he said, his voice panicked and quick. "You have to know that. Everything inside of me is fighting it…but that's the thing about fights, I guess. They can only last for so long before something eventually wins."

Her lips moved, but no sound came and that alarmed her more. She started struggling, her blond hair whipping him in the face and flooding him with that scent as she beat her hands against his chest and tried to wriggle free. But something inside of him, the darkness, the *predator*, liked the struggle, thrived on it. He shifted their bodies toward one of the buildings and pinned her against it. Without a second thought, he crushed his lips against hers and let the feeding begin.

The strength that flowed from her lips to his overwhelmed him. A fire ignited beneath his skin, spreading through his face and quickly down each limb and filling him with a sense of power he'd never known he craved. He couldn't stop, couldn't break his lips away even though she struggled between his body and the jagged bricks. As the predator thrived, the human in him died.

Suddenly, a bone-shattering pain shot through his head, forcing his body to jerk back on reflex. The pain intensified, urging him to his knees. The streetlamps began to flicker on and off as he felt another presence, a stronger one, enter the alley. Through the flickering light, he could make out Charity's figure moving toward him with elegant, graceful strides. As she came closer, one hand outstretched, her lips murmuring words in a language he didn't recognize, the pain intensified.

The pain ripped through his body, disabling him while Charity ordered the girl to run. The girl scrambled away and tore out of the alley. Once they were alone, Charity turned a furious look to the monster on his knees. "Who are you?" she demanded. "What did you do with Brad? How do you look like him?"

He gripped his head and tried to fight through the pain. "It's me."

"You were attacking that girl," she shouted, twisting her hand. He felt his right arm jerk behind his back, the bones stretching at a very uncomfortable angle. "Brad would never do that."

"I wish this wasn't me but it is."

"No," she whispered, her hand falling.

As her hand dropped, the pain ceased, allowing him a moment to catch his breath. While he tried to recover, she stared at him and tried to figure out if he was telling the truth.

But before he could gain a full minute of relief, another type of pain tore through him like a tornado, from the inside out. As the hormones he'd absorbed took full effect on his body, he let out a ragged, tormented scream. Spots all over his body started to ache: his hands, between his shoulder blades. Something was growing inside him, tearing its way out.

***

Charity stared in shock and awe as Brad's body changed before her eyes. Dark-as-night veins bulged and rippled beneath his skin. His fingernails sharpened into talons and with another scream of total agony, he slammed his fist down into the ground, creating a chasm at least two inches deep.

A fierce gust of wind whipped around them as Brad's screaming finally stopped. He stayed there, hunched forward on the ground, breathing heavy and ragged. She watched his back rise and fall with the heaves and slowly reached out to touch him.

In a flash, he was on his feet, his arms thrust out and his face turned toward the sky as his desperate shout echoed in the alley. "No!"

A spontaneous burst of lightening allowed her to take in the view of huge, dark wings coming from behind Brad. His head slowly lowered to look at her, and she saw his eyes were glowing bright red and ravenous. His t-shirt hung in tattered pieces around his shoulders and his lips were pulled back in a vicious snarl, revealing two rows of razor-sharp teeth.

Falling back a step, Charity stared in fear at the winged creature with Brad's face. Seeing her, the animal snarl disappeared, replaced by a look of bewilderment and shame. The red glow faded and his eyes returned to their normal steely color.

He dropped to his knees, hunching over once again. He grunted in pain as the wings burrowed themselves back into his flesh. When his body finally looked human again, he let out a shaky sigh of relief and cautiously looked up at her.

Her expression must've revealed her utter confusion and bewilderment, because taking one look at her, the shame swarmed his face. "Oh no," he whispered, falling back on his hands. His voice was barely audible and shocked as he murmured, "What have I done? What have I done?"

In that moment, the compassion and heartbreak washed over her, drowning out any fear she'd felt before. She dropped to her knees in front of him and reached out, placing her hand on his. The second she touched him, she could feel his fear and anguish. More than anything, she just wanted to help him. "Tell me what's happening to you," she whispered, locking eyes with him and urging him to confide in her.

But he was still panicked and upset. His words came out in jumbled, barely comprehensible fragments. "I never wanted this. This wasn't supposed to happen. I was supposed to die. *That's* what I wanted."

"Calm down," she said, squeezing his hand for comfort. "I don't understand."

"I gave up my humanity," he blurted out, still rambling. "I didn't mean to but I guess...just for a second, I wanted it....and now..." his eyes widened and his head shook gently from side to side. "Now..."

He stood to his feet, stumbling back and away from her. "I'm so sorry," he said, whispering still. "I'm so sorry, Charity."

"Maybe I can help you," she started, but he violently shook his head and backed further away.

"No, you can't help me," he said. "No one can."

Turning, he took off in a run. She started after him, but the second she did, those expansive black wings sprouted from his back and his feet left the ground. Amazed, she watched as Brad's body soared high into the air, those wings flapping him higher and higher, carrying him away from her. She watched as he blurred across the night sky like a dark angel.

***

"You set me up." Mykaela looked across the dungeon-like room to her older brother, who did nothing to stop a fellow hunter from chaining her up like a prisoner. "You were never going to let me help you."

There was a flash of guilt in Jared's dark eyes, but in an instant it was gone.

"You just wanted me to trust you." She swallowed a lump of tears as the realization fully dawned on her.

Jared glanced over at Mr. Evans, who sat in a fold-out chair in front of Mykaela, watching the charade play out. "I need a minute alone with my sister."

Mr. Evans looked back and forth between them, then stood. Jared stepped away from the door to let him out. And for a second, just a second, she was sure he'd help her escape. He'd only been playing along, he hadn't really betrayed her. Then he locked the door again.

She couldn't even look at him now. Lowering her gaze to her lap, she tried to blink back tears. For the longest time, neither of them moved, or spoke, or attempted to offer comfort or explanations. There was only heavy, unbearable silence.

Finally, she heard Jared's work boots scuffle across the floor as he came closer to her. He grabbed the fold out chair with one hand and turned it around, sitting in it backwards.

Resting his arms on the back of the chair, he looked at her closely. "I'm so sorry it had to come to this."

"Then let me go," she said, her voice barely above a whisper.

He sighed. "I can't."

Her only reply was a disgusted scoff. When she lifted her head to look at him, a few tears escaped and rolled down her cheeks.

"You won't stay out of it any other way," he said. "You know that."

"So this is some kind of punishment?" she asked, her voice harsh and bitter. "Are you just going to kidnap me every time I don't do what you say?"

"This isn't a punishment," he said. "This is tough love."

She shook her head at his delusional display of affection. It was probably the most ridiculous thing she'd ever heard, and she'd heard many ridiculous things.

Reaching to the floor next to him, he picked up the journal Mykaela had written in 1847. "You weren't kidding when you said I didn't know the whole story." He opened it up to find the photograph Mr. Evan's had used as a bookmark. Looking down at the picture, he wore a subtle look of awe. "I've seen a lot of things, but reincarnation? That's one I never would've believed, if the whole prophecy wasn't playing out before my eyes."

She shifted in the chair, looking away from him, to one of the four stone walls.

"And I knew this...thing between you and Dylan was unhealthy, but I had no idea it was so twisted." He locked eyes with her again. This time, he was the one who looked disgusted. "The things you did... just to keep him with you. The lives you were willing to sacrifice."

"That wasn't me," she said, her voice shaking under the shame. "Not really."

"How do I know that?" he asked. "Because I feel like I don't even know who you are anymore."

"I'm your sister," she said, the frustrated cry echoing in the cold, dark room.

"Are you?" he asked, narrowing his eyes in confusion. "Or are you just the reincarnation of someone I'll never understand?"

"Is that why you've got me locked in here?" she asked, trying in vain to brace herself against the sting of his words. "You see me as the enemy now."

"No. No, of course not," he said, looking frustrated. He kicked the chair back as he stood up and paced across the small room. "Look, I don't know what to make of all of this okay? It's just...it's too much."

She nodded slowly, staring at him the entire time. "Welcome to my life."

"I mean it's too much for *you*," he said, pointing at her with the journal in his hand. "This wasn't supposed to happen to you. You were going to grow up and go to college. Meet a great guy and have kids. And now, what? You're supposed to lose everything because of something that happened over a century ago? It isn't fair!" He screamed the last bit and the sound echoed back at them from the cement walls as he hurled the book across the room. The hardcover smacked against the wall with a loud *thunk* and hit the floor.

Mykaela jumped in her seat at the sound.

Quiet, his breathing forcedly slow and even, he allowed his body to fall back and lean against the wall. "I don't know how to get you out of it yet," he said finally, returning to the point he'd been trying to make all along. "So you're just going to stay here until I do."

"Listen to yourself, Jared," she reasoned. "This is crazy. If you'll just think about it a minute, you'll see that."

"It's no crazier than anything else lately."

"It's no secret you've been a control freak since mom got hurt, but this time you've gone overboard. Big time. You can't do this," she said. "In here, I'm a sitting duck. I won't even be able to defend myself." She yanked at the chains to show him that she could barely move. "If you want me protected, you need to let me go."

He studied her for a second, taking his time looking from the chains and back to her face before he answered. "Tell you what," he said finally. "Promise me you won't leave this room, and I'll untie you."

"Fine," she said, deciding it was a start at least.

He untied her arms, and then handed her the key so she could unchain her legs. "So tell me," he said as she worked to get her last leg free. "How does this all work? Do you remember what you did back then? Have you always known what you were supposed to do?"

Though she was still angry with him, she decided she owed him a couple answers. "No," she said slowly, reluctantly. "Not really. At first I didn't remember anything. But lately, bits and pieces have been coming back. And, for whatever it's worth, the part of me that did this…created the curse…it's gone now. I mean…I can't believe I…" she let her words trail off.

As she freed herself from the last chain, she stood, prompting him to stand quickly and brace himself.

"Relax," she said, shooting him a look as she walked over to the far side of the room. "I'm just stretching."

He nodded, but didn't sit back down. Instead he just kind of lingered by the two chairs, watching her. "Now, what can you tell me about the souls? Do you know where they're stored?"

She turned to him as she stretched her arms up over her head and pressed her palms together. "Why do you want to know?"

"So we can end this, once and for all."

"And who are 'we'?" she asked. "Whoever owns this place?"

"Mykaela, I can't answer any of your questions," he said. "I'm sorry."

"So am I," she said, and then she rushed at him. Grabbing him by the shirt, she hurled him across the room. As he smacked against the cold stone wall, she fled for the door and flung it open. She made a mad dash for the hallway outside, but ran straight up against something solid and bounced right back into the room. Puzzled, she tried to step over the threshold again, but it felt like she was bumping into some sort of invisible barrier.

What the hell? she thought as her fingers pressed up against something she couldn't see. Behind her, she heard Jared stand to his feet, chuckling softly.

"You remember that room I told you about?" he asked, coming closer.

The one that could hold any supernatural being, she realized with a sickening, suffocating feeling. Even though she knew it was futile, she kept pressing up against that invisible barrier and attempting to escape.

"Like I said," Jared's voice came from behind her.

She turned an enraged glare to Jared as he approached.

He looked winded and a little hurt as he came toward her. "Until I figure out how to kill the sea-witch, you're staying here." Then he lunged at her with another syringe.

***

The door to Brad's apartment flung open without being touched. Charity used her newly endowed magic to turn on the lights, as well, and then moved around the small living room in a violent search for answers.

With a flip of her finger, she sent couch cushions flying into the air, but she found nothing important hidden underneath them. She turned to Brad's desk in the far corner of the room and began searching wildly through the mess of papers and notes. There was no information on a creature with wings that preyed on women in dark alleys.

Kneeling down, she yanked open a drawer and rifled through it. She found some highlighters, a few knives and a first-aid kit. Moving on to the next, she found a small, weathered book. Reaching out, she picked up and knew instantly that had belonged to Brad's mother. Opening the leather cover, she scanned the first page, and her attention was hooked from the very first line.

I can't believe what I've done.

She wasn't sure how long she sat there, reading the secrets on those ink-stained pages. But she made no effort to move from Brad's desk chair once she'd finished the last journal entry. In a stunned daze, her mind tried to wrap itself around the story of Brad's origin.

His mother had been so desperate to have a child that she'd made a deal with the devil. As a result, Brad was half-siren, half-human. A dangerous incubus that fed on human hormones and left their victims as nothing but drained corpses. And now that his transition was complete and his human side was gone, there would be nothing to stop him from hurting people.

***

It wasn't strange to find the Seaside Inn empty these days, so at first Dylan thought nothing of it when he went to visit Mykaela and no one was home. But as he was leaving her bedroom, he noticed the sword he made her was sitting on her desk. She never went anywhere without it, and she usually at least kept it in her car.

He had an uneasy feeling he couldn't shake, so he decided to retrace the route she usually took when she patrolled. When he came upon her Jeep abandoned on the side of the road, he knew something was seriously wrong. He took out the cheap, prepaid phone he carried and tried to call her, but her phone went straight to voicemail. Jared's did, too and no one answered Brad's number.

Where is everybody? he thought. He needed help, and he could only think of one person who might be able to help him.

The door to Brad's apartment was standing open when Dylan arrived. He cautiously looked inside to find the place ransacked. Among the scattered rubble and debris, Charity sat at the desk. Dressed in a long white dress, her platinum blond hair hanging straight down either side of her face, she looked ghostly and ethereal. A numb and vacant look was on her face, causing him to step inside cautiously.

"Are you okay?" he asked, taking a tentative step toward her.

She didn't move even a muscle to acknowledge his presence. Her gaze stared, hard and unyielding, at something hidden beneath her hands folded on her lap. "What are you doing here?" Her voice was shaky and quiet.

Concerned, he looked around awkwardly and realized this was a bad time to ask for a favor, especially one from Charity. But he needed to ask. "I need your help."

She scoffed.

"Actually, Mykaela does," he said, coming a little closer. "I think something bad might've happened to her."

"Bad things keep happening everywhere," she said.

"I know you're angry with her," he said. "No one can blame you for it. But are you just going to keep acting like all of those years of friendship mean nothing to you?"

Charity's gaze moved to meet Dylan's in a cold stare. In it, he could see she was nowhere near forgiving Mykaela, yet. But he hoped he could do something to shed light on Charity's misconceptions. "Did you know Mykaela tried to go back in after you?" he asked, and Charity looked away again. But he could hear in the way her heartbeat sped up that she was listening to him. "After I pulled her out of the ocean, she tried to run back in after you. She was crying, fighting, screaming your name, all the way up until she passed out. She would've drowned herself looking for you."

Charity stood to her feet in a sharp, swift movement that cut Dylan's words short. "I'm not in the mood to relive history."

He held her gaze a moment before speaking. "Are you sure? Because it looks like you're just sitting here, feeling sorry for yourself."

"How dare you?" she asked, tilting her head in a glare to size him up. "You have no idea what I've been through tonight!"

"You're right, I don't." He motioned around the apartment. "But from the looks of things, you could use something to keep your mind busy."

With a small sigh, she crossed her arms and surveyed the room casually. As if concluding he was right, she said, "What makes you think I could help you, anyway?"

"Because I know what you are," he said, taking a step closer. "And I know what you can do."

She narrowed her eyes, just enough to let him know he'd struck a nerve.

"I won't tell anyone," he assured her. "Your secret is safe with me. I just need you to help me find Mykaela."

She stared at him a minute before dropping her arms. "Fine. But we can't do it here. We need to go to the beach."

***

The half-moon overhead lit the way for Charity and Dylan as they approached the beach outside Mykaela's house. The sounds of the water echoed around them like static.

"I need to find a few things." Charity crouched by the shore and motioned to the deserted inn behind her. "Can you run inside and grab a tourist's map from the front desk? And something that belongs to Mykaela. Something she wore."

It only took him a second. With a loud swoosh, he left and came back with the map before the wind around him had settled. The cool, calm tide flowed against Charity's ankles as she searched the wet sand at the shoreline until she found a seashell. She used the pointed tip of the small cone-shaped shell to draw a circle in the sand.

Watching her, Dylan saw an entirely different side to Charity. She no longer seemed like the angry victim who'd drowned a horrible death and came back to a harsh and cruel world, instead, she seemed serene and comfortable with herself. As if this, the beach, the ocean, was where she belonged.

"Where did you learn all of this?" he asked.

She glanced at him a moment before answering. "Witches have complete dominion over the other side. When I died, I was reunited with my ancestors. They taught me." Each movement was assured and confidant as she dipped the laminated map and the lightning bolt necklace he'd given her into the ocean. Once they were damp, she sat down in the middle of the circle and laid the items out in front of her.

"So you were a witch before," he concluded.

She nodded. "And I came back as a white sea-witch."

"Like Nerina," he whispered, feeling a small, but undeniable, spark of hope. Of course, he realized. Nature always found a balance—that was the first rule in any type of magic. When Nerina was killed, it tipped the scales in Narissa's favor too much, so the witches found a balance. It was one tiny, but significant, step toward victory. It also meant, he hoped, that Charity was sent back to help them.

When he looked up at Charity, he found her staring at him, studying him. He didn't know what made her look so closely, so he asked, "what?"

"I'm ready to do the spell," she said, recovering from whatever the stare was about. "But I need you to stand back so your power doesn't interfere with mine."

He moved back until she signaled him to stop, then watched from the distance. She lowered her head and brought her hands together prayer-style, with Mykaela's necklace dangling between her interlace fingers. After a moment of concentration, she scooped up a handful of sand and held it up in the air as far as she could reach.

A subtle but forceful wind whipped around her in the circle as she chanted. It blew her hair around her face like a flickering candle flame. Opening her hand, she let the sand fall in a slow, steady stream. The tiny grains formed a small tornado in the wind, swirling them around until each one landed gracefully on the map.

Then the wind died down, and Charity motioned for him to come over. As he came inside the circle, he felt a chill of power ripple through him and knew it was coming for her.

On the map, a trail of sand marked a path from the Seaside Inn to a spot on the outskirts of town.

"The locator spell found her at the Harmony plantation," she said, pointing to a spot on the map where the sand was the thickest.

"Thank you," he said, starting in that direction.

"Wait," Charity called, leaning over to examine the map closer.

Dylan hesitated at the edge of the circle, looking back at her.

"This place...it's one of the only places in town that isn't around the ocean. There's no water around for miles," she said, standing.

He stared blankly at her. "Okay..."

She sighed impatiently. "It means that whoever has her isn't drawing power from the ocean the way we do. They must be human—hunters, I'm guessing. And if you get hurt with their favorite little glass knives, you won't be able to heal yourself."

"Thanks for the tip," he said, "But if they have Mykaela, I still have to go."

"*We* have to go," she said reluctantly. When he looked at her, she said, "Oh, don't look at me like that! I might be mad at her, but I'm not going to let her get hurt. I'm just suggesting that we go about this in a smart way."

***

When Mykaela finally awoke from the drug-induced stupor, she was chained to the chair once again. She felt weak and dizzy as she lifted her head to look for Jared.

He was sitting in the fold-out chair, positioned in the corner of the room. He looked tired and worn down as he sat in silence.

"Again with the chains?" she asked, her voice shaky and weak. Looking down, she saw there was something else in her arm. A needle and tube hooked to an IV bag pumped medicine into her veins. It stung and burned and she pulled at her arm, trying to break free. What was in that needle? And why was Jared doing this to her? Whatever drug was going into her system was making her feel lightheaded and sluggish.

"It's just a sedative," Jared said softly, his indifferent voice coming from the dark corner of the room. "Just to make sure you don't hurt anyone," he said.

"Is that really what you think of me?" she asked.

He was quiet, thoughtful. "I don't know what to think anymore."

"Then let me fill you in," she spat venomously. "I would never hurt anyone. I would never put my debt above someone else's life and I would *never* do *this* to *you*."

"Do you think I like this?" he asked, standing. He looked down at her, his face a mix of conflicting emotions. "I don't! But you're too strong and iron-willed. There's no stopping you when you set your mind on something and I can't let you give Narissa those souls. It'll be the end of all of us."

"I would never give them to her," she started to protest, but Jared cut her off again.

"Not without something really important to you at stake," he said. "So far you've managed to hold on to your resolve even through massacres and magical comas and resurrected friends. But how long do you think you can keep that up? How long before Narissa threatens to take something you just can't live without? How long before she finally breaks you?"

Her mind was still clouded, so although she heard him, his words had no affect over her.

"You can hate me for this all you want." He bent in front of her, bringing them eye level. "But you're going to stay here until I kill the sea-witch, and if you know where the souls are, don't say a word. To anybody. No matter what."

The desperation behind his words caught her attention, and she looked at him in confusion and fatigue. Finally, she nodded. "I won't."

His heavy work boots thumped against the floor as he walked over to the door and opened it, flooding the room with light. She squeezed her eyes shut as the brightness of it overwhelmed her senses, and when she opened them again, she caught a glimpse of Jared looking back at her from the doorway. As the door closed, darkness fell over the room again.

She didn't know how much time had passed before the door opened again. All she knew was that she was tired, and her muscles were stiff and sore and she was bored out of her mind.

Her neck ached as she lifted her head up to look at her visitor. Mr. Evans carried a small lantern inside and let the heavy door swing shut behind him.

"Let me save you some time." She shifted in her seat to sit up straight. "I'm not going to answer any questions."

"I didn't come to ask any." Sitting the lantern on the floor beside them, he took a seat in the foldout chair still in front of her.

Narrowing her eyes, she wondered what he'd meant, but she didn't ask. Instead, she waited, watching him carefully.

"In all this time that beings—supernatural and human alike—have been searching for the vault of souls, I'm surprised no one's figured it out." He leaned an arm against the back of his chair as he spoke to her, his eyes filled with amusement and triumph.

A feeling was nagging at Mykaela's gut, telling her he knew way too much. She hoped she was wrong.

"Let's think about it a minute. Of all the things on this earth, what has the power to contain a human soul?" He waited, then framed his ear in a mocking gesture when she didn't respond. "The human body."

Her heart gave a wild thump in fear as his eyes lingered wickedly on hers. She swallowed hard, pressing herself further back into the chair. Her senses became acutely aware of the chains binding her arms and legs.

"And out of the people who cast that tragic spell in 1847, which was human?" He leaned in, bringing his face closer to hers as his lips spread in a proud smile. "In exchange for saving your fiancé, you agreed to let Narissa store all of those cursed souls in your body, didn't you?" he asked, his voice a taunting whisper. "That's why you're so strong, so fast, so quick to heal. That's why you lure supernatural entities to our town like a beacon."

She tugged at the chains around her arms in hopes she could break free, but her arm could barely move, and the drug moving through the IV tube was making her weaker by the second. As she stared him down, she knew her once-kindly and supportive English teacher had just turned into her most dangerous enemy.

"There's only one way to stop this before Narissa uses you again." Standing, he moved the chair, sliding it across the floor and out of the way with excruciatingly slow movements. "There's only one way to set those souls free and end the reign of terror you brought upon us all."

He stopped in front of her once again, and in the blue-tinted light from the lantern, she saw something metal glint. Realizing he had a knife, her heart started thumping in her chest. It was beating so hard it felt like it would burst through her chest like some old-fashioned cartoon. Yanking her arms as hard as she could, she struggled and writhed against the heavy metal keeping her captive in the chair.

"To break the curse…" Stepping forward, he brandished the knife, causing a blue beam of light to bounce around the room. "You have to die."

Chapter Fifteen

The Harmony plantation house stood, each massive brick wall casting looming shadows over the field around the old building. It was so old that Dylan could remember attending a party or two there in the 1800's with Mykaela and her family. But now, each window was boarded up and no light came out of the house, making it look like a giant, shadowy mass in the night.

"That's creepy," Charity said, taking a moment to look at the house. She ran her fingers along the strap of her messenger bag nervously, then dropped her hand to pat the bulk of the bag, as if reassuring herself of what was inside. Inside, they'd brought everything they needed to protect themselves.

They'd spent a good twenty minutes getting bottles of seawater and sand and collecting seashells, and although Dylan didn't know exactly what Charity planned to do with those items, they seemed to make her feel better about coming.

"That's a really big house," she said, still lingering in the shadows of the woods. "I doubt we'll have time to search the whole thing. Can you narrow it down, a little?"

He nodded, and then focused all his attention on listening carefully. Inside the house, he could hear the heavy footsteps of several men. From the sound of heartbeats, there were at least four of them on the first floor. He ignored them and instead listened for the familiar sound of Mykaela's heartbeat. Finally, he found it, dull and faint, coming from seemingly under the house. He could tell her breathing was labored and slowed, as if she was in pain. "She's in the basement," he said. "And she sounds hurt."

They found a door on the side of the house. It was set at the end of a dark, narrow staircase. As Charity and Dylan descended the steps, suddenly Charity said, "Wait."

Dylan stopped, looking back at her.

"At the bottom of the steps," she said, pointing. "Look."

He adjusted his vision to the darkness and took a closer look. Right after the last step, on the small slab of stone before the door, there was a small circle of blue and purple chunks of glass.

"Fulgurite," he said. "That was a close one."

"Yeah." She squeezed past him and stepped down into the center. The trap did nothing to her, so she picked up one of the chunks and broke the circle. She stepped out of the way, slipping the piece of glass down inside her messenger bag.

Dylan used his heightened strength to break open the door and then led them inside a cold, dark hallway. Inside the house, Dylan followed the faint sound of Mykaela's heartbeat to a bulky metal door. Charity hesitated outside the door, suddenly going perfectly still, but Dylan was on a mission.

He yanked open the door, breaking the chain lock right off it and saw Mykaela chained to a chair. In front of her, a tall, dark haired man stood with a knife in his hand. He turned when the door opened, raising the knife in the air.

With a flick of his wrist, Dylan sent the man hurtling across the room. He smashed into one of the hard stone walls and fell to an unconscious heap on the floor. His knifed clattered to the ground next to him.

Mykaela's eyes widened when she saw him, relief flooding her face. "Dylan," she whispered.

He rushed inside without thinking first and knelt at the edge of the chair. He was horrified to see she was hooked up to some kind of IV and her arms were bound by thick heavy chains. Her eyes were still wide and horrified. He carefully pulled the needle out and then cradled her face in his hands so he could look into her eyes. "Hey, look at me," he said, trying to get her hazy eyes to focus on his, but she was weak from whatever had been in the IV bag. He dropped his hands to the chains and pulled each one at once, causing them to break.

Now that the needle was out of her arm, Mykaela's head seemed to be clearing. "You shouldn't have come in here," she said, clinging to him to support her weight as she stood.

"We have to get you out of here," he said, wrapping an arm around her waist. He pulled her toward the door, but she was fighting him. He didn't understand until he tried to step over the threshold…and couldn't.

"We can't leave," she said, her voice sounding weak. "Nothing supernatural can. It's some kind of spell."

"What?" he asked, a sudden rush of panic flooding over him. Who had locked her in a room that nothing supernatural could escape? His gaze flew to Charity, who was still lingering outside the room, looking just as panicked. "Can you break it?"

Her eyes were wide and full of fear as her gaze darted from the door, to the hallway where the exit was located. For a second, Dylan thought she might leave them both here.

"What?" Mykaela asked, sounding confused as she looked back and forth between them.

"I don't even know what the spell is," Charity said, her voice shrill. "How can I break it if I don't know anything about it?"

Upstairs, he heard heavy footsteps coming closer. "Someone's coming," he warned. "There's got to be something you can do!"

"I can't lower the barrier," she snapped, her voice frantic. For a second, he was sure she'd bail. Then, realization and hope dawned on her face. She started digging through her bag, whispering, "But maybe I can *rip* it."

She came out with a bottle of sea water and another cone-shaped sea-shell. "Stand back," she ordered as she opened the bottle.

As they fell back a few steps, Mykaela's gaze focused on something across the room. Suddenly, she broke away from him.

Charity thrust the open bottle toward the door, splashing its entire contents against the invisible barrier. The water clung to it and she started to chant as she dug the very tip of the cone shell into her palm until it drew blood. Then she stepped forward, pressing the bloodstained tip against the barrier and moving downward, as if she was slicing something with a knife.

Before their eyes, the seashell left a pale yellow glow in its path. Then, the barrier ripped open. Mykaela returned to Dylan's side clutching a large hardcover book against her chest. Seeing that the glowing light, she looked at Charity in confusion.

"Hurry," Charity said, "it won't last for long."

They dashed through the door and into the hallway.

"How did you do that?" Mykaela asked, staring at her friend in awe.

"There's no time." Charity grabbed Mykaela's wrist and pulled. "We have to get out of here."

The three of them hurried down the hallway, with Dylan leading the way. They turned down another long corridor, heading for the exit. One of the doors to their right opened, and Jared came into the hallway, looking alarmed to see the three of them.

"Jared," Dylan said, relieved to see him. "Do you have any idea what your hunter buddies were —"

Mykaela grabbed Dylan's arm, her fingernails digging in tight as she pulled them both back a couple steps. He saw her cheeks had gone ghostly white again and she watched Jared with a braced look. "He knows," she said, her voice a hoarse, fearful whisper. "He did it."

Dylan's eyes narrowed into angry slits as he turned to look at Mykaela's older brother. Before he could act on any of the anger he was feeling, though, Charity stepped up and blew something off the palm of her hand. Tiny grains of sand flew into Jared's face as Charity whispered, "Sleep."

Jared's eyes rolled back in his head and then closed. His legs buckled, his body slumping to the floor with a thud.

"What did you do?" Mykaela asked, her eyes wide with panic. She knelt at Jared's side, her fingers feeling for a pulse.

"He's just sleeping," Charity said. "He'll be fine."

"I've heard that before."

Her eyes narrowing into a glare, Charity grabbed Mykaela's hand and pulled her to her feet. "Do you want out of here or not?"

Reluctantly, Mykaela nodded, and the three of them took off again.

***

Later, after they'd escaped to safety, Mykaela paced nervously across the floor of Dylan's warehouse. Looking out the windows that overlooked the field, her eyes searched for signs of movement along the edges of the woods, anything to indicate the hunters were coming after her again. "You're a sea-witch," she said, after Charity had finished explaining. She still couldn't believe it. This was Charity. She'd grown up with her and not once noticed anything magical about her. "A sea-witch."

Charity, sitting on one of the bar stools across the room, sighed. "Yes. For the thousandth time, yes."

"A white sea-witch," Dylan added, as if it made the situation less mindboggling. "Like Nerina."

"But Nerina was thousands of years old," Mykaela said. "I just assumed she'd always been a sea-witch. How do you get turned into one?"

"I have no idea," Dylan said.

They both turned to Charity. Her attention was focused on an assortment of seashells spread out in front of her. As if sensing their stares, she looked up, then widened her eyes at them. "Really? We're going to do the expositional thing right now? When those hunters could be coming after you two?"

"I've had enough hunter drama to last a lifetime," Mykaela said.

"Fine." Charity lifted a seashell and a small knife and began carving something into the smooth inside of a shell as she spoke. "It turns out I come from a long line of witches. Dying at the hands of an element is a very powerful thing for a witch...it's like our spirit gets bound to it. Connected to it. So for a while I was just...a water sprite, I guess. Not really alive, just haunting the water. But when Nerina died, white magic needed a new representative. So they chose me."

"Who?" Mykaela asked.

"The witches on the other side."

"And it's that easy to just bring someone back to life?" she asked.

Charity was quiet a moment, obviously thinking about something before she replied. "No, not usually," she said. "But there was a huge massacre not too long ago—at the beach, remember?"

"How could I forget?" Mykaela shuddered at the memories of all those dead bodies and the evil energy left behind.

"While that many souls were crossing over, I slipped through the open door. Well...the witches gave me a little push."

"But...you told me you didn't remember anything between drowning and waking up in your coffin," Mykaela said.

"And you told me you didn't know why Narissa was after you." Charity caught Mykaela's gaze as she tossed the seashell to her. "Guess we've both been keeping secrets."

Mykaela looked down at the seashell she'd caught in her hand. There was a symbol carved into it.

"That'll keep you hidden from Narissa." She picked up another seashell and began to carve the symbol again. "She won't be able to sense you as long as you have that with you. The downside is, neither will I."

"Why did you help me?" she asked suddenly, unable to hold the question inside any longer. "I thought you hated me."

"I don't hate you," she said simply. "But, as a servant of nature—of good magic—I don't approve of what you did."

"No one approves of it," Mykaela retorted. "That's why it's a *curse*."

Charity shrugged, keeping her attention focused on her task.

Turning back to the window, she slipped the seashell in her pocket. "Do you know how to stop Narissa?"

"No," she said without missing a beat. "Not exactly."

Mykaela looked over at Charity again, trying to read her. For what had to be the hundredth time, she examined Charity's aura. Like that night in the cemetery, she was surrounded by a hazy white mist. It seemed Charity was who she claimed to be, but why was she being so secretive? "Meaning?" she prodded, turning to look out the window again.

"Meaning the spirits are all about 'when the time is right'. They'll reveal the answer when they're ready."

"Wait, the spirits?" she asked. "You mean the witches? They're still helping you?"

With a sharp sigh, Charity swiveled on the stool to look at Mykaela. "Do I ask you all the ins-and-outs of being...whatever the hell it is that *you* are? Have I asked you a single question about it?" She shook her head as her words quickened with stifled anger. "And, P.S. you're not the only one who's had a night from hell. So if you wouldn't mind being *quiet*, I'd like to finish these sigils and go home."

Mykaela nodded, wondering what Charity had meant by a night from hell.

"Do you trust me?" she asked, her gaze lingering on Mykaela's.

Last year, she'd have said yes without hesitating. But after everything she'd been through, she wasn't sure. Every time she trusted someone, she ended up burned. Even her own brother had betrayed her, held her hostage and spilled her secrets to God knows who. Still, Charity had saved her life tonight, or at least her sanity. That would be enough to make a normal person—one without all of these hang-ups—trust her. Keeping that in mind, she nodded.

"Then trust that when I know how to stop Narissa, you'll be the first to know." She turned back to the counter. "After all, this is *your* problem. Not mine."

Starting to pace again, Mykaela kept her gaze on the spotted glass window. Outside, clouds covered the sun, making it a dreary overcast day. It somehow made the field outside look creepy and desolate.

At the very edge of the woods, she saw something move. It was quick, just a blur, but she caught it. Stepping closer, she peered through the window. Whatever was out there didn't have an aura, so it was likely Jared. He knew about the warehouse and Mr. Evans had probably followed her here more than once.

She gave a slight jump as she felt Dylan come up behind her. He placed his hands on her shoulders, pressing his lips against her ear. "It's just a deer."

Her body relaxed, just a little. "We can't stay here. It's the first place someone would look."

Charity stood from the stool and crossed the room to them. "You remember where my parent's cabin is?"

Mykaela nodded.

Charity handed Dylan the seashell. "Take her there, then wait for me. I have a few things to take care of here, and then I'll tell you everything I know. Okay?"

As Charity started to leave, Mykaela found herself moving forward, arms stretching out. She pulled Charity into a tight, grateful hug. "Thank you," she said, her voice shaky with emotion.

Charity was stiff and surprised against the hug, but then she gently brought her arms up to embrace Mykaela. Her voice was soft and delicate. "You're welcome."

Mykaela stepped back and let Charity leave, then turned to Dylan. "We should get going, too. I need to stop by home and get a few things."

"You haven't sat still for two seconds, Mykaela," he said, his voice taking on his concerned tone. "You're obviously shaken up. I think we should talk about what happened."

"I can't," she said, stepping back. She raked a hand through her hair. "I can't think about it. We just need to get somewhere safe, okay?"

"He would be stupid to come after you again," he reasoned.

"Alone," she said. "But what if he came with his hunter buddies and fulgurite and more drugs? We wouldn't stand a chance, Dylan."

He looked at her a second, his eyes studying her carefully. Finally, he nodded. "Okay. Let's go."

***

When Charity arrived back at Brad's apartment, the place was cleaner than when she'd left. It wasn't completely disaster free, but the books were back on the shelves and the cushions were back on the couch.

As she was shutting the door behind her, Brad came out of the bedroom with a pile of laundry in his arms. Seeing her, his footsteps slowed and a cautious look crossed his face. "Hey," he said slowly, taking a small step closer.

"Hi," she said, dropping her messenger bag by the door. "What a night, huh?"

He nodded.

"I guess we have a lot of catching up to do." She sat down on the couch and patted the space beside her. "I managed to find most of the answers about you. But I'm sure you have questions of your own."

"Only one." He dropped the laundry to the floor at the end of the hallway and stepped into the living room. He shoved his hands in his pockets and kind of hunched his shoulders, reminding her of a meek little boy. "How much do you hate me?"

"Hate you?" she repeated, tilting her head to look at him with undeniable compassion. She stood, moving a little closer to him, but still kept her distance. "Brad, I feel *sorry* for you." For a moment, her gaze searched his as she gathered words. "I read your mother's diary...and the records you kept. You had no idea what was happening...it was so sad."

As he looked at her, his almond-shaped grey eyes were every bit as tumultuous as the storm clouds outside.

"You didn't have to keep it from me," she said, "but I understand why you did. The only thing I'm concerned about is what you plan to do now. I mean...last night was the first time you fed, right? Your notes were clear about fighting it...all the way up until two days ago."

He nodded, staring at her in awe. Finally, he managed to speak, but the words were broken and unsure. "Uh...yeah, last night was the first time."

"After you left," she asked cautiously, afraid to hear the answer. "Did you hurt anyone?"

He looked down at his hands, then stuffed them in his pockets. "I don't know," he admitted finally. "I blacked out, I think. I woke up outside in the parking lot this morning."

Taking a deep breath, Charity told herself this was okay. Just a hitch in the road, nothing they couldn't conquer together.

He took another step closer, clearing his throat. "But nothing's been reported. I've been keeping an eye out."

"How do you feel now that the transition's complete?" she asked, hesitating before continuing the question, "Do you feel like…"

"A monster?" he asked, with a small, weak laugh. "I thought I would, but surprisingly…I feel like *me*. Unless you count the constant feelings of self-loathing and disgust."

"Good," she said, smiling, coming closer. "That's good, because as long as you're still *you*, we can fight this." She took his hand, lacing their fingers together as she added, "*Together.*"

Chapter Sixteen

"Wow…I haven't been here in years." Mykaela dropped her duffel bag by the door and took a look around the small but quaint cabin. Somehow, even though so much had changed, the place felt just as cozy and homey as when she'd been a kid.

The kitchen was still over-decorated in a country apple theme and the living room had a set of glass doors that overlooked a calm, shallow piece of the ocean. There wasn't a neighbor around for miles. It was the perfect hideout.

Dylan placed a bag full of books — some she'd stolen from Jared's room — on the kitchen table. "Nobody will think to look for us out here," he said. "That's for sure."

"Good." She knelt by the door and unzipped her bag, then reached under a stack of clothes to find the book she'd stashed inside. Pulling out the large, thick book drew a curious look from Dylan.

"Okay, you almost ended up staying trapped in that room to get that thing and you haven't let it out of your sight. What is it?"

Carrying the book over to the table, she took a deep breath and set it down between the two of them.

"It's...well...it's hard to believe, really," she began. "It's the diary I kept in 1847."

His eyebrows lifted in an intrigued look.

"Apparently it was enough to tell Jared everything," she said. "He knew about you and me and the siren. He knew about the deal with Narissa, too." Looking down at the book again, she ran her fingertips over the elegant gold trim. In the sunlight from the windows, it glinted against the dark black hardcover. "Maybe there's something else in here, too," she said, hoping this was true. "Something that will help me get out of the deal."

Dylan reached out and placed his hand on hers, giving her a reassuring smile. "Looks like you've got some reading to do, then." He nodded his head toward the couch. "You go get comfy. I'll make you some tea."

The offer brought up bittersweet memories about her mother. Blanche was always offering some sort of herbal remedy or comfort food, and right now it was exactly what she needed. She tucked the diary against her chest and headed toward the couch, but as she passed him, she stopped. She reached up, wrapping one arm around his neck and pulled him into a hug. With the book pressed between them, he wrapped both arms around her in a bear-tight hug.

"Thank you for saving me," she whispered, tears clinging to her throat. "Again."

She felt his head move up and down against hers in a nod, and for a second, no one needed any words. The way his arms stayed tight around her, protecting and adoring, resonated with her more clearly than anything he could've said. She knew that he would *always* come save her. When she pulled away, she saw his eyes were damp so she planted a kiss on his cheek.

Then she made herself comfortable on the couch and draped an afghan over her lap. Dylan moved around the room like a silent helper, closing all the curtains and turning on lamps, checking the locks. Once they were safely hidden inside, he went to the kitchen and began making tea.

Her heart started to thump with anticipation as she turned her attention to the diary. Turning the cover, she traced her fingertips over the inscription of her name.

She flipped the page and began reading.

Dear Diary, (December 4th, 1846)

Mama and Papa have started their talk of suitors again. And even though I roll my eyes and brush them off, they still won't take the hint. They say people will start to talk if I don't at least make an effort to find a husband.

That's the most important thing in the world, don't you know? Finding a respectable young man and producing a bunch of strong, healthy children. If I refuse to fulfill that crucial task, my life will mean nothing and I will leave no mark on this earth. At least, that is how they see it. With every day I avoid doing what they want, I see that slight look of panic in their eyes. The problem is…there's nobody in Harmony Harbor I can picture myself with. But they will be so very embarrassed if they don't marry me off soon.

They don't understand that I haven't found "it" yet. That feeling described in every romantic story I've ever read and every fantasy I dreamed up as a little girl. Your heart is supposed to thump with joy, not quicken with dread. And when I see the man I'm going to marry, my eyes will go all swooning and doe-like, not squeeze shut in annoyance. When I finally meet him, I will feel it in every part of my body and I will not settle for anything less.

She'd been expecting a play-by-play of how the gruesome deal went down, but she'd never suspected she'd catch a glimpse of the girl she'd been before all of that happened. Before she'd ever met Dylan.

Dear Diary (December 5, 1846)
The most astonishing thing happened today. I was enjoying the last of the warm weather by reading Macbeth on the front porch, when a man stumbled out of the woods. It startled me and I almost screamed for Papa, but then I was filled with this overwhelming urge to help him.

I've never seen wounds like the ones that were on him. His bare feet were blistered and bloody and infected, and there didn't seem to be an inch of his body that wasn't covered in dirt or scrapes. And even though it was the most gruesome thing I've ever seen, when he looked up at me from the ground, our eyes locked and...I felt "it."

At least I think I did. It all happened so quickly and then he passed out from exhaustion. But I remember thinking that his eyes are like emerald jewels and there was this spark in them, this life.

Papa and his servants whisked the boy away and cleaned him up, and now he's sleeping in one of the servant's rooms downstairs. It's late and everyone else is asleep, but I couldn't stop thinking about his eyes. They were so deep and green and I want to know the person behind them.

I couldn't think of anything else, so I snuck into his room. Right now, in the dull candle light, I can see parts of his sleeping form. He looks so much more handsome now that he's cleaned up. His face is long with sharp angles and a strong jaw, but softness around the eyes. And though he's thin, he's not as frail looking as I remember outside on the beach. His arms are strong and muscular and the length of his body is lean. His hair has a tint of red to it, but is mostly blond. He looks so handsome and peaceful, like he's an angel. I just want to touch him to make sure he's real.

Just look at me, rambling like a fool over somebody who's been asleep since I met him earlier today. It's so silly, but I can't seem to stop.

Dear Diary, (December 6th, 1846)
He woke up today, barely — just enough for me to get his name.
Dylan.

Dear Diary, (December 7th 1846)
Dylan and I talked for hours today. He told me his entire story. He was orphaned when his family migrated from Ireland and he travelled all the way from Boston on foot. Can you believe that? I told you he was a survivor.

Over the next month's worth of entries, Mykaela gushed about Dylan on every page. It was clear she'd fallen head over heels for him. So engrossed in her reading, Mykaela barely glanced up and murmured a thank you to Dylan when he brought her a cup of hot tea.

After a while, she took a break and stretched.

***

The next afternoon, Charity entered Brad's apartment with two shopping bags in tow. The first two rooms were empty, so she shut the door and walked down the dark hallway.

In Brad's bedroom, she could hear the sounds of heavy, ragged breathing, and she didn't know what to expect. But when she stepped inside, she saw Brad huddled in the farthest corner of the room. His knees were pulled against his chest, with his arms wrapped around them. He was wearing only a pair of gym shorts and his body glistened with sweat as if he had a fever. His skin was pale and clammy and his limbs shook with frayed nerves and struggling self control.

"What's happening?" she asked, hurrying across the room. Kneeling in front of him, she set the shopping bags on the door and placed her hands on his.

"It's wearing off already," he said, his voice shaky and tense. "The hunger is setting in again, I can feel it. Where were you all night? I could barely keep myself in here."

"I'm sorry," she said, squeezing his hand. "I was out researching and I just lost track of time, but it was worth it, Brad."

But he was barely listening to her. His body continued to shake as he pressed himself further into the corner. "I don't know what to do. My body needs those hormones to survive, but I can't get them without killing people. I'm going to die, aren't I?"

She shook her head, scooting closer to him. "No, that's what I'm trying to tell you," she said, her lips spreading in a hopeful, relieved smile. "I figured it out. I found a way to save you."

He tilted his head, his hazy and fatigued eyes narrowing in confusion. Breaking her hands from his, she reached into one of the shopping bags and pulled out a box. "Those rules that say you have to kill or die are so ancient and dated. I started thinking…in this day and age, there has to be another way. And then it occurred to me. Hormone *supplements*."

That caught his attention, and he leaned forward, his attention drawn toward the box she was opening.

She lifted the flap to reveal several jars of clear serum, each one marked with a white label. "I was out all night looking for just the right ones, but I managed to find all the hormones the books say you need. Oxytocin, estrogen, testosterone, adrenaline. It's all here, Brad."

"Will it work?" he asked as hope sparked in his eyes.

"It should," she said. She reached into the other bag and came out with a package of needles. Taking one out, she prepared his first injection. "We'll have to experiment with the doses a little, but I really think this is the answer."

He stretched his arm out for her and tightened his hand into a fist to make a vein bulge. In his hunger, it wasn't hard to do. Though he'd always been squeamish of needles, the sharp prick didn't seem to bother him now. He watched with hungry, anxious eyes as she plunged a syringe full of oxytocin into his system.

Almost immediately, she could see his eyes soften. A rosy color returned to his cheeks and his back relaxed against the wall. She injected the estrogen next, and then the testosterone. By the time she got to the last one, Brad's posture had relaxed and his color returned to normal.

"It worked," she said softly, smiling. There was nothing to keep them apart now. The relief was so overwhelming it caused tears to sting her eyes.

He smiled, then started chuckling lightly as if a huge weight had been lifted from his shoulders. Reaching out, he cupped her face in his hand, then leaned in and kissed her. When he broke his lips away, he let his face linger close to hers, whispering, "I'm so glad you're here." His eyes were moist with emotion and relief. "Living without you...it was..."

She brought her lips to his to cut him off, and then said, "I'm never leaving you again."

He rested his forehead against hers, closing his eyes.

She gave him a minute to calm down before she told him what they needed to do next. "But we do have to leave together."

"Leave?" he asked, pulling back a little.

"Just to my parents' cabin for a few weeks. This apartment is smack in the middle of town," she said. "It might be easier for you to adjust to the supplements if you weren't around so many humans."

"Okay. You're right." He nodded and pushed himself up off the floor. Walking over to his closet, he pulled out a suitcase and started to pack. "Good thinking. It's less risky that way."

"There's just one...tiny little detail you should know before we get there," she said.

He paused as he placed a shirt on top of a pile in the suitcase, waiting for her to continue.

"Dylan and Mykaela are going to be there."

***

An hour later, even though the back of the truck was loaded down with groceries and clothes and they were only a few minutes away from the cabin, Brad was still having doubts.

"Are you sure it's a good idea?" he asked as he drove his truck down a twisting dirt road shrouded with trees. "The four of us staying at the cabin together?"

"I think it's a better idea than you staying in town, surrounded by all of those humans," Charity said. "The supplements will sustain you, but you've still got to control the urge to kill. And that's easier to do when you're not running into your food every time you step out the door."

"But Mykaela's human," he said.

"And super powered," Charity added. "She'll be fine. Besides, she's the only human out there and I'll take those odds over staying in town." Suddenly, as if sensing that he was keeping something from her, she turned to face him. "What's with the second thoughts? Is there something I don't know?"

He was quiet a minute, then finally admitted, "It's Mykaela."

Charity raised an eyebrow, waiting.

And just as he was about to confess to all the sexual tension and budding feelings that had been building between her best friend and him, he found himself saying instead, "She doesn't know...about the incubus thing. I never told her."

"But she's dating a soul of the sea and her best friend is a sea-witch," she said. "I think she can handle it."

He nodded, knowing Charity was right. And since she was now referring to Mykaela as her best friend again, he didn't want to do anything to jeopardize that. Still, the four of them staying in some secluded cabin gave him the creeps.

***

The log cabin had been built at the edge of the woods, overlooking a shallow part of the ocean. It looked just as she remembered, with the dark wood color and the hand-carved patio set on the front porch.

Across the sand, a dock led to the ocean, but she suspected she wouldn't be using it. Lacing her fingers through Brad's, she prepared herself for the blast from the past.

Inside, Mykaela was reading on the couch. Charity told her they needed to speak in private, so the girls headed upstairs.

"It's all so...surreal," Charity said, as she lingered at the dresser in her old bedroom. She was looking over a collection of small troll dolls, running her fingertips along the fluffy points of colorful hair. "If I stop to think about it for too long, I start to think I'm in some kind of nightmare."

"Yeah," Mykaela said as she sat down at the foot of the twin-sized bed. "Let me know if you find out the key to waking up."

"I think I know," she said, doing a half-turn to look at Mykaela. "But...I need to make sure I can trust you first."

"Then we have a problem," she said, "because I have no idea how to prove that you can trust me."

"You can start by being honest about how you're mixed up in all of this," she said.

In Charity's indigo blue eyes, Mykaela could see that her friend already knew much more than she was letting on. But Charity was the type who could keep a secret.

"Okay, fine." Mykaela took a deep breath and stood as she prepared herself for what came next. "I have a past life. Back then, I made a deal with Narissa. She created a curse that would steal Dylan's soul back from a siren, keeping him immortal. What she didn't tell me was that anyone who died the way he did is affected by the curse too, and the souls are stored somewhere only I can access. And she wants me to give them to her."

Charity kept an even-keeled gaze on her friend. She didn't so much as blink at the confession, which confirmed what Mykaela had suspected. Charity had already known. "Good job. I wasn't sure you had it in you."

She gave Charity a wry smile. "See? You can trust me. Now what do you know?"

"Every spell needs a power source. For the curse, it was your love for Dylan. For my resurrection, it was the massacre on the beach." Charity turned and walked over the set of double doors that enclosed a small deck just outside Charity's room. Opening the doors, she stepped out into the cool night. "Narissa wants the souls to power a spell."

"What kind of spell needs thousands of human souls to power it?"

"A very dangerous one." Charity placed her hands on the rail and looked out at the calm, serene ocean view. "How much do you know about Narissa's origin?"

"I know she's Poseidon's daughter and she had a twin sister, Nerina."

"Right," she said. "Enter Delphinus. Poseidon's fiercest and most-trusted warrior, god of the dolphins."

This made something in Mykaela's mind click, and an old memory resurfaced. Brad, consumed with grief and desperate to know why Charity had died, had arrested Mykaela and shown her crime scene photos from the beach where Charity's body washed up. On her right wrist, there was a dolphin symbol burned into the skin. Mykaela reached out and took Charity's wrist to see if it was still there, and it was. Though now the thin, dainty outline in the shape of a bottlenose dolphin was just a faint scar.

"This can't be a coincidence," she said, still holding on to Charity's wrist.

Charity's eyes shone with the hint of tears. "It's not. But you're skipping ahead. Delphinus and Narissa fell in love and together, they planned to overthrow Poseidon. They gathered followers, like *armies* of them. Then Nerina, being the faithful daughter she was, warned her father what they were planning. Poseidon was furious. He scattered their armies, exiled Narissa and sent Poseidon to a prison in another dimension. It's a world of complete and total torment. The only portal is the constellation Delphinus." Pulling her hand from Mykaela's, Charity pointed to a spot in the sky.

Just above the trees, Mykaela could make out three stars in the shape of what looked like a triangle. If she tilted her head just right, she could make out the vague form of a dolphin, and suddenly, a cold chill ran down her back.

"Narissa wants to open the portal and free Delphinus," Charity said, looking a little pale at the thought. "If she succeeds, his followers will rise with him, and they'll try to do what they wanted to do all along. Except now they have thousands of years worth of rage fueling them and all of us here on land…we're all at the mercy of their war."

"So we just have to keep the souls hidden from Narissa," she said, fighting another shiver.

"No," Charity said. "We can't. While she's doing the spell to release him, she'll be at her weakest. Think about it. It takes a lot out of a witch to do certain spells, especially the powerful ones. If her magic is channeling all that power, her body is completely vulnerable."

Mykaela tilted her head, listening while Charity explained.

"If you let her start the spell, I can kill her."

"But if she starts the spell, Dylan will die," Mykaela said. "And the souls…they'll just get used up. They'll evaporate into nothing. No afterlife, no heaven or hell…that's not right."

"None of this is right," Charity said, resting her hand on Mykaela's. "And I know you don't want to lose Dylan, but the truth is, he's gotten longer than most people get. And it's just…it's not a good enough reason not to go through with it."

Mykaela leaned her elbows on the banister and took a deep breath as she brought her hands to cover her mouth. It was all so much to take in, so unreal and yet it was all happening. The thought of facing the aftermath without Dylan's help was terrifying. But Charity was right. Mykaela couldn't choose to spare Dylan while throwing potentially everyone else to the sharks. "How can you kill her?" she asked finally.

"With this." Charity snapped her fingers and a ball of light appeared in the palm of her hand. As the light faded, Mykaela could make out a dagger the size of a butcher knife. Taking a closer look, she could see the handle was made up of dozens of sparkling seashells and liquid flowed inside of the clear double-edged blade. "They say the heart of the sea is as cold as ice," Charity said, "But they have no idea. This blade was carved out of an ice-crystal found at the bottom of the ocean. It's the most powerful sea magic and earth magic rolled into one weapon."

"That's the heart of the sea?" Mykaela asked, remembering that Nerina had used her dying breath to tell them to search for it.

Charity nodded. "Nerina knew that her father, though he was powerful enough, could never kill Narissa. She also knew that that was exactly what needed to be done. So she sought out the most powerful earth witches and found a coven here in Harmony Harbor — the Cavanaugh's."

Mykaela recognized the last name as Charity's. "Your family," she said.

"Together they combined all the elements into this one dagger. It's strong enough to kill her," she said. "But only a descendant of theirs, a true Cavanaugh witch, can use the dagger and survive."

"So they brought you back," she said. "So you could use the knife on her."

She nodded. "But Narissa's no fool. She knew exactly what her sister had done. A few years later, she got her revenge on the coven by manipulating one of their descendants into creating an abomination of nature. The curse of the sea. The start of her plan to bring Delphinus back."

It took a minute for Charity's words to sink in. When they did, she could only stare dumbly at her. "Wait...you're saying that I'm a descendant of the witches who made that dagger?"

"We both are," she said. "When we were doing the séance that night I died, we tuned in to the supernatural world and announced to it that the Cavanaugh coven was still alive. So Morrigan came to kill us both." She raised her wrist in the air for Mykaela to see. "She left this dolphin on my wrist as a reminder that Narissa will stop at nothing to bring Delphinus back."

Mykaela felt like her entire world was spinning. She staggered over to a wooden deck-chair and sat down. "We're both witches?" she asked. "And no one ever told us."

Charity nodded, turning to face Mykaela. She leaned up against the banister. "That's why she killed my mom, and why she's trapped yours in a coma. She's afraid they would've tipped us off, or taught us about our magic. I mean, it never occurred to you how you could've cursed Dylan if you weren't a witch?"

"No," she said, and now she wondered why it hadn't.

"They wanted us dead because only a descendant of the coven can use the athame. But Narissa has caused too much carnage, so the spirits sent me here to find the dagger and kill her."

Charity snapped her fingers again and the knife disappeared.

"I don't understand," Mykaela said, still stunned by this new information. "Why wouldn't anyone tell us about this?"

"To protect us?" Charity offered. "Does it really matter? They're all gone. We're the only two left."

"So, when is she going to do the spell? How much time do we have?"

"She needs to harness the power of the blue moon. That's in a week."

"A *week*?" she asked, her heart filling with fear. "That's it?"

She nodded. "When the time is right, you have to give her the souls," she said desperately, "So we can end this, once and for all."

As Mykaela studied her friend, she realized that Charity was the only one to never ask where the souls were. It seemed odd to her now, since Charity's entire plan hinged on relinquishing the souls to Narissa. Leaning an elbow against the banister, she locked gazes with Charity. "You know where they are don't you?"

A hint of acknowledgment flickered in her eyes. "I haven't told anyone and I won't."

"But how do you know so much?" Mykaela asked, remembering how Charity, although she had a golden heart, had never quite been the brightest crayon in the box. Now, she seemed like an all-knowing, all-powerful witch. It was a hell of a transformation in just under a year.

"I told *you*," she said.

Again, Mykaela was confused. After a minute, she realized what Charity meant. "The visions," Mykaela said. "I haven't had one since you came back."

"Time is fluid on the other side, bendable. Sometimes I could catch glimpses of the future. I used our connection as witches to send them to you."

"You were helping me, even back then."

Charity seemed to debate this a moment, and then nodded. "Well, now you know everything that I do."

"And this will work?" Mykaela asked. "You trust the spirits that have been telling you all of this?"

"Absolutely," Charity said. "It'll work."

Mykaela nodded, considering this. Now, at least, they had a plan. Granted, she still hated the idea of losing Dylan, but she didn't see another choice.

"We should probably go downstairs," Charity said. "Make sure those guys don't have the rulers out."

She chuckled and looped her arm through Charity's as they headed back inside.

***

They found Brad and Dylan in the kitchen, arguing over the stove.

"They're not done yet," Brad was saying, reaching past Dylan to turn the stove burner back on.

"Yes, they are," Dylan argued.

In a large skillet in front of them, several steaks simmered. It smelled delicious, but it was more entertaining to see the boys bicker, so Charity and Mykaela lingered at the edge of the kitchen.

"No, they're not. Look, read this chart." Brad plucked a magnet from the refrigerator. "It says right here steaks have to be at least 145 degrees before they're done."

"I don't think any of us are susceptible to food poisoning," Dylan said, starting to sound annoyed as Brad jammed the pointed end of a thermometer into one of the steak cuts.

"Oh, funny." Brad cracked a smirk as he asked, "Do mer-zombies even need to eat?"

"I am *not* a mer-zombie." Though he sounded insulted, there was a glint of humor in his eyes. "And…technically, no. I don't really *need* to eat. You girls enjoying the show?" he asked without looking at them as he flipped one of the steaks with a fork.

"Oh yeah," Charity said, stifling a giggle.

"Hey, I'm just glad the two of you stopped trying to kill each other," Mykaela said.

"Desperate times," Brad said.

Mykaela walked up to Dylan and looped an arm around his waist as she looked over his shoulder at the sizzling skillet of food. "I never knew you cooked."

"You never asked," he said. Using a fork and a knife, he cut her a bite and fed it to her.

"Mm," she said, giving him a coy smile. "So many talents."

"I just lost my appetite," Brad said, turning to Charity. She punched him playfully on the arm.

"Just be happy for them," she said. "We could all die tomorrow."

"Nice outlook you've got, Char," he said, bringing his lips to her cheek. "You know I'd die before I let anything happen to you."

A knock at the door interrupted them. Mykaela met Dylan's gaze with a wide-eyed, fear-filled one. "Who could that be?" she asked, her voice tense.

Brad returned to the stove and turned the burner off. "That's just Jared."

Mykaela felt her cheeks go pale and her heart went off-beat in dread. Charity, Dylan and Mykaela turned to look at Brad with perplexed expressions.

"What?" he asked with a shrug. "He called and asked if I'd seen you," he added to Mykaela. "So I told him where to find us."

"Didn't you tell him?" Mykaela asked Charity.

"Hey, I've had to convey a lot of information in the last 24 hours. You can't blame me for forgetting something."

Dylan shook his head. "We really need to work on our communication skills." He nodded his head toward Charity, signaling for Mykaela to go over by her, while he went to the front door. He opened it and stepped outside, closing it behind him again without letting Jared inside.

"What?" Brad asked, looking at the two girls, now standing side-by-side. "What am I missing?"

"We're here *because* we're hiding from Jared," Mykaela said.

Charity looked at Brad and gave him an innocent shrug. "By the way, honey, we're hiding from Jared."

"Why?" he asked, his gaze focused on Mykaela. "He's your brother."

"Yeah," she said, "and his little band of hunters kidnapped me and held me in some kind of creature torture room. Charity had to cast a spell to get me out."

"What?" he exclaimed, turning to the front door just as it opened again. Dylan came inside, followed closely by Jared.

As the three gaped at him, Dylan held his hands up in a peacekeeping attempt. "We need to hear him out," he said. "He's figured something out."

Chapter Seventeen

Standing outside on the porch, Jared leaned against the rail and looked at Mykaela in sympathy and regret. But she couldn't look at him. Keeping her arms crossed, she stared up at the sky instead.

"I had no idea what Mark was planning to do," he said. "I never would've put you in that kind of danger..."

"But you did," she said. "I trusted you and you led me into a trap."

"I was trying to keep you safe," he said. "I had no idea that I was being played by him."

"That's kind of your thing, isn't it?"

"Did he tell you why he tried to kill me?" she asked cautiously, still not looking at him.

"It doesn't take a genius to figure it out," he said, following her gaze to look at the sky. "You can't lead anybody to the vault if you're dead."

She breathed out a slow, inaudible breath of relief. At least he didn't know where the souls were located. Mykaela loved her brother, but his mind was weak, which meant anybody with a little bit of power could dig around inside his head for answers.

"I wanted to protect you," he said. "But I put my trust in the wrong people."

She couldn't hold that against him.

"Please let me stay and help."

She was quiet as she thought about what he'd said. Finally, she turned to him and said in a warning tone, "Do you promise to play nice? Everyone here is an equal, human or not?"

He chuckled. "I promise."

"Cross your heart?" she asked. "Pinky promise?"

With his forefinger, he made an X over his heart and then held up his pinky. They looped their fingers together and squeezed in a pact. Before she let go, Mykaela added, "One more thing."

He raised an eyebrow in response.

"Charity and I already have a plan," she said. "So I need you to honor that."

"What kind of plan?" he asked, letting his hand fall to his side.

She considered telling him, but she knew he wouldn't like the idea. So she gave him the same answer he loved to give her. "It's on a need to know basis. When you need to know, I'll tell you."

He looked skeptical, but nodded.

"Dylan said you found out something," she said.

***

A few minutes later, he was spreading a town map out over the coffee table and the group gathered around it. "Did you know those stains you keep referring to also show up as EMF?" Jared asked.

"Wait," Charity interrupted, turning on the couch to look at Mykaela. "You can see EMF?"

She shrugged. "Apparently."

"Anyway," Jared continued, "The whole town is marked with these hotspots. Mr. Evans has been doing research for the council for years and he says that right now, they're useless, but if a witch is powerful enough, they can turn these hotspots on. Think of it like flipping a switch."

"Okay," Brad said, obviously concerned. "The switch comes on and..."

"The spot will literally start radiating evil," he said. "And everything around it becomes unholy ground."

Mykaela leaned closer to look at the map. A red dot marked an evil hotspot, and there were red dots from Dylan's warehouse all the way to Hunter's Point, on the opposite side of town. At least half a dozen areas would be affected.

"It gets worse," Jared said.

"How can it get worse?" Mykaela asked, dread in her voice.

"Once these hotspots are on, they can't be turned off. For the rest of time, they'll draw creatures to town. Harmony Harbor will be this giant, supernatural beacon."

"What would Narissa want with these spots?" Mykaela asked, mostly to herself.

"Some spells are so dark they can't be done on normal ground," Charity explained. "They need a place just as dark to cast the spell."

As Mykaela studied the map, she saw something. "Does anybody have a pen?" she asked.

Jared pulled one out of his pocket and handed it to her. Clicking it open, she brought the tip of the pen to the paper and started connecting the dots. She began with the killings out toward the warehouse and worked her way toward the other side of town. By the time she was done, there was a clear outline of a dolphin spanning most of the small city. The cliff were Dylan died marked the very tip of the back fin, and Hunter's Point was at the nose.

"So everything inside this dolphin would turn to unholy ground," Brad stated as they all stared at the map.

"She's not just breaking him out," Mykaela said. "She's creating him a kingdom of his own."

"Whoa," Charity whispered, sounding a little intimidated. "She really has thought this through."

"Our house is right here." Mykaela pointed to a spot on the map about where the dolphin's eye would be. "Practically right in the middle."

"In fact, the only spot in town that would be protected is the cemetery," Charity said. "But even then, it would be one good patch in a bunch of bad."

"We have to stop her," Brad said. "We can't let her do this to our town."

Mykaela and Charity exchanged a look. They both knew they didn't have a choice.

"What is it?" Dylan asked.

"We have a way to take down Narissa," Charity said.

"But she has to be doing the spell while we kill her," Mykaela finished.

The boys stared back at them with blank faces, as if waiting for the punch line.

"You can't be serious," Jared said. "Even knowing what you know about these hotspots?"

"It's the only time her body will be vulnerable enough for the attack," Charity said. "I don't like it any more than you do, but I don't see another option."

"I do," Dylan spoke up. "We find the vault and I drain it before Narissa does."

"And we're back to this again," Jared said, rolling his eyes. "Dude, there's no way we're letting you have a nuclear weapon. Get that through your head already."

"Can you think of another way to kill Narissa before she can flip these switches and turn the whole town into unholy ground?" he asked, holding Jared's gaze in a challenge. "I'm the only one here with the ability to take the souls. That's why it has to be me, not because I *want* it to be me."

"No one is changing the plan," Charity said, her voice sounding surprisingly bossy and demanding. "Mykaela and I have it worked out. Whoever wants to come along for backup is welcome to do so as long as you keep it in your heads that this is *our* destiny. Not yours."

"Charity, listen to yourself," Brad said. "Even if you take out Narissa, these hotspots create a whole new threat once she's gone."

"Then we'll just deal with those threats as they come," she said. "Isn't that what the hunter's council is for?"

Dylan stepped up to Mykaela and pulled her aside. "Let me help you," he whispered. "If I take the souls, I can kill her and spare all of you from this."

"We don't even know the vault will make you powerful enough to kill her," Jared said. "It could backfire and then we'll have a raging sea-witch on our hands."

"This plan was set into motion long before we were born," Charity said. "If we tempt fate, who knows what will happen?"

Dylan shook his head. "What do you think will happen if Narissa activates these hotspots and gains the power from the vault?"

"This is exactly what you wanted to do last time," Jared pointed out. "And you almost killed Mykaela."

"I know you're afraid I'll become some loose nuke, but I won't," he said.

This arguing went on for at least ten more minutes before Mykaela finally pulled Dylan aside to talk some sense into him. Alone in a bedroom upstairs, she closed the door.

"None of them have even seen Narissa," Dylan said, turning in the center of the room. "But you know what I'm talking about. You know we can't let her have access to that much power. We *have* to find the vault before she does."

This seemed really important to him, and she couldn't help but feel suspicious. After all, he'd starved for decades and then got a major power boost by feeding on her. After that, he'd gone straight to starving himself again. She wasn't naïve enough to think that had been easy. "Are you feeling okay?" she asked. "I mean…is that power boost still lasting?"

She didn't have to say anything else for him to understand her worry, and he came forward and took her hands. "This isn't for me. This isn't because I want the power," he said, holding her gaze. "But we have to find someone more powerful than Narissa. And maybe with the souls, I can…"

"We found another way," she blurted out, desperate to make him stop. She'd seen what power had done to people like Morrigan and Kerr, and she didn't want him to be anything like them. "Charity has a way."

He squinted, his protests quieting. She could see now he was ready to listen. She began to explain the basics about their plan in a low, quiet voice. She told him about the dagger, about the coven and the witches on the other side.

"Jared was right. We don't even know if your powers will kill Narissa, even if they're boosted by all of the souls. But we know this dagger will work. The most important thing is timing," she finished, delivering the next part as delicately as she could. "We have to wait until she's doing the spell before we can kill her. She'll be vulnerable, distracted. Then Charity will use the dagger to kill her."

He eased into a seating position at the edge of the bed, keeping his blue eyes on hers in a blank stare as this information sank in.

"I've been thinking about it," she said, "And maybe since your soul was the first one cursed, it'll be the last to leave. Maybe if Narissa is killed before your soul comes out of the vault, you'll be okay."

"That's a big if," he said. "There's just one thing I don't understand. If you're a descendant of the Cavanaugh coven, why aren't you the one using the dagger? Why resurrect Charity?"

"Because it's going to take both of us." She hesitated, tucking a strand of hair behind her ear. "I'll be providing the distraction."

"But you said she was going to be distracted by..." his words trailed off. She could see the pieces click in his mind. He looked her up and down, his mouth agape, as the realization dawned on him. "Wait...you're..." He shook his head to deny it, his expression pleading for her to do the same. "The souls...they're in...*you*?"

She nodded slowly, remaining silent while he processed this.

"Mykaela..." he stood, taking her hands. "If you let her take that much power from you, it could kill you."

"I know," she said, blinking back tears. She knew very well how this would turn out for her—she'd foreseen each vivid detail and she knew exactly how this love story would end. But at least now she knew it was a love story. "But...it's the only way to weaken Narissa enough to use the dagger. If we kill her...all her spells are broken. The one on my mom, the one on you. My mom will finally be free, and I wish I knew what was going to happen to you, but I—"

Bringing his palms to her cheeks, he held her face close to his to drive his point. "I don't care what happens to me," he said, "but you deserve to walk out of this alive."

She opened her mouth to protest, but he interrupted her.

"Charity's going to have to be fast. Narissa isn't an idiot; she knows we'll try something. But if Charity gets to her quick enough, you'll be okay."

She nodded, trying to be brave, but then she remembered her last vision. She remembered how badly it'd hurt, how deep the torment had gone, how she'd been utterly helpless. Suddenly, she felt like she was surrounded by an abyss with nothing but darkness and pain all around her. No matter what choice she made, someone wound up hurt. Always. Blinking, she tried to keep the tears back, but she couldn't, so she buried her head in Dylan's chest and let a few escape. Resting his chin on the top of her head, he wrapped his arms around her, one hand sliding through her hair to cup the nape of her neck.

"You're going to be okay, darling," he assured her in a soft, gentle voice. "You're going to be fine."

"I don't want to die." She lifted her head to look at him through blurry, teary eyes. "I don't want to lose you, either."

His lips tried to form words, but for once he was at a loss.

"I never even appreciated you," she continued. Odds were one of them, if not both of them, would be dead by this time next week and she needed to get this out before that happened. "I spent so long blaming you, being confused and angry. And now, just when I'm realizing how much you mean to me…" she shook her head, the next part hurt too much for words.

"Mykaela…"

"I love you," she said, the words tumbling out of her lips for the first time in this lifetime. Holding on to her bravery, she made no attempt to take them back. Looking at him, she remembered everything she'd loved about him. His strength, his faith, his survival and even overprotective instincts. Overwhelmed by these feelings, she threw her arms around his neck in a tight hug. With their bodies touching, his arms wrapped around her, she felt complete. Safe and still and peaceful. Closing her eyes, she treasured this feeling and let it linger. "I need you to know how much I love you, Dylan. I know I said I hated you, but I never did. I was just — "

As if those words overwhelmed him, he crushed his lips against hers in a deep passionate kiss. Holding her tightly in his arms, the kiss spoke all the words they couldn't say.

***

Charity slipped into the bedroom and found Brad unpacking his suitcase. He looked over his shoulder at her as he took a stack of t-shirts to the dresser. "Hey," he said.

"Hey," she said as she headed over to a large free-standing cabinet and opened it. "It's nine o'clock. Medicine time."

"Is that what we're calling it?" he asked, the self-loathing evident in his voice. "Besides, you don't have to tell me it's feeding time. I've been feeling it for hours."

Charity thought about this as she prepared the first syringe. "Maybe going eight hours between doses isn't such a good idea."

"No, it's fine." He took a seat on the bed. "This is about sustenance. I want to get by on as little as possible."

"Just remember that the hungrier you get, the more chance you'll have of blacking out again. If you black out, you'll feed. Probably even kill."

"You should just put me down," he said, shaking his head.

She gave him a scolding look as she sat down on the bed across from him. "I'm not going to put you down like some animal, Brad."

"No, like a monster."

"That's not what you are." She grabbed his hand and stretched out his arm, taking a close look at the inside of his elbow for a vein. Finding one, she eased the needle into it and injected the adrenaline. "This is...a genetic mutation and nothing else. You can manage it."

He closed his eyes as the hormone went into his system. Immediately, she could see a change of attitude, and because the first hormone was adrenaline, it wasn't exactly a positive change. "Now I'm a mutant?" he asked, still moody.

"And I'm a resurrected witch," she pointed out as she prepared the estrogen and testosterone injections. "Dylan's been cursed for the last hundred years and Mykaela's got superpowers. You blend right in."

"Is that how the witches feel?" he asked. "The ones you answer to?"

She hesitated with the needle in his arm. "Why do you ask?"

"You said witches keep the peace, right?" he said. "You're like hunters, but with different methods and abilities. Something crosses the line and witches show up to kill it."

"Or punish." She nodded, turning back to the vials to pick up the last injection.

"I doubt they'd like the idea of their great white witch shacking up with an incubus."

"We're hiding out," she said with a laugh. "And I *am* keeping the peace by helping you save yourself from this."

"But you were supposed to stay in the cemetery for your training," he said as she continued the injection. "Then I found you and blew your cover and now, here you are taking time away from your responsibilities to help me. I'm sure they don't like me much. My point is…I don't want you to get in trouble because of this."

"I won't," she promised.

"I mean it," he continued. "It's bad enough this ruins my career as a deputy. It shouldn't ruin your life, too."

"It's not," she said. She put the syringes and medicine away and scooted closer to him, taking his hands. "I know how much you miss being human, but if it helps, I'll let you in on a little secret."

He nodded, his eyes narrowed slightly in curiosity.

"If I succeed in killing Narissa," she said, "then my place as the 'white witch' becomes permanent. *Forever.*"

His head tilted a little, like he just wanted to make sure. "Forever?"

"I'll never have to worry about dying again," she said, feeling the warmth of hope rush over her at the thought. "And as long as you take these supplements, you won't die either. So can we please just forget about being human and actually embrace *life*? However it happens to come to us?"

Looking at her, his eyes were full of emotion. He reached out to touch her and solidify their connection. "We can," he said with a hint of a smile. "We will."

***

Late that night, fierce gusts of wind woke Mykaela from her sleep. Still dazed, she was on the verge of drifting back to sleep when the wind howled again. Sitting up, she turned on the bedside lamp.

Dylan was awake, sitting in a wooden chair in the fair corner of the room, keeping watch.

Rubbing her eyes with her fists, she yawned. "What time is it?"

"Just after four," he said.

She shivered as an ominous feeling swept over her. "Does that wind sound…creepy to you?"

"It's just wind," he assured her.

But still, something didn't feel right so she slipped out of bed and grabbed her thin cotton robe. The hem of it dusted the floor as she wrapped it around herself. "I think I'm going to check out the house anyway."

"I'll come with you," he said, standing from the chair.

They left the room together, going into the hallway. Past the railing, she could see the first floor below. It was dark, without even the dull light from a TV. Everything seemed quiet except for the wind slamming against the house, but Mykaela still couldn't shake the feeling that something was wrong. She descended the steps smoothly, taking a look around.

With the heavy curtains to the window shut tight, the room was a giant shadow, swallowing the furniture and making objects undecipherable. The more she searched, trying to keep her attention on every corner, the more the nervous feeling inside her grew.

The light in the kitchen flashed on, washing the room in a dim, yellow glow. She gave a frantic look over her shoulder and found Dylan by the switch. He gave her a curious look. "You're jumpy," he said.

In the living room in front of her, she saw Jared asleep on the couch, flat on his back. The way the light cast a glow on the sharp angles and planes of his high-cheek-boned, stern-chinned face made him look softer, somehow. Kinder. His brown hair was short and thick, and probably would've had a curl to it if it'd been long enough. He looked so normal, the kind of guy that could be found on a college campus or working behind the register at the local video store. If he hadn't been born a Whindom, trained by a secret society that was founded to erase the stains of her mistakes. She wondered how he would've turned out if their father hadn't been a hunter, and if he hadn't molded Jared to be the same since the age of five.

Suddenly, that feeling washed over her again. It was cold, powerful, like there was something she needed to be paying attention to, but wasn't. It was almost like her instincts were screaming at her. "Something's wrong, Dylan," she said, unable to fight the feeling anymore. "I can *feel* it."

A loud crack of thunder rang out, illuminating the room with a flash of pale blue light. She jumped, her heart thumping, and looked up at the ceiling, although she wasn't sure why.

Dylan walked over to the kitchen window and looked out at the sky. "It's starting to storm," he said.

"But is it a natural storm?" she asked.

"I don't know," he said. "You're the one who can see magic."

She joined him at the window and peered out. In the sky above, thick dark clouds rolled as far as her eyes could see. And around the clouds, like a silver lining, were the ebony black colors that served as Narissa's signature.

"It's Narissa," she said, shoving away from the counter. "Go get Charity."

He nodded and followed the order, zipping up the stairs in the blink of an eye. She rushed over to the couch to wake Jared, but as she arrived at the edge of it, a fierce gust of wind shattered the picture window, sending shards of glass whipping around the room. At the sound, Jared bolted off the couch, his gaze immediately scanning the room and landing on her.

"It's Narissa," she said as he jumped over the couch to take her side. If they could just get upstairs to Charity, they might stand a fighting chance. Grabbing his hand, she turned, ready to dash up the stairs, but she ran smack into something.

Slick, black fabric was inches away from her face, and the smell of the sea-water and sand filled her senses. Frozen, she looked up into the stunningly beautiful and chillingly evil face of the sea-witch. Before she could scream, Narissa's arm lurched out and her cold fingers clamped around Mykaela's throat. Tightening her grip, she lifted her feet off the ground, leaving nothing to support her weight but the hand around her neck.

Jared, moving swiftly, pulled out his fulgurite knife and slammed it into the witch's side, but the blade shattered on impact. With her free hand, Narissa made a flinging gesture. As if being struck, Jared soared off his feet and tumbled through the broken window.

Upstairs, Charity woke the second Dylan barged into the room. Brad, who'd been sleeping beside her, jumped out of bed. Downstairs, she could hear the sounds of broken glass and wind and she knew something was wrong.

"It's Narissa," Dylan said, his voice frantic. "She's here."

Her heart leapt in fear and she lunged out of bed, but lingered behind it. "What? She wasn't supposed to find us."

"She did," he said. "You have to come help."

"I can't," she said desperately. "It's too soon. I'm not ready!"

As Dylan gazed at her in disbelief, she felt completely ashamed and unworthy of her new life. Terror crippled her, snaking into her heart and stealing away her breath. She wanted to gasp, to cling to something and just let the tears run free. She tried to be brave, to move forward and go downstairs to confront the sea-witch, but her feet just wouldn't budge. Downstairs, the crashing sounds were so loud and she could literally feel Narissa's power resonating through the house like a radioactive wave.

"Charity," Dylan called, his voice loud.

"Give her a minute," Brad snapped, coming to her side. He took her face in his hands and looked into her eyes, trying to get her attention. "You can do this."

Downstairs, she could hear Mykaela scream and her heart started thumping wildly. Pulling away from Brad, she walked quickly toward the door. But as she reached it, at the last second, she picked up the pace and made a dash for the adjoining bathroom, closing herself inside. With her hand gripped tightly around the knob, she sank to sit on the floor and collapsed against the door. Tears festered in her eyes, swelling like a volcano that would erupt any second as she desperately tried to breathe. But the simple action of inhaling a breath seemed too difficult to accomplish. On the other side of the door, she heard Brad pleading for her to come out, but she couldn't. There was no way she could use magic in this state of mind; she would likely level the entire house. So she hid, crumpled against the bathroom door, listening to the chaos downstairs.

***

Downstairs, Narissa still held Mykaela by the throat, with her feet suspended and her legs dangling.

"You dare to test me?" Narissa spat, her voice venomous and wrathful. "Did you really think there wouldn't be a price to pay for it!"

She had no idea what she was supposed to be paying for this time, and she had no way of conveying that to Narissa. The crushing force was blocking her windpipe and the room started to blur in and out around her from lack of oxygen. She kicked her legs and squirmed, trying to break free.

"Where is she?" Narissa hissed, bringing her face dangerously close to Mykaela's.

"Who?" She finally managed to squeak out the word. Before the witch could answer, a bolt of blue lightning zipped in from the left, striking Narissa in the head and sending her body hurtling toward the wall. Mykaela landed on her hands and knees and brought a hand to her throat, coughing. Looking up, she saw Dylan rushing to her side.

Brad hurried down the steps toward them, lunging for Narissa. But she flung him aside like he was a ragdoll, knocking him unconscious and rendering him useless.

As Dylan helped Mykaela to her feet, his attention was focused on Narissa, who was now standing up. "I was being kind by leaving your mother in your care, and now you've cloaked her from me? How'd you do it?" she demanded. "Who do you have doing magic?"

"I don't know what you're talking about," Mykaela said, her hand still around her aching throat. "My mother went missing from the hospital. You took her."

"Don't play games with me!" she yelled. "You think you can sabotage me? Have some ace up your sleeve? Well I've worked too long and too hard to be undone by a teenager!"

Mykaela didn't understand what was happening. She'd been so sure that Narissa had kidnapped her mom, but obviously that hadn't happened. So what had happened to her?

Just then, Jared climbed in through the broken window. This time, he had his gun out and managed to fire off two rounds before Narissa dashed to his side and yanked the gun out of his hands. She wrapped her hand around his throat and squeezed tight, forcing him to his knees. Mykaela lunged for the two, but Narissa flicked her hand and slammed her into the furthest wall, delaying her long enough for one last warning.

"I've had it with your stalling," Narissa said. "You've proven to be really stupid, so let me spell it out for you."

Huddled on the floor, Mykaela tried to stand, but her body refused to cooperate with her. Her legs felt like gelatin and her arms wouldn't support her weight. While she was busy fumbling to her feet, Narissa was choking the life out of Jared.

Narissa's eyes were cold as ice and dead serious, her voice unmistakably a last chance warning, "Meet me on the bluff where Dylan took his swan dive on Friday at sunset. Come alone and don't put up a fight. Or your brother dies."

The black smoke started at Narissa's feet, swirling up her body and engulfing Jared's, too.

"No!" Mykaela saw what was coming and ran forward, trying to latch onto her brother. Just as she reached out, her fingers grasping for his shirtsleeve, they both disappeared, leaving only traces of the black smoke in their wake.

Every muscle in her body jerked into terror-mode. Her heartbeat slowed to a stop before it bucked into a rapid pulse, the beating sensation jarring her entire body. Butterflies squirming in her stomach, she took a slow, thorough look around. The room was a mess, the coffee table was broken. And Narissa had just kidnapped Jared.

Chapter Eighteen

"Let me get this straight," Mykaela said, pacing across the messy living room floor. "My brother was just kidnapped and you were upstairs. *Hiding*."

Charity was sitting at the kitchen table, her knees pulled up to her chest. She was looking down at the floor, her lips set in a shamed frown. Brad had pulled a chair up next to hers and had his arm wrapped around her shoulders. "Mykaela, I'm so sorry," she said, her voice quivering. "I don't know what happened."

"What happened? Our secret weapon was MIA and now Jared's being ransomed, that's what happened!" she cried. She knew she was lashing out unreasonably, but she couldn't stop. The fear was swallowing her in its shadow now, leaving nothing but hysterics. "Do those sea-shells you gave us even work? I thought she wasn't going to be able to find us!"

"Jared didn't have one," Brad spoke up. "She must've followed him here."

"That's just great," she spat. "He came here to protect me and winds up—"

"I froze," Charity snapped, looking even more ashamed. "I'm sorry. She caught me by surprise and…I just froze."

"You're the key to taking down Narissa," Mykaela said, "You can't freeze! How do you expect to be able to —"

"Mykaela, calm down." Dylan came to her side, taking her by the shoulders to get her to pay attention. "She took him as leverage, which means she needs him alive."

"Is that supposed to make me feel better?" she asked, pulling away from him. Raking a hand through her hair, she blew out a frustrated breath and tried to calm down. "What happened to my mom? That's why Narissa was so upset. And if *she* didn't take Mom, then who —"

"I did." Charity stood from the table to face Mykaela. "I didn't think she'd be safe in the hospital, so I hid her. I had no idea Narissa would…"

Mykaela studied her friend, her thoughts finally calming down so she could think.

"I just couldn't tell you because you didn't know I was a witch," Charity quickly explained. "But I hid her in a safe place. I can take you there right now if you want. I know it won't make what happened to Jared any less horrible, but just in case it helps at all."

Finally, Mykaela nodded. "Take me to her."

***

Charity opened the heavy stone door to the Cavanaugh crypt and turned on the flashlight to light the way. She'd been completely silent the whole way over, urging Mykaela to do the same. Once they were closed inside the crypt, however, Charity finally sighed. "Now we can talk freely," she said. "The building is cloaked, so even if Narissa followed us here, she'd pass right by like the crypt wasn't even here."

"Why didn't you use that spell on the cabin?" she asked, following Charity to the furthest corner of the room.

"Because it only works on hallow ground." She stopped and pulled at a latch on the floor, pulling up a small door and revealing a narrow staircase underneath. Mykaela followed Charity down the steps to a secret, underground room.

Several battery operated lanterns lit the room from every corner. By the farthest wall, she saw her mother sleeping on a twin-sized bed. The feelings of relief and hope that sprang to her were indescribable and overwhelming as she rushed to her mother's side and grabbed her hand. Feeling her flesh, solid and real, she squeezed her eyes shut in a feeling of gratitude. "You really did keep her safe," she said to Charity.

"Of course I did." Charity pulled up a metal foldout chair and sat down. "She was innocent in all of this…she doesn't deserve what happened to her."

"You can't wake her up, can you?" she asked, looking down at her mother's frail and limp hand.

Charity shook her head. "It's a sleeping curse. Killing Narissa is the only way I can break it."

Mykaela nodded. She'd suspected as much and was already prepared for the answer. "I just wish I could get her advice before I agree to be nearly killed in Narissa's ritual."

Charity nodded in understanding, then her expression lit up. "Maybe you can." She stood suddenly and headed over to the table stacked with supplies. She took a white candle and a bundle of sage from the table. Using a lighter, she lit the end of the sage wand and handed it to Mykaela. "Spread the smoke around the room and I'll explain."

Mykaela did as Charity instructed and waved the smoke in every corner of the room.

"While she's affected by the curse, her body is asleep but her spirit is awake," she said as she lit the candle and moved it to Blanche's bedside. "It sounds bad, but it's good news because I happen to talk to spirits all the time." She reached for the sage wand and motioned for Mykaela to sit. Leaving the sage burning on the table, she took Blanche's hand and reached for Mykaela's. "Maybe this time I can take you with me."

Mykaela placed one hand in Charity's and the other one on top of her mother's. Between the three of them, they formed a tight-knit circle by bed. Closing her eyes, Charity took a few slow, deep breaths.

She looked peaceful, serene, as she made the connection between their minds. Soon, Mykaela felt the outside world falling away. It was like falling into space. Soon, they found themselves surrounded by brilliant white light.

Looking next to her, she saw Charity. "It worked," Charity said.

"What is this place?" Mykaela asked, feeling a chill of wonder as she turned in a circle, taking in nothing but white light from every direction.

"We're inside your mom's mind," she explained. "Not physically inside…it's hard to explain."

"But it's…blank."

"This is what the mind looks like while you're asleep. A blank canvas," she said. "Now be quiet so I can contact your mom."

Mykaela was quiet, watching as Charity dipped her head. A few seconds later, like magic, someone stepped out of the light. The soft brown hair ending just around the shoulder, the kind eyes and bright smile undeniably belonged to Mykaela's mother. Blanche's eyes brightened in relief when she saw Mykaela and she rushed forward, her arms outstretched.

She ran to her mom, diving gratefully into those warm arms and enjoying the comfort of her embrace. It filled her with strength she didn't even know she possessed, and it made her feel like she could conquer anything.

When Blanche pulled back, her eyes were damp. She looked back and forth between Mykaela and Charity with a teary smile. "I'm so proud of you girls," she said, stretching one arm out for Charity.

She moved closer to them, giving Blanche a tight squeeze before stepping back again to give Mykaela some time. But Blanche held on to Charity's hand, looking at them both now. "Be strong and have faith. If you do that, you can use the dagger to kill Narissa and finally end this war."

Mykaela studied her mother in awe. "How did you..."

"I've been watching over you," she said, cupping Mykaela's cheek with one hand. "I can only catch glimpses."

"Then you've seen how I've been treating Jared," she blurted out, tears springing to her eyes. "Mom, he was just trying to protect me and I've been giving him such a hard time. And now..."

"You can still save him," she assured, without even a hint of anger in her voice. "As long as Narissa is convinced you'll do what she says, Jared's safe. Don't lose hope, Mykaela. It's all you have left."

She nodded, reminding herself to be brave for her mother's sake. She pulled her into another tight hug. "I'm going to save you, too," she promised, emphasizing it with a squeeze.

"I know you will," she said, "I believe in you."

"I hate to interrupt," Charity said gently, looking at Mykaela. "but I can't keep this up much longer. We'll have to leave soon."

"One last thing," Blanche said, taking Mykaela by both hands. She cupped her face, speaking quickly. "Go into my bedroom, move my dresser and pull up the loose floorboard. In there, you'll find one of my family's spell books. It could help you make this right with Dylan before he dies."

Confused, Mykaela opened her mouth to question, but Charity interrupted.

"I'm sorry," she said, "the spell's weakening."

Mykaela felt a strong tug, like something was yanking at her, but she grabbed her mom one last time. "I'll see you soon," she said.

And then they were gone. The light was gone, Blanche was gone. And they were sitting underneath a tomb, the three witches still holding hands. Mykaela released her mother's hand and looked at Charity in awe. "Thank you," she whispered, wiping her damp cheeks with her palm.

"I'm sorry I couldn't do more," she replied.

"You did plenty."

Before they went back to the cabin, Mykaela and Charity made a trip to the Inn to get the grimoire that Blanche had told them about. The dusty old book was hidden exactly where she'd told them to find it.

"I never even knew my mom practiced witchcraft," Mykaela said as they drove down the dirt road that would lead to Charity's place. The first hues of the sunrise started to streak the morning sky. Night was over, and a whole new day was beginning. Now there were four days until Friday, until the blue moon and Narissa's ritual.

Her friend was in the passenger seat, leafing gently through the spell book. "There's some good spells in here. To create a door, to find a lost child. There's even a glamour to change your appearance," she said, flipping another page. "I wonder how many of these Blanche wrote herself."

"Any sign of the spell she was talking about?" she asked, feeling eager to get to the cabin so she could look over the book herself.

"Not yet," she said. "We'll keep looking."

And they did. For the next few hours, they holed up in the kitchen and searched through the thick spell book. Around mid-morning, after her fifth cup of coffee, Mykaela was getting too restless to sit at the table and read. She decided to leave the studying to the magic experts, Dylan and Charity, and joined Brad in the living room. He'd pushed the couch out of the way and cleaned up the broken coffee table. All morning long, he'd been doing pushups and sit-ups and more complicated push-ups. It was clear for Mykaela to see that he was worried about Jared.

"You've been at that all morning," Mykaela said. "Is it making you feel any better?"

"Not really." He stood from his position on the floor and grabbed a nearby towel to wipe the sweat from his forehead.

"I didn't think so." Reaching to the other end of the couch, she grabbed his sparring gloves and tossed them to him. "Let's spar."

He caught the gloves effortlessly, but looked unsure. "I don't know..."

"It's more for me than it is you," she said, just in case it helped tip the scales. "I really need to hit something, and no one thought to bring a punching bag."

Chuckling, he looked down at the gloves in his hand, debating. Finally, he slipped one on. "Did you bring your gloves?"

Nodding a quick yes, she jumped off the couch and ran upstairs to get her sparring gloves. She pulled them on her hands as she headed back downstairs and took her stance in front of Brad.

She swung the first punch, which he blocked without a problem. Moving to his side, she tried to drive her fist into his ribs, but he tucked his elbow into his hip and blocked her again.

"You've gotten better at this," she commented, throwing a couple practice blows into the air to loosen up her shoulders.

"And your style is as sloppy as ever," he said. "All passion and no focus."

"You still think I can't focus?" she asked, throwing a swift, solid punch. This time she nailed him right in the chest with more force than she should've used on him. Brad barely made a grunt in response, and Mykaela's fist felt like it'd collided with cement. "Ouch," she said. Pulling her hand back, she shook it and then wiggled her fingers as if to shake off the pain.

The more they continued to practice, the more relaxed Mykaela felt. It felt good to move and get her blood pumping. Before long, they were working up a sweat. Lost in their work-out, she didn't notice when things started to get a little too rough. She'd swiped her legs under his, causing him to fall to the floor. It'd taken her half-an hour to get him off his feet and she wasn't going to let him back up, so she straddled him, pressing her hands on his shoulders to hold his body against the floor.

"And that's how it's done," she said, breathless. She gave a triumphant smile that wounded Brad's pride.

"You think?" He grinned, giving her a push. Just a little one, that felt like barely a nudge, but the force behind it sent her soaring across the room, over the couch. Her back smacked against the banister to the staircase and she fell back to the floor, landing on her knees.

She was too shocked and stunned by what had happened to form any coherent thoughts. Dylan and Brad got to her at the same time, but Brad hung back as Dylan helped her to her feet.

"Are you okay?" he asked, shooting Brad a glare.

"I'm fine," she said, turning to Brad. "How did you do that?"

"You could've killed her," Dylan said, his voice scolding. "Don't you think it's time you tell her the truth?"

Mykaela looked back and forth between them. They were keeping something from her? Those two, who could barely be around each other without arguing, were keeping a secret together? What was going on?

Brad opened his mouth, then closed it again. Finally, he spoke. "Kerr was my biological father," he explained. "I'm half-siren. An incubus, technically."

For a minute, she didn't know what to say. She'd suspected he was something, but Kerr's son was nowhere on her list of suspicions. "Wow," was all she could think to say in response.

"There was a transition period," he explained. "I had a choice to feed or die, and I chose to die but at some point...I guess the hunger took over and before I even really knew what was happening, the transition was complete. I tried so hard not to."

"You killed someone?" she asked, feeling like the image of her hero had just been shattered.

"No," he said. "The girl lived. But it was enough to activate the change, I guess."

"Not to interrupt this long awaited discussion," Charity spoke up from the kitchen table. "But I think I found the spell we're looking for."

Mykaela pushed the questions about Brad aside. He'd had months to talk to her about this and chose not to, and right now, she had more pressing matters to address. She went over to the table and leaned her palms on it, stretching over to take a look.

"I'm not sure you're going to like it." Charity pushed the book across the table.

Mykaela picked it up, reading aloud. "To release a loved one," she said. At the top of the page, there was a list of ingredients for the spell. It seemed simple enough; they just needed a personal object of Dylan's and few herbs. "This looks like it's used to put a ghost to rest. I don't understand how this will save Dylan."

"Blanche mentioned making things right," Charity pointed out, "Not saving him."

Mykaela looked up, catching her friend's gaze. "What will the spell do, then?"

"I think..." Charity looked over at Dylan, breaking the news gently. "It'll release his soul from the curse. It'd be like...you letting him go. His spirit would be free to move on and wouldn't be obliterated by Narissa on Friday."

"Move on?" Dylan asked. "To where?"

"The afterlife," Charity answered gently.

"So I would die," he said.

She nodded. "Instantly."

Mykaela looked over at Dylan. From the looks of things, he would die anyway, and at least this way, she knew his spirit would find peace. This way, she knew he wouldn't be channeled into power and used up until there was nothing but a puddle of water to mark his existence on earth. It seemed like their only shot at a happy-ish ending. "You would find peace," she said.

"I'd die before Narissa's ritual," he told her. "And what if something goes wrong? You might need me there."

"We're talking about being zapped into oblivion, Dylan," she said. "I think this is the better option."

"I wouldn't be able to protect you," he said. "And I'd rather get the extra few days and be zapped into oblivion than risk the chance that something bad happens to the two of you because I wasn't there to help."

"I know you want to protect me," she said, "but I want to protect *you*."

He just stared at her, his blue eyes filled with so many questions and so much confusion that it stunned her. Finally, he shook his head and walked across the living room, leaving out the front door.

She waited a second, looking over at Charity. Then she went after him and caught up with him on the beach outside the cabin. He was looking out at the ocean, his posture rigid and stiff. His eyes were cloudy and dark.

"Dylan," she said, trying to get his attention, but he didn't look at her.

"I can't believe you're even considering this," he said.

"I can't believe you're *not*."

He bit his lip, trying to keep from saying something.

"What?" she prodded, confused as to where his anger was coming from.

"Nothing."

"No, say it," she demanded, studying him carefully. "I want to understand."

Turning to look at her, he kept his voice low but she could still see his anger. "You turned me into this without giving me a choice," he said. "And I wound up stuck on this godforsaken planet without you for *a hundred years*, Mykaela. Just wandering and remembering and longing for you."

She opened her mouth to say something, offer him some comfort or apology, but she knew no words would console him for this. How could she make up for such pain?

"And now, again without giving me a choice and listening to what I *want*," he said, emphasizing the words,

"You want to just...release me? When you need me the most."

"Dylan, I don't *want* to lose you," she said, stepping close to him so he would see her sincerity. "But I'd like to know that after everything you've gone through, you'll be able to find peace somehow."

"And I'd like to know that you'll survive to see Saturday morning."

"But then I'll lose you *forever*," she said. "And if I release you now...then maybe there's a chance we can meet up again. In the spirit world...or wherever we end up."

"I don't know if it even works like that," he said.

"Maybe it does," she said weakly, clinging to this hope. Maybe someday, after she died, they could be together again. "But if you let Narissa take your soul with all the others, I *know* I'll never see you again."

"And I know you need me *now*," he said. "The last time Charity had to go up against Narissa, she froze. And Brad is still adjusting to his change — he's hardly reliable. Who knows what's going to happen to your brother? I can't leave, knowing this is the situation I'm leaving you in. I won't."

He made good points, but in her mind it hardly made his case. But, somewhere deep down, she knew she owed him the respect of letting him make this choice. Maybe that was how she could set things right with him. "I don't like this," she said slowly. "Not even a little. But you're right about one thing. This is a decision you deserve to make for yourself."

"Then I choose to stay," he said without hesitation. Reaching out, he took her hand in his, giving it a tight squeeze. "To stay with you until the very end."

"But it will be your end," she said, tears clinging to her throat. "We know that for sure."

"I know you want to save me from this, but you just can't. I'd rather stick around and protect you."

"That's all you've been doing since we found each other again." Moving closer, she slipped her arms around his waist and pressed her forehead against his chest. "I just wish I could protect you for once."

***

Things were quiet for the next few days. Charity practiced using her magic to levitate tables and used the trees outside for target practice with those light-beams. Mykaela and Dylan squeezed in as much time as they could together, always inseparable. On Thursday night, they cooked a feast of their favorite foods and deserts. Cheesecake and lasagna for Charity, cheeseburgers for Brad. Mykaela made her mother's chicken casserole and banana bread, and Dylan made the best mashed potatoes and skins she'd ever tasted.

No one had said it, but they all knew this was their last time as a group together. Not everyone would make it back to the cabin tomorrow, but instead of talking about that, they chose to stick to lighter subjects. They laughed and played a TV marathon in the background. For just a few hours, it seemed like everything was normal. Mykaela only wished her brother could be there to join them.

After dinner, Charity and Mykaela started to clear the table. But Brad stepped up, took the plates from Charity's hand, and placed them back on the table. "Let's go outside," he said to them. "Enjoy the fresh air."

Outside, the wind was cool and still, the perfect summer breeze — except for in October. The moon was high in the sky, nearly full. The four of them walked along the beach, looking out at the calm, still waters.

Mykaela slipped off her shoes, carrying them in one hand, and dug her toes down into the grainy sand. After a little while, Brad finally stopped the stroll by turning to Charity and stopping in front of her.

"I keep waiting for the right time to do this," he said to her. "And now...it seems like we're running out of time, so..."

Mykaela and Dylan glanced over at the other two just as Brad went down on one knee.

Charity hissed in a gasp of surprise. "What are you..."

"I know it's crazy," he blurted out, reaching into his pocket. He pulled out a small box and Mykaela just watched in awe, her fingers interlaced with Dylan's. "But we've been through so much together — just since you've been back, even, and I don't want to take another second for granted. I don't want to go another second without knowing having the guts to ask you this question."

On cue, he popped open the box. Mykaela couldn't see the ring, but she could tell by the way Charity's face lit up that she loved it.

"It was my mom's," Brad explained. "My dad gave it to me after she died. He always told me that when I found the right girl to give it to, I'd know. And I did. I've wanted to give this to you for the last two years," he said with a soft chuckle. "For a while, I thought I'd never even get the chance. But now you're back. And I want to marry you."

Charity brought her hand to her mouth, speechless. Her eyes were wide and teary, and she still hadn't said a word.

Brad waited, looking nervous. Then he prodded, "So...if we don't die tomorrow, will you be my wife?"

She was crying now. Dropping her hand to his, she pulled him to his feet, waiting until she could look into his eyes before she said, "Yes."

As they kissed, Mykaela squealed and clapped her hands in excitement. "I'm so happy for you two," she said, rushing up as they parted to throw each arm around one of them. "If anybody deserves it, it's you."

"Thank you," Charity said, sounding emotional.

Mykaela stepped back. "We'll just...give you guys some privacy," she said, turning to Dylan. "Let's go."

They walked back toward the cabin, but after a few steps Dylan stopped, looking at her with a mischievous grin.

"You know what? If it's my last day on earth, there's something I've always wanted to do with you."

She raised an eyebrow suspiciously. "Oh, really?"

His lips slanted in a lopsided grin, then he grabbed her arm, tossed her onto his back and sped them into the ocean together. The water splashed up around them as he drove them out further and further, until she was sure the water was over her head. He was moving so fast that everything around her was a blur of blue hues and splashing water. She wasn't exactly sure where they were when they finally stopped. All she could see for miles around was the calm, pure ocean water.

At first she was afraid. She'd never learned how to swim, and had spent much of her life avoiding stepping foot in these waters. Then she reminded herself that she was with Dylan, who'd lived in the ocean for a long time. She knew he wouldn't let anything happen to her, and in his arms, she was as safe as if both feet were planted firmly on land. Even though she'd always been taught to fear the ocean, now that she was surrounded by the water, she saw things differently.

It was beautiful, the way the water waved up and down as far as the eye could see. Everything was so quiet, so peaceful. Out here, it seemed like the entire world had faded away and it was just the two of them.

"Wow," she whispered with a smile of awe. "So this is your definition of ocean-view."

"Absolutely," he said, but he was looking at her.

"I can see why you stayed for so long," she said, turning her attention back to him. This close to the ocean and his eyes, she could see they were the exact same shade of blue. It should've been freaky, but it was beautiful. "You know...it was kind of romantic," she said, wrapping her arms around his neck. "Brad proposing to Charity."

"It was sweet," he agreed.

"I've heard we were engaged once," she said, taking her time to beat around the bush with her question. "But I haven't gotten that far in the diary yet."

"Ah," he said with a teasing grin. "You want to hear how I did it."

"I really love hearing you tell me these stories," she confessed, twining her fingers through his damp hair. "Even if I can't remember, it feels like I do when you tell me."

"Well, it wasn't as pretty out as it is tonight," he began. "It was in the middle of a horrible blizzard. We were snowed in the house for weeks. Most people started to go stir-crazy, but not us. For hours, we'd just sit by the fire, sharing a book or discussing poetry. You used to ask me to tell you stories about the migration, or my trek down south. Seems like that part hasn't changed."

"I guess I've always found your life fascinating," she said. "And besides, I just *love* to hear you talk. Your voice is beautiful."

"My voice?"

"Your accent," she explained. "It's....charming. I could listen to it for hours. And while I'm confessing guilty pleasures," she added, a flush creeping to her cheeks. It was embarrassing, and a little unnerving, letting him in like this, but she wanted him to know these things. "I'm also crazy about the pet names: love, darling. They make my heart go all…offbeat."

He chuckled, one arm tightening around her waist. "Then allow me to entertain you, *darling*."

She gave an exaggerated and swooning sigh, resting her head against his shoulder.

"Once the snow started to melt, we were both a little disappointed. We were standing by the window in the dining room, looking out at everything all melting and gross. You looked at me and you said 'I wish I never had to leave your side' and I said, 'then don't.'" He looked down at her as he told the story, keeping both arms tight around her as they drifted in the open water. "I hadn't planned on it. Up until that moment, a future with you just seemed like a fantasy. I never thought you would want it, too, but when you said that…my bravery just kicked in. I took off my grandmother's claddagh ring and I told you the story behind it. She always said the ring was lucky, and it had a way of bringing couples together. Before we left Ireland, she gave it to me and told me it'd lead me to the girl of my dreams, and that if I gave it to her, I'd get to keep the dream."

She wished she could remember this happening, and hoped she'd written every detail in her diary. "How did you ask?"

"I said, 'Miss Whindom,' and then I had to clear my throat because I was so nervous," he said, doing a comical imitation of clearing his throat. "Then I said, 'Let me be your husband. Let me spend every day of the rest of my life striving to be good enough to look into your beautiful eyes and call you mine.'"

Even hearing it now made her go weak in the knees. "You really said that?" she asked, blushing. "Without practicing at all?"

"Well...I may have practiced once or twice," he admitted.

She laughed lightly, dipping her head. "I am yours," she whispered softly. "And I always will be."

Chapter Nineteen

As the sun dipped beneath the horizon, Mykaela and Dylan walked out of the woods and onto the cliff, their hands interlaced. Brad and Charity were hidden in the trees just before the clearing, waiting for the right moment to come out.

Narissa stood at the edge of the cliff, with the massive ocean view behind her. The waters were calm and still, and it gave Mykaela chills to look at it. The woman, normally cloaked in black or silver, was now wearing a stunning white dress that, at times, looked like it was made of pearls. Seashells and jewels adorned her hair, too. Clearly this was a big day for Narissa.

"I'm here," Mykaela said as she and Dylan crossed the clearing together. "Just like you asked. Now let my brother go."

Her lips curved in a proud, smug grin. "A deal's a deal." She brought one hand out to her side and made a big deal of snapping her fingers. Jared appeared beside her, surrounded by traces of that thick, black smoke. His wrists and feet were bound some kind of twine. His eyes went wide when he saw his surroundings.

Mykaela rushed forward to untie him, but in one swoop, Narissa stepped into her path. "Not so fast."

"You said if I came without a fight you'd let him go," Mykaela reminded her, a warning in her voice.

"And let him go I shall." Turning, Narissa kicked Jared in the stomach. His body soared off the cliff and then dropped, hurtling toward the ocean below. Mykaela and Dylan ran after him, but once they reached the edge of the cliff, they ran up against a barrier.

Mykaela screamed, slamming her fist against the force field as she searched the water for any sign of Jared. But it was so far down, and with night falling, she couldn't see a thing.

She whirled around to face Narissa. "Bring him back up," she demanded.

"Consider his death the price for your disobedience."

***

Brad ducked back down behind the shrub, where Charity was knelt on the ground, preparing an extra injection of adrenaline for a boost of power. "She just sent Jared into the water," he said, his voice panicked. "Juice me up and I'll fly around the barrier. Maybe I can still save him."

Without a word, Charity grabbed his arm and plunged the needle into a vein. With one swift push, she plunged the fluid into his system. He started to scream, his flesh sizzling and burning. Smoke started to rise from his skin and he cried out in pain.

Confused, she tried to look in his eyes. "What's happening?" she asked, desperate. This was off plan. This wasn't supposed to happen.

"That's not adrenaline," he said, feeling his body grow weaker and weaker.

In horror, she looked down at the needle in her hand just as a loud bellowing voice shouted from the clearing in front of them, "You can tell your friends to come out now."

Their cover was blown and their team was compromised, so Charity surrendered and helped Brad stagger out of the woods and into the clearing.

"Mykaela, you've been hiding a secret weapon," Narissa scolded as she turned to look at Charity. "I should've known those pesky witches would send another one in my sister's place."

Next to her, Brad cried out again, clutching his chest as he dropped to his knees on the ground. His breathing was ragged and labored, his body growing weaker by the second. He slumped forward, his eyes closing. Charity dropped to her knees beside him and felt for his pulse, thankful to find his heart beating slow and steady. "What did you to him?" she demanded, a venomous look fixed on her opponent.

"Did you know that holy water is poisonous to an incubus?" Narissa asked simply, her eyes glinting with pleasure. "The hormone supplements were genius, by the way. It gave me the perfect opportunity. All I had to do was sneak in and exchange the vials. I needed your lover boy out of the way for a few hours."

Charity looked around the clearing, feeling her heart fill with fear. Across from them, Dylan was leading a silent and grief-stricken Mykaela across the field. She was leaned against him, as if she couldn't even stand on her own. Jared was probably dead by now, Charity realized.

"You thought you could crash my party," Narissa gloated, looking at Charity. "But it turns out, I have a use for you after all. The spell demands I sacrifice a witch, and I was going to choose Mykaela, but you'll do nicely."

With a menacing smile, Narissa raised her hands in the air, palms facing the sky. Suddenly, the cliff started to shake and tremble. Slowly at first, but then the motion became faster and the ground shook with a violent earth quake.

It knocked Mykaela and Dylan off their feet and they clung to each other to brace themselves against the motion. Charity leaned forward, covering Brad's body with her own as she felt the cliff break off from land. The chunk of rock slid down the side of the cliff, in a jagged freefall toward the water.

***

It felt like forever before Mykaela had the courage to open her eyes again. She clung to Dylan, hiding in his arms with her face buried in his chest, afraid to face the situation around her. When the rockslide stopped and the land went still again, she finally lifted her head.

She saw that they were trapped on the broken part of the cliff, adrift in the middle of the ocean. Immediately, she began to hyperventilate. Besides last night, she hadn't even been on a boat since before her father died, and now there was nothing but ocean water all around her. Before, it had been exciting and adventures, venturing into the deep with Dylan. But now she was terrified. For miles around, all she could see was the blue waters, the darkening sky. Her friends were hurt, one of them unconscious and the other petrified. At the other end of the rock, Narissa was preparing an altar.

Suddenly, their plan seemed a lot simpler in theory, and now she was overcome with fear. Dylan tried to calm her, speaking soft words of comfort, trying to make her look at him and not the scene, but all she could do was take in the view with an impending feeling of horror.

"I can't swim," she whispered to Dylan finally, even though it seemed so stupid, right now it was all she could think. "I never learned how. Even if I survive, how can I get home?"

Dylan was close to her, his arms still wrapped around her and his head tilted down. "Charity can control the water," he said. "She'll get you out of here."

"But look at her," she whispered. "She's terrified. She can't do this."

He looked over, where Charity was still knelt beside Brad's body. She'd moved him to his back, now, and was trying to shake him awake. "She'll be fine," he said, though he didn't look convinced. "She has to be."

Narissa came up to them and grabbed Mykaela's arm, pulling her to her feet. Dylan jumped up, his arm latched onto Mykaela's in defense.

"Easy, Prince Charming," Narissa said, holding up one hand to stop him. "I just need something from the two of you." She pulled them toward the other end of the tiny island, where there was a cup and an athame laid out on the grass.

Looking down at the grass, Narissa frowned. "This will never do," she said, mostly to herself. Then she snapped her fingers and the ground underneath them turned from grass to stone in an instant. Mykaela almost slipped on the slick surface, but Dylan steadied her.

"There we go." With a satisfied sigh, Narissa stooped down and picked up the dagger and the cup. She turned to the couple. "Each of you hold out a hand."

Reluctantly, Mykaela did as she was told. Dylan followed suit, keeping his eyes on Mykaela the whole time. Using the dagger, she cut a line down the center of both their palms and held out the cup to catch the trickling blood.

"I need the blood of soul mates to consecrate my circle," she explained, looking at Mykaela. "It's a shame you never embraced your roots as a witch. Magic can be so freeing."

"You don't look very free to me," Mykaela said, watching as her blood and Dylan's mixed in the silver cup.

"I've been a slave to time," Narissa admitted. Looking up at the sky made her smile again. "But soon…Delphinus and I will be free at last."

"You think that," Mykaela said, shaking her head gently. "But even if you save him, you'll spend the rest of your life fighting to keep him."

She caught Dylan looking at her out of the corner of her eye.

"I've got what I need." Narissa set the cup down at her feet and held up both hands, each palm pacing one of them. The sky above them turned instantly cloudy and dark. With her magic, she shoved them over toward the other side of the stone and then created a raincloud above each of their heads. As the water trickled down in a small circle around each person, they were trapped.

***

The stone slab was about the size of a baseball field and floated smoothly on the surface of the roaring seawaters. A few miles off the coast of town, the unlikely group of friends were trapped on the small island made of rock.

Storm clouds rumbled above, as violent and turbulent as the waters. Every now and then a bolt of lightning would streak through the silver clouds, leaving a trail of pale light behind them. Though the sky was overcast, the blue moon shined clearly through them, a bright beacon of tinted light in the darkness.

At the far end of the slab, Narissa prepared her ritual. She'd used the blood she'd drawn from Mykaela and Dylan to paint a circle around herself. The bright red stain encased her as she closed her eyes and chanted, channeling power from the hotspots all over town. Mykaela could see the colors floating across the ocean and gathering around the circle, reinforcing it. It looked like the dark side of a rainbow, the way the purple and blues mixed with each other around the witch.

On the other side, Mykaela, Charity, Dylan and Brad were all encased with circles of rain they couldn't break through. The raindrops fell in steady, constant streams, surrounding them like bars on a jail cell. They poured from clouds positioned over each of their heads, trapping them in a circle no larger than parking space.

From inside her rainy prison, Mykaela looked toward the space next to her, where Dylan was trapped. It was just Narissa's romantic heart, she guessed, that led her to imprison them so close together. If it weren't for the magical barriers, they would've been able to hold hands.

He was looking at her, too. His body leaned against the barrier, he peered through the rain at her with his intense blue eyes. She stared at him, drinking in every detail. Soaking wet from the storm, his hair was finger-combed back in spiraling blond wisps and the water drops clung to his fair skin. Though he didn't say a word, Mykaela could read the signs of remorse on his face and she couldn't bear to watch him blame himself.

"Don't," she called, hoping her voice would reach him. When his eyes shifted, just enough to let her know he heard her, she scooted closer to the edge of the rain, so close it was splattering back at her. "Don't blame yourself. This is *my* fault."

He shook his head, his eyes remaining steadfast in his belief. "No, it's not," he said, his voice just a dull whisper by the time the wind carried it to her. "You don't deserve this."

"You don't, either." Tears mixed with the rain on her cheeks. "It seems like your entire life was one giant struggle.

You left Ireland for a better future and all you found was...*this*. You never even got a chance."

"You were my chance," he said, locking eyes with her once again. A bittersweet smile curved his lips. "I had *two* chances with you, with lifetimes in between to ponder and reflect on how things would be different...and somehow it's still not enough."

"That's not true," she insisted. "It was enough. You loved me in a way I never even knew existed. I'll never forget that, Dylan. *Ever*."

"Then I'm being selfish right now," he said with a heavy-hearted laugh. "Because I want a thousand eternities with you."

Dylan's words tugged at her heart, making her tears flow as steady as the rain. Blinking them back so she could see, she kept her gaze locked on him as if he was the only one in the world. She pressed her palm up against the watery barrier; it was the closest she could get to touching him. He raised his hand, too, lining their palms up with each other. If she closed her eyes, she could almost feel his fingertips brush against hers.

"This can't be the way it ends," he said, and Mykaela wasn't sure, but she thought she saw tears on his cheeks. "Not after all this time..."

"Maybe it's not," she said, clinging to her hope. "Stranger things happen every day, just look around." Through her tears, she laughed, but it wasn't a joyous sound. It was one of soft hope and great sorrow. "Maybe it's not the end."

***

Charity sat directly under the center of her thick, grey cloud. Her legs crisscrossed in front of her, with her hands rested on her knees, she kept her eyes closed in meditation. With slow, steady breaths, she prepared herself for what was to come next. This was her defining moment; the reason she was given a second chance. If she succeeded in stopping Narissa, she'd be allowed to stay and live out the rest of her immortal life as a protector of white magic. But if she failed…it was back to the spirit world. Back to always watching, unable to communicate or interact with anything real. With a shiver, she tried not to remember that horrible year that had stretched on forever. She never wanted to go back to the other side, at least not yet. She was determined not to fail.

Drawing power from the water around her, she focused her attention inward. Bit-by-bit the outside world began to fall away. Peaceful and calm, she focused only on her connection with her ancestor's spirits. Soon, she had no awareness of the stormy ocean all around her, or the powerful dark magic taking place just yards away. All she heard was the powerful voices of the spirits, disembodied sounds coming from every direction, all around her. From within her.

"Are you prepared to do what is necessary?" they asked—at least a hundred voices, echoing and intermingling with each other.

"Yes," her mind whispered, and it was enough. The words didn't have to leave her lips for her family to hear her.

The voices began to whisper affirmations and blessings, and among the voices, she heard her mother's. "You can do this, Charity." It was faint, but the kind reassurance was unmistakably from her mother.

Opening her eyes, Charity knew she was ready.

***

When the time came and the moon rose high above the ocean, Narissa came to get Mykaela. With a wave of her hand, she made the raincloud above Mykaela's head dissipate.

Freed from her prison, Mykaela stood and looked over her shoulder at Dylan. Keeping her gaze locked on his as Narissa took her by the arm and led her across the stone slab to the altar.

"We made a deal," Narissa said. "Do you willingly surrender the souls to me?" She waited for an answer, her eyes sharp with warning.

Mykaela looked at her friends. At Charity, waiting patiently for her cue, at Dylan, watching with dread. Brad's unconscious body was lying at the farthest end of the slab, and beyond him she could see the constellation Delphinus.

She remembered the vision Charity and sent her, and remembered just how much this soul-draining hurt. But it was necessary, so Mykaela nodded her head just once, reinforcing her decision. She practically had to shout to be heard over the sound of the wind, and her voice echoed around her as she said, "I do."

Narissa's lips curved in a smile of delight and without another word, she raised her hands in the air, lifting Mykaela up off her feet in the process. Narissa closed her eyes and began to chant, and Mykaela felt the sharp stings of pain, felt her power begin to fade. Light erupted from her. Rays of all colors flowed from her body and into Narissa's, just like she'd seen in her vision. Except this time, instead of the power flowing straight into the witches' body, it hovered over her hands and veered off toward the sky instead. Mykaela realized the beam of light was aimed right toward the constellation. All this time, they'd been assuming breaking open the door was a two-step process...which meant the timeline of their attack was devastatingly off.

Opening her mouth, she tried to scream a warning to Charity, but no sound came out. If this kept up, the door to the other world would soon open and they would all die.

***

Maybe it was their connection as witches, or their lifelong bond of friendship, but Charity could feel Mykaela's panic and follow her train of thought. She realized the time to strike was *now*.

Lifting her hand, she threw a blast of light from it and destroyed the prison that held her, then she did the same for Dylan and Brad. More than anything, she wanted to check on Brad but there wasn't time for that now. She could only have faith that he would be alright.

The bright glow of power masked their escape and Narissa was too distracted with her ritual to notice that Charity and Dylan were loose. Snapping her fingers, Charity made the dagger appear in her hand. Clutching her fist tight around the handle, she crouched forward, slinking toward the witch unnoticed.

Dylan was next to her and she whispered, "Once Mykaela's body falls," she said, "Take her and *swim*."

He narrowed his eyes at her. "But you'll—"

"Just do it," she hissed. Then without another word, she sped toward her foe. Her body moving as fluid and swift as the ocean itself, she reached her in a split second and raised the dagger in the air, ready to plunge it into Narissa's chest.

Narissa dropped her hands. Her face full of anger and wrath, she brought one to Charity's throat and curled her fingers tight around it. With her focus interrupted, Mykaela's body fell. Dylan rushed forward, jutting his arms out. He caught her body right before it smacked against the rock.

Dylan gave Mykaela a gentle, but firm, shake to wake her up. If he was still alive, that meant she was, too. Now, he just needed to get her out of here.

"Did you really think you could get the jump on me?" Narissa spat, the gusts of wind picking up speed with the witches' outrage. Still clutching the dagger in her hand, Charity fought to shove it into the witches' heart, but her arms just weren't long enough.

Above, Dylan watched the stream of light soar through the sky into the constellation of the dolphin. The three stars that made up each point of the dolphin's nose, fin and tail began to glow brighter and brighter until the form of the animal was clear and visible in the sky.

Narissa smiled at the glowing stars and turned her attention back to Charity. "You're too late," she said menacingly. She flung Charity across the platform, clear across to the other side. The dagger skidded across the stone a few feet away from her, but Narissa paid no attention to it. She spread her arms up and out, palms facing the sky, and bellowed in a booming voice, "Come, my love! I've waited far too long already."

In the sky, Dylan saw the portal rip open. Right in front of his eyes, he saw the fabrics of the universe part, and in the glowing triangle of space he could make out a dark and stormy world. And something from that world—the darkest of shadows—was rushing straight toward their floating platform.

Mykaela started to stir finally, and he could tell she was disoriented and weak. He helped her to her feet and rushed her over to Charity. Charity was sitting up, holding a hand to her head. The three of them crouched in a small circle, and Charity looked at Dylan in aggravation. "I told you to take Mykaela and leave!"

"It's a good thing I didn't," Dylan said, his eyes quickly scanning his surroundings.

Narissa turned a ravenous gaze on the three of them. "Now all that's left to do is kill you pesky girls...*again.*"

He looked at Charity. "Take Mykaela, swim her to shore."

The girls looked confused and started to protest, but Dylan wasn't paying attention. He saw the enchanted knife, just a few inches away from Brad's body. The blade was dangerously close to skidding off the edge and tumbling into the waters below. He gave a frantic glance toward the other end of the stone, and saw Narissa still marveling in her moment of victory as she came toward them. He didn't have much more time, but he needed to say one thing first.

He took Mykaela's face in his hands so quick and unexpectedly that she jumped in alarm, then her eyes softened into a questioning gaze as he peered deeply into them, driving his message home. "I need you to know something."

Her eyes widened, as if reading between the lines and she began to shake her head in denial. "No, Dylan—"

"I never stopped loving you," he said, cutting her protests off. His fingertips drank in the feeling of her soft skin, for what he feared would be the last time. "Not for a second."

She opened her mouth to plead with him, but he stopped her with a quick, desperate kiss.

Then, he focused all of the power he'd been saving and channeled it, forcing his body into super-speed mode. He made a quick lunge toward the edge of the stone. With his right hand, he picked up the dagger and then zipped back across the platform. He moved faster than Charity—so fast that everything around him was a blur of stormy blue colors and loud, whooshing sounds. Narissa barely even knew he was coming. Pointing the tip of the dagger outward, he drove the crystal blade straight into her heart.

Her eyes flew wide open and she let out a shocked scream. She looked down at his hand in horror as he twisted the knife in deeper, smiling in relief and triumph when he saw her eyes grow weak.

Then the knife in his hand started to glow, dimly at first, then bright. And brighter and brighter. He tried to let go, but it felt like his hand was fused to the handle, and he couldn't separate himself from it. Panic sank in and he pulled, trying to free himself. The ball of pale light glistened all around his hand now, and he looked back at Mykaela in fear. But seeing her beautiful face, the concerned expression on it, eased his worries and gave him a sense of peace.

***

Mykaela tried to rush forward to help Dylan but Charity grabbed onto her arm and held her back. She wasn't sure why at first, and then she saw the ball of pale light expanding. It was huge now, and glowing between the sea-witch and her killer. A bright flash blinded them, and when the light faded out, Mykaela saw Narissa's body sprawled out on the slab of stone. Blood stained the front of her dress, the crimson color a bold contrast to the white silk. A trail of blood leaked onto the stone, trickling down toward the girls. Right in front of their eyes, Narissa's skin crackled and frosted over. Her skin was coated in the cool blue color; like her body was frozen from the inside out. The handle of the dagger poked out of her frozen chest, and her body was lifeless. Defeated.

And Dylan was gone.

Turning, Mykaela looked all around but could find no sign of him. She ran to the edge of the slab and screamed out into the still roaring waters. *"Dylan!"*

With Narissa's death, the storm around them began to fade. The clouds rolled away and the waters calmed. Under the light of the blue moon, Mykaela cried out into the sea, hoping to summon Dylan, but he didn't come.

She dropped to her knees at the edge of the rock, her chest heaving with grief and sadness. She felt like there was a gaping hole in her chest that nothing could ever fill again.

Looking over her shoulder, she saw Charity knelt by Narissa's body. Wrapping her fingers around the sea-shell covered handle, she pulled the knife out and looked at it. "They warned me," she whispered, her voice hoarse. "They said only a descendant of the coven could use the athame."

"What does it do to someone else?" Her voice sounded shrill and panicked. She rushed over to Charity and grabbed her by the shoulders, shaking her. "What did it do to him?"

"I don't know!" Charity cried, slapping Mykaela's hands away. "It was never supposed to be him. He was supposed to take you and run!"

"He can't be dead," she whispered, then she repeated it louder. "He's not dead or there would be a puddle of water here and look, it's completely dry. So dig through your witchy little brain and tell me what happened to him!"

They were distracted by loud squealing sounds. Looking around, they saw they were surrounded by dolphins. Their sleek, shiny skin reflected in the moonlight as far as their eyes could see. Hundreds of them flanked the stone platform. They were doing flips and jumps, almost as if they were...rejoicing.

"Oh my God," Charity whispered, looking toward the other end of the stone.

Mykaela followed her friend's gaze and saw a huge tornado of navy blue and black smoke. It swirled down from the sky, spinning faster and faster, heading straight for them.

Charity turned, examining Narissa's body and the area around it. "He killed her on the altar," she said, her pitch rising with fear. "He sacrificed a witch."

"Does...does that mean..." Feeling a sudden chill sweep over her, Mykaela looked at the ominous black smoke rushing toward them.

"He's coming," Charity whispered.

Like that bitter moment back on the cliffs, they stood powerless and still while the spinning cyclone of smoke swirled down toward Brad's body and engulfed it. Charity screamed, diving toward the billowing plumes, but Mykaela grabbed her in a bear-hug and pushed, forcing her in the other direction. Everything was so loud; the sounds of the wind, the shrieking from Charity's lungs, the joyful squealing of the dolphins. Then, suddenly everything went eerily silent. All sounds cut off, leaving Mykaela with a ringing in her ears.

Charity stopped fighting and Mykaela turned to follow her friend's gaze. The smoke had vanished. At the end of the platform, Brad stood at the same time fountains of water sprouted up from the dolphins. Charity rushed to make sure he was okay, but Mykaela lingered, her eyes scanning at the calm ocean and the spurts of water. Looking at Brad, she saw he was surveying the scene, too, with the strangest expression on his face. Almost as if...it was all new.

Suddenly, all the missing pieces started clicking into place. She remembered how avidly Narissa's foot soldiers had gone after Brad. Morrigan and Kerr had torn everyone he loved away one by one. Even before that, he was genetically engineered to be something...and they had made sure he had little to claim in the human world. Now, she could see why. An incubus was the only creature with a soul to surrender, an empty vessel. And after centuries of being tortured in a spirit world, Delphinus would need a body.

"Charity, don't!" Mykaela shrieked, stopping her friend to a sudden halt. She ran over to her, meeting her just feet away from him. She grabbed her friend's hand and held it tight, her voice a desperate warning, "That's not Brad."

Charity went utterly pale, her mouth dropping open as she turned a fearful gaze to her boyfriend's body.

He smiled back at them with Brad's lips, but it was chillingly different from anything they'd ever seen Brad do.

"Delphinus?" Mykaela whispered, the sound coming out so quiet she wasn't even sure he'd heard her.

He craned his neck left with a loud crack and then right with another pop, settling in. Then he gave them that smile again. "Call me Finn."

Chapter Twenty

Both girls fell back a step, perfectly in sync. In Charity's hand, she clutched the dagger, the heart of the sea. "What did you do to him?" she asked, her voice quivering.

"Him?" he asked, looking confused. "Oh, you mean this?" He tapped his chest with two fingers.

"He was the love of my life," she said. "Where is he?"

"He's *gone*." He came a step closer, his silvery eyes boring down on them. "He was only temporary…someone to train the body before I came. This vessel was always meant for me…and Narissa took such care in crafting it." Finished with them, he stepped back and turned in a half-circle, surveying the scene. "She should be here. Narissa!"

They looked at each other, silently asking each other the same question. What would he do when he realized what they'd done to her?

His body stiffened when his gaze landed on the altar. Eyes going wide, his mouth dropped in a gasp of denial. His head shook from side to side as he pushed past them, whispering, "No. *No!*"

In front of him, the sun was rising over the horizon and casting orange and pink glows over the water. Mykaela noticed how rigid and precise each movement was, and how regal he looked as he knelt by the frozen corpse of his beloved. Even after everything that'd happened, she felt a little sympathy for him as he picked the body up and cradled it against his chest in a bear hug. After all, having a broken heart and being separated from a loved one was something all three of them had in common now. Bending, he kissed Narissa softly on the lips and then eased her body back to the ground. While his back was turned, Charity and Mykaela started moving backwards slowly toward the edge.

With a heartbroken, guttural scream, Finn stood to his feet, the dolphins crying out in mourning around him. "Are you happy now, oh great and powerful god of the sea?" His voice radiated with sarcasm as he shouted into the ocean. "Your daughter is dead because of you — before we got even a moment of happiness. I'd wager that brings you a great deal of pleasure, does it not? You call yourself a king! You send children to do your dirty work," Finn's voice was quieter now, but still marked with disdain and defiance. The dolphins joined his rebellion by doing flips and shouting along with him, sending up splashes of water rippling across the surface. "But her blood is on your hands, Poseidon! Come and face me yourself you coward!"

Please, please don't, Mykaela thought as she and Charity backed toward the edge of the broken cliff.

But nothing happened. Wherever Poseidon was, he wasn't answering.

"Of course you do nothing," he whispered. "To show your face would require a shred of honor."

They were at the edge now, but before Charity could swim them to shore, Finn turned to face them so quickly they jumped. Mykaela lost her balance, teetering off the edge of the cliff. Her heart leapt into her throat, but Charity gave her a good tug and pulled her to safety.

"Before you go." He held out his palm, revealing a burn in the shape of a dolphin on his wrist. The dagger flew out of Charity's hand and hurtled through the air into Finn's. He curled his fingers around it and held tight. "This belongs to me."

Charity stared down at her hand, looking completely confused, but before either one of them could say something, the rock began to shake and tremble. Then it broke apart, separating the girls from Finn. With the wave of one hand, he sent their small wedge of stone soaring through the waters. The rock slammed against the shore and tossed the girls onto the beach. Scared and shaken, but unharmed.

Face down on the beach, Mykaela's entire body was shaking as she placed her hands on the sand and tried to push herself up. She was still weakened from losing the souls, and adjusting to not having powers and the exertion left her dizzy. Sitting up, she looked next to her, where Charity sat, still and stiff, her vacant and numb gaze fixed on the ocean.

"Tell me that didn't just happen," Charity whispered, a tear rolling down her cheek.

But it had. They'd just lost Brad, Dylan, and Jared in one horrible night. How had things gone so terribly wrong? Raking a hand through her wind-tossed hair, she scanned the beach, not really sure what she was looking for. But then she spotted something on the shoreline.

A damp, unconscious body.

Standing, she ran over and knelt by the body, turning it over. Realizing it was Jared, tears stung her eyes and she dropped her head to his chest. She started sobbing and she couldn't hold it back. Her entire plan had hinged on keeping everyone safe, and now hardly anybody she cared about was left standing. Now, things seemed more hopeless than before.

Then she heard it, dull and faint, but a spark of hope in the darkness. Jared's heart was still beating. She sat up, calling out, "Charity! Come look." She started shaking him, trying to stir him, but he didn't open his eyes.

Charity came over to them, dropping to her knees by Mykaela's side.

"His heart's still beating," she said, shaking him again. "Is there anything you can do?"

"Because my magic came in so handy before," she said bitterly.

"I've seen you put him to sleep before," she said, ignoring Charity's self-doubt. "Can't you wake him up?"

"Maybe." Charity reached down and scooped up a handful of sand. Holding it in her palm, she blew the grains gently into Jared's face and whispered, "*Wake.*"

Mykaela waited, each second passing excruciatingly slowly. Finally, Jared's eyelids fluttered open and his pupils expanded. Taking in a sharp breath, he sat up, startled. Looking at both of them, he seemed a little relieved. "You're okay," he whispered.

"So are you," Mykaela said, throwing her arms around him in a tight, grateful hug. "I thought you were dead."

"Are you kidding?" He chuckled softly, wrapping one arm around her in a weak hug. "Dad used to tie me up and toss me into the water as training."

"For once, I'm glad he was a twisted freak." She let him go and sat back.

He looked from Mykaela to Charity, and then past them, as if searching for more survivors. His face fell and he looked back to his sister. "What happened? Where's Brad?"

"Delphinus took over his body," Charity said, finally looking up from the sand. "He's possessing it."

"No." Shaking his head, he stood, looking outraged. "Damn it." His gaze landed on Mykaela, and his expression changed to concern again. "And Dylan?"

Dipping her head, she took a slow breath as she remembered that blast of light that'd been Dylan's demise. "He used the dagger to kill Narissa," Mykaela said. "But he wasn't a member of the coven, so it...did something to him. He just...*vanished*."

He reached out, placing a hand on each of their shoulders as he looked at both of the girls. "We'll get them back, okay?" His eyes locked on Mykaela. "*Both* of them."

"Where do we even start?" Mykaela asked, her voice breaking.

"We start by going to find Mom," he said. "And then...we'll figure it out, like we always do."

Looping his arm around Mykaela's shoulder, he gave her a reassuring squeeze and started to lead them away, but Charity stayed at the shoreline. She was looking down at her hand, and the delicate engagement ring on it. "We were supposed to get married," she whispered. "He was all I had left."

Mykaela extended her hand toward Charity. On her wrist, she still wore the beaded friendship bracelet. "You have me," she promised. "And I'll help you save him. It's the least I can do."

Looking out at the ocean, Charity was silent as she debated about this, as if weighing which world to align with. Then she turned, stretched out her arm and took Mykaela's hand.

Epilogue

When Dylan's emerald green eyes opened, the first thing he saw was that everything around him was white. The brightness of it blinded him, causing his eyes to sting and tear. The cold pierced his clothes and skin, chilling him to the core. A thick, white sheet of snow covered the ground. White-capped mountains surrounded him in every direction, their peaks stretching toward the cold, grey sky. Wind howled around him, making the land seem desolate and lonely. There wasn't another soul in sight.

He stood, searching for anything that would indicate how he'd gotten here. The last thing he remembered was using an enchanted dagger to kill Narissa. What had happened after that? Had the witch died? Did Mykaela survive? He needed to find her, make his way back to her somehow. Then, he noticed something strange: white puffs of breath were coming from his nose and mouth.

He took a deep breath and blew it out as a test, staring in disbelief and awe when the breath turned white against the cold again. A strange feeling of joy filled him and he started laughing in excitement. He could breathe, he could *sigh*.

It'd been a hundred and more years since his lungs had felt the pleasure of fresh air. But now, the curse that'd kept him frozen in time was broken with Narissa's death. Pressing a hand to his chest, he felt his heart beating sturdy and persistent. *Amazing*, he thought with a feeling of hope. It couldn't be…

Was he *human* again?

Just in time to freeze to death in an arctic wasteland, he realized with a dreadful look at his surroundings. Again, there was nothing but snow, ice, and mountains all around him. It was startling, just how cold he felt. He'd spent over a century immune to both cold and heat, and the sensations were more intense than he remembered. Now, they were downright crippling.

He shivered, wrapping his arms around himself in a bear hug for warmth. Moving quickly, he trekked through a few feet of knee-deep snow, growing more chilled by the second. Something glinted up ahead. Taking a few steps forward, he peered into the distance.

Ice crystals reflected off the dull light shining from the sun (lost somewhere in the thick grey clouds). Hundreds of them, huge and massive, formed a castle in the wilderness, at the foot of a large snowy mountain. Their panes formed towers that stretched up toward the empty, bleak sky, each point of the crystal peak sparkling like a star. A few slick sheets of ice-formed steps that led up to an alcove, where there was a set of frosted double doors framed by stunning swirls of ice. The castle was the most beautiful thing he'd ever seen. And somehow, also the loneliest.

The way the beautiful structure was hidden in such a horrid place was the strangest part of all. Did anybody live in there? He wondered. So far, it was the first sign of life he'd seen so he decided to check it out. As he stumbled toward the castle, he wondered again…*Where was he?*

More importantly...how could he return home to Harmony Harbor? To Mykaela?

Succumbing to the cold, he took a few more staggering footsteps toward those icy stairs. Just short of them, though, his knees buckled. He could no longer feel his toes or his fingers, and the breath he'd celebrated only moments ago now pierced his lungs like sharp knives with every inhale. Shivering, he curled up into a ball at the foot of the stairs in hopes of protecting himself against the harsh lash of blustering winds.

With a loud scraping sound, like an ice-scraper gliding across a frosted windshield, the double doors to the palace opened. Looking up, Dylan squinted against the brightness of the snow.

At the top of the steps stood a gorgeous woman clothed in a shimmering blue gown. Her hair was ghostly white and flowed down her back in a braid. From the top, she looked down on Dylan with an unreadable gaze. "Who dares to disturb my fortress?" the woman bellowed, her voice chilling him every bit as much as the wind and snow.

"Help," he pleaded, his voice a low whisper among the howling wind. As he felt his body growing weaker, he thought of Mykaela. Oh, how he hoped she'd survived the whiplash of that powerful dagger. He longed to see her again, but he feared that after a hundred and eighty years, his number was finally up.

He could still see his soul mate as clear as day in his mind. In her first lifetime she'd been a delicate but brave southern belle, and in this current one she was a spunky, and also very unlikely, hero. He clung to the image of her as his body grew weak. Picturing her delicate green eyes punctuated by the dramatic curves of her eyebrows, arching up to just a few inches below her dark cascade of brown curls.

Closing his eyes, he thought of her bravery and strength and the lengths she'd endured to protect the ones she loved. It started in the 1800's, when she'd worked with a sea-witch to curse Dylan in order to save him from the clutches of a dangerous siren. And in this lifetime, she'd delved into the mystery behind her friend's death and nearly agreed to join a siren king to protect her mother. Most recently, she'd allowed a thousand souls to get sucked from her body, draining her of all her superpowers and leaving her merely human. She'd done all of it to protect Dylan, her family, Harmony Harbor, and as she called it "the greater good." That was Mykaela. Fiercely protective, hopelessly heroic and loyal to the very end.

His heart ached, he missed her so much. The last time he'd seen her, they'd been floating adrift in the middle of the ocean on a broken cliff while Narissa was in the middle of freeing her long-lost lover from a supernatural prison. When he'd used the dagger to kill Narissa, he'd thought he'd die as a result. Only a Cavanaugh could use the blade — and though there had been two Cavanaugh witches at the ritual — Charity and Mykaela — neither had been strong enough to get the jump on Narissa. So he'd prepared himself for a sudden death to protect the woman he'd loved for lifetimes. He never imagined he'd end up transported to some strange and cold land and wind up separated from Mykaela yet again. This — not knowing whether she was alive or dead or safe — was absolute, utter torment.

If he didn't love Mykaela so much, if he wasn't so concerned about her safety, he would've let himself die there on the spot. After all, it had been a very long and lonely hundred years in between his relationships with Mykaela and after all the bloodshed, battling and disaster, he was exhausted. Weary and discouraged. It would be easier to stay in the snow and allow the thick, crisp flurry cover him while he waited for death to come at last, than it would be to keep fighting. But Mykaela's safety was uncertain, and he couldn't lie down and die without knowing what had become of her.

Rolling over, face down in the snow, he planted his palms on the ground and channeled every ounce of love for her into strength and pushed himself to his feet. Each step was a triumph and he finally made it to the bottom step of the castle.

Looking up, he saw the woman still watching him. There were only about six short planks of steps between them, so she was close enough for him to look into her eyes.

"Help me," he shouted a desperate plea into the wind, "I beg you!"

Her cold blue eyes watching him with the strangest expression, she stepped down onto the first plank of ice. Her shimmering azure gown gliding across the ice as she moved, she came a little closer.

"My soul mate is in trouble," he explained, though with every breath he took it pained him to speak. "I can't explain how, but I know she is. You have to help me get back to her." While he desperately tried to speak to the strange and aloof woman, he moved up another two steps. There was now only one plank of ice separating them.

His tattered t-shirt was now stiff and frozen, and the icy breeze cut right through his jeans. Shivering, on the brink of death, he looked up into the woman's eyes and begged one last time, "Save me," he whispered, "so I can save her."

He collapsed again, landing on his hands and knees on the ice. Weakened and disoriented, he was sure the woman would leave him to die in the storm. She startled him, though, when she reached down and took his arm in her icy cold grasp. She pulled him back to his feet, and then led him inside the ice castle.

MORE BOOKS BY JASMINE DENTON

CURSE OF THE SEA
Soul of the Sea
Song of the Sea
Heart of the Sea

FROM THE DAMAGE (CO-AUTHORED WITH GENNA DENTON)
Opposites Attract
Coming Clean
Collateral Damage

ANOTHER LIFE
Another Life
Past Indiscretions: The Prequel
Forgetting Yesterday (Coming Soon)

FATED SISTERS TRILOGY
DIVIDE

STAND-ALONES
Inner Demons
Saving Hannah

About the Author

Jasmine Denton started writing when she was ten, authoring a series of short stories about a line of princesses who find themselves in similar forbidden love scenarios. As a teenager, she wrote stories filled with angst and growing pains. Now, she's found a genre that allows her to tell forbidden love and teen angst stories against a paranormal backdrop. Jasmine's published works include Soul of the Sea, the first in the Curse of the Sea series and Inner Demons, a modern day retelling of Dr. Jekyll and Mr. Hyde.

To learn more about Jasmine, you can follow her on Twitter (@JasmineLDenton) or visit her blog @ jasmineldenton.wordpress.com

www.ingramcontent.com/pod-product-compliance
Lightning Source LLC
Chambersburg PA
CBHW020257200626
46816CB00001BA/338